Crumbling Bones

Mary Coley

Published by Mary Coley, 2024.

Table of Contents

Dedication

I dedicate this book to the people in my hometown of Enid, Oklahoma, the setting of this book.

My years in Enid during the Fifties and Sixties began to mold me into the nature-loving writer that I have since become. I have thought about writing a book set in Enid for many years. It took a while for the story to take shape.

My brand of mystery story is family oriented and often has to do with lost memories or family secrets. The main characters or protagonists are women. Once my overactive imagination dives into a story, I am influenced by everything I've ever done and every person I've ever known, every place I've ever visited, and probably by every book I've ever read and every movie I've ever watched.

Crumbling Bones is no different. You may recognize the setting, but I assure you that nothing that happens in this story ever happened to anyone that I know. I struggled to get it right. I hope I've done that.

Enjoy this Enid adventure. Thank you for your support.

And as Bob Hope sang when I was a kid, "Thanks for the memories."

Crumbling Bones
Mary Coley

A SPOOKY MANSION, a decades-old body, even a ghost dog, *Crumbling Bones* has everything it takes to keep you awake at night and turning pages. - Marcia Preston, Mary Higgins Clark Award winner for *Song of the Bones*.

This character driven mystery will keep you guessing. No one is who they seem to be in *Crumbling Bones*. Mary Coley's characters are real and you'll love the extraordinary house set in her hometown. - Peggy Chambers, author of *Blooming Greed*.

Mary Coley taps into her Oklahoma roots and takes the reader on a harrowing journey to discover the truth hidden in a historic mansion. With a riveting cast of characters and a determined heroine, the story will draw you in and carry you to a shocking conclusion! - Jude Bayton, author of *The Secret of Witch Haven Lane*

This is a work of fiction. All of the characters, organizations, and events portrayed in this novel are either products of the author's imagination or are used fictitiously.

Copyright 2024 by Mary Coley. All rights reserved. No part of this book may be reproduced or retransmitted in any form or by any means without the written permission of the publisher.

Published by Mary Coley, Moon Glow Books

Printed and Distributed by: Draft2Digital

www.marycoley.com[1]

www.facebook.com/MaryColeyAuthor[2]

https://www.goodreads.com/search?q=marycoley&qid=YzEpg50sr9

---

1.   http://www.marycoley.com

2.   http://www.facebook.com/MaryColeyAuthor

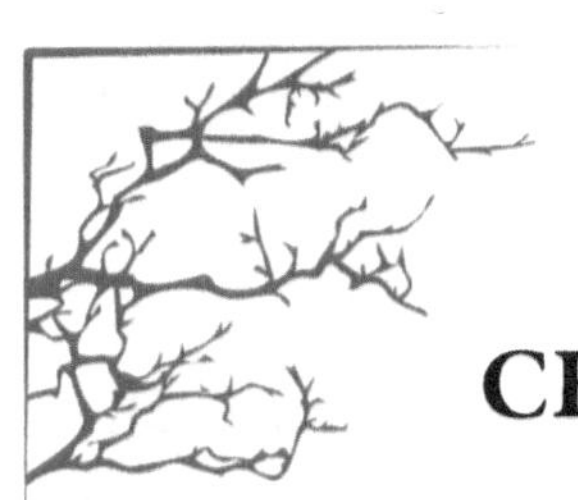

CHAPTER 1 - KYRA

Smiling, Kyra Blackwood flicked on her turn signal and exited the highway at the small park in Enid, Oklahoma. The once familiar swings, so tall, still stood guard over the grassy park, the merry-go-rounds, and the newer slide forts made of brightly colored plastic.

A mother and child, hand-in-hand, skipped as they neared the pad where a zebra, frog, and duck perched at child height on top of their coiled springs. Orange October leaves quivered around them in the tall trees.

Those elms and oaks partially hid the lines of the historic Kamber mansion. But Kyra knew the house was there.

She thought of her kids, Robbie, Declan, and Skye, and warmth spread through her body. She'd told her children goodbye this morning when they left the house to catch the school bus and promised she'd see them tomorrow evening. She would only be gone one night, but Skye had stiffened, her 8-year-old brain unable to accept that Mom might go anywhere without her. She never had.

Kyra cherished the good life she had built at the ranch with Dawson. They had a loving family. Her heart pounded in her throat as if the hooves of a horse were running there. She had not thought this through. This visit might disrupt everything she loved about her life. Why hadn't she been able to resist the lure of returning to her hometown?

Fighting nausea, Kyra turned the aging Ford Bronco to the curb and parked. She pushed the button to roll down her window. The mansion was a half block away. Seconds away. When she closed her eyes, her brain bombarded her with a dark, suffocating silence, and memories—her stomach aching with hunger, her dry mouth craving moisture. She opened her eyes to stare at the house. She traced the lines of the roof, and focused on the slate shingles, the lightning rods, and the chimneys. A silent scream hung in her throat. Dread and fear slithered through her veins along with her icy blood at the sight of those beautiful leaded windows sparkling in the mid-afternoon sun.

Entering the community lottery to spend a night in that house had been a bad idea.

"Contribute $50 to a local charity for a ticket. The holder of the winning ticket number is entitled to tour the fabulous Kamber mansion in Enid, spend a Friday night in the house, and attend a Saturday afternoon pre-Halloween costume party." The raffle advertisement on the library's bulletin board had lured her.

The minute she had seen the promotional poster, her brain had buzzed. Afterward, Kyra had been unable to get it out of her mind. It niggled at her every minute of the day, when she was feeding the chickens, letting the horses out to pasture, making lunches for her children, or even sipping coffee on the broad front porch of the farmhouse while staring out at the orchard next to the house, where the apple trees hung heavy with red fruits.

A week later, her community's winner was announced. She'd won.

The air thinned. She pulled in breath after breath, until her brain nudged: *you are hyperventilating.*

A horn honked behind her.

She shifted her foot from the brake to the gas pedal and the Bronco rolled on toward the mansion. Dread and fear ballooned in her stomach.

She pulled into the long driveway that crossed the mansion's front lawn on the east side, facing the park. Before she could step out of the car, a young man jogged toward her, waving. Kyra unrolled the window.

"No parking here today. We're unloading for the party tomorrow. Drive around the corner and turn in at that driveway to park. Thanks." He waved one hand in the air.

An old pickup truck pulled in behind her.

Kyra did as the young man said and drove back out onto the street, turned the corner, and went up a second drive on the west side of the house. Several other vehicles were already parked in designated spaces. She pulled into a space, grabbed a small carry-all from the back seat, and started for the house, leaving her hanging clothes on the hook above the back side window.

A middle-aged man smoking a cigar leaned against the driver's side of a black Lexus SUV. "Are you one of the lottery winners? Spending the night here tonight?" The man called.

Shading her eyes from the mid-afternoon sun, Kyra peered at the man. Stocky with a ruddy face, not a hair of his thick silver hair was out of place. His mustache was perfectly trimmed. Tiny red capillaries meandered across his cheeks and prominent nose. He grinned and tossed his cigar to one side, perused her from head to toe, and settled his look on her eyes as he approached.

"Who are you?" She asked the inquisitive man, not ready to be social but knowing that she had to be, at least for the next 24 hours or so.

"Matt Cleary. I'm with the local news. Writing a story about the mansion and the first big party the Kambers have hosted since Nicholas Kamber took over the leadership of the Kamber Company. Lots of locals will be in attendance here tomorrow. Nick invited me to get a head start on the story and to talk to the four raffle winners. So, tell me, why did you buy a ticket for a chance to come to the mansion and attend the party?"

A wave of dizziness engulfed her. It wasn't a matter of just being social. She had not anticipated and did not want to be part of a story in the news. "I'm not newsworthy." She turned toward the house. "Thanks anyway," she muttered.

"I've already got the list of names. I know you're not the mayor or her husband, or the store owner, and you don't look like the history professor. That leaves Kyra Blackwood, the rancher's wife. Right?"

"Not now." She hurried toward the back door.

"So, Kyra. Am I saying that right? Long I on Kyra? You don't look like a typical farm wife, at the mercy of wind and rain and heat. Sort of letting herself go *Au natural*?" He snickered as he followed her. "You look great, trim and athletic. Pretty hair. Makeup. You've come to town! I don't think this a rare trip for you."

She jabbed the doorbell button and ignored the man.

"Have you met the Kambers or been in the house before?" He stood directly behind her.

When a woman about her age opened the glass storm door and smiled, Kyra let her shoulders relax.

"Welcome. Come in." The woman held the door open. Kyra and Matt Cleary stepped into a small mud room and then into the adjacent kitchen. The afternoon sun filled the room, shining off aluminum fixtures, countertops, and a table with chairs. "Matt, I hope you're not bothering our guest. I need to show her the basics. Come with me." At close to six feet tall with almond skin and black hair streaked with white, the woman expected to be obeyed. "I'm Zia, Mrs. Kamber's assistant." She led Kyra out of the kitchen and into a hallway.

"Pleased to meet you." Kyra put one foot in front of the other and followed, blinking. The world around her shifted and then shifted again. She kept one hand on the wall as she moved.

Matt Cleary stayed in the kitchen.

Her head buzzed. In a brain fog, she navigated the hallway and climbed the wide oak staircase. On the second floor, Zia walked a few steps down a long hallway and then opened one of the doors. "Here's your room for the night. After you've settled in, come back downstairs. I've brewed some iced tea, or we have soda pop. Mr. Kamber will start the tour at 3 p.m. He'll meet your group in the front hall." With a smile, Zia left the room, pulling the door shut behind her.

Kyra stepped into an elegant bedroom. Light green walls and plush linens welcomed her. A wide window let in the glorious autumn light and offered a view of the front lawn and the park across the street. The buzzing in her head eased. Her shoulders relaxed.

Maybe it would be all right after all.

She opened her amber-flecked brown eyes wide. The bedroom was three times the size of the bedroom she shared with Dawson at the ranch house. Light streamed through the sheer curtains on the wide window, and the scent of lavender wafted from a bowl of potpourri on a table beneath an air vent.

A dragging noise sounded as something moved across the floor above her.

Kyra glanced up. She rubbed her forehead. Something to do with the party. None of her business. She thought of Matt Cleary. This party would make the news, and she did not want to be part of that feature story. She'd avoid the man, whatever it took.

Dawson had wondered why she'd accepted the ticket to the mansion shindig in the first place. He was an introvert too and didn't mind missing parties in their rural community. He'd nuzzle her neck and say, "I'm happy having you all to myself."

Last week when she told him she'd won the raffle drawing, he'd raised his dark eyebrows. "Didn't think you liked parties. And a rich guy's mansion? This isn't some mid-life crisis you're having, is it?" He peered at her with his brown eyes to search her face before his look caressed her thick shoulder-length hair. A few premature gray strands glistened among the dark ones.

Kyra had turned her back on her husband of fifteen years. She couldn't explain. He'd never asked about her past. He'd been happy she'd accepted his marriage proposal and settled down on the ranch to build a family. Why should he care what had happened in her life before they met?

"Not early menopause?" he'd asked when she didn't respond to his question.

She heard the frown in his voice. Again, she shook her head and added a drawn-out sigh.

"Pregnant?"

She imagined his eyes going wide and his skin turning pale as he asked. She managed to keep the grin off her face as she pulled a plate from the sudsy water in the double sink, rinsed it under the faucet, and dried it with the striped dish towel. "For heaven's sake, Dawson. You took care of that after Skye. We agreed that three kids were enough. I want to see that mansion. That's all."

Her words echoed in her memory. She'd been as truthful as she could have been. She'd lived five years alone and on her own before she met Dawson, years that her husband knew nothing about. She'd worked at a café, lived in a ratty trailer at the edge of a tiny town, and studied for her GED. Kyra had expected to go to her grave without talking about either her teenage years or the years after she ran away. All before she and Dawson met.

But winning the raffle supplied an opportunity she couldn't ignore. Kyra would slip in and out of the city with no one the wiser about her history, who she was, and what had happened decades ago. To put to rest her continuous bad dreams, she had to revisit the place where they might have happened.

Above her, the sound came again, a dragging noise and a final faint CLOMP.

She listened for more sounds, lulled into a stupor by the lavender fragrance and the soft comfortable chair she'd dropped into. Outside the window, yellowing leaves clung to tree branches that jerked in the breeze. She glanced at her Apple Watch. Nearly 3 p.m.

In a few minutes, she'd meet the other winners. She was sure that they, like her, had bought their tickets never expecting to win.

Kyra crossed the large room to the cedar closet where she had stashed her carry-all and dug out her cosmetic bag. After freshening her makeup in the bedroom's adjacent bathroom, she headed downstairs to meet the others.

Four faces looked up as she stepped off the front staircase and into the hall. It was obvious who was who, but she joined in when they introduced themselves.

Jerry Newcomb, the shop owner, was forty-something with a muscular physique and a slight limp. His heavily scarred face didn't prevent her from thinking that he was handsome in a familiar way, with intelligent, inquisitive hazel eyes. Kim Spaeth was the mayor of her town, a red-haired slightly overweight woman with laugh lines around her eyes and mouth. Kim pointed to her husband, Richard, and said he'd tagged along with permission from the Kambers. Richard studied the wall art in the front hall, arms crossed, frowning, also slightly overweight and far-sighted. His thick glasses magnified his eyes so that he looked like an alien.

Kyra had never considered asking Dawson to join her. Work was nonstop on the ranch, weekend or not.

The last person in their group was Andrea Watts, a willowy blonde with shoulder-length hair pulled back into a low ponytail, black glasses, and red lipstick. Kyra wondered how Andrea had gotten interested enough in history to teach it at the college level. Kyra's education in history—or anything for that matter—had been eclipsed by her home situation and the need to leave town even before graduating from high school. This other winner had not only graduated from high school but earned a bachelor's and probably a master's degree in history.

Matt Cleary, the local journalist she'd met earlier outside, walked in through the front door. "Hello, raffle winners," he said, grinning. When his look landed on Kyra, he winked.

"Hey Matt." Kim Spaeth spoke up. "Should have known you'd weasel your way into an invite for this event."

"Ah, Kim. And Richard. Nice to see you again. Yes, couldn't miss the chance to see this house after all these years. They've kept this place buttoned up tight, with no social events, and little news. According to the morgue at the newspaper, the last article about the house appeared twenty-plus years ago, when that local kid disappeared. I was teaching at the time." He paused, glanced around the group, and then blurted, "The kid was a delinquent. Got in trouble at school. Off the record, the story was that Old Man Kamber—Nicholas' father— or maybe even Nicholas—had something to do with his disappearance. School gossip mill."

Kyra listened with the others, and then Kim sputtered, full of questions when Matt stopped talking. Before Kim could ask anything, a tall, athletic, middle-aged man with a shaved head came in through the hallway that led off to the kitchen.

Arms crossed, he looked at them with tired eyes. "Welcome to my home." He glanced at the group, and then his look settled on Matt.

The local journalist crossed the room to shake Nicholas Kamber's hand. "Nice to see you, Nick. This is going to be fun. Looking forward to it." Matt Cleary stroked his neatly trimmed beard.

Kamber nodded, unsmiling. "Glad to hear that, Matt." He turned away from the journalist and his look skirted the four raffle winners.

"I'm Nicholas Kamber. Welcome," he said in a low voice. "Our tour—four floors, 40 rooms, and 20,000 square feet—will take about an hour."

Kyra smiled. Good. They'd see it all. The weekend would be well worth the $50 from her savings that she'd spent on the ticket, a donation to her town's small medical clinic.

She stared at Nicholas Kamber's face, seeking the features she had once been familiar with. She found them in his gray eyes, his thick eyebrows, and his ears. But when his look passed over her, there had been no recognition.

A pang pierced her heart. As a teen, so many years ago, she had idolized him, seen a possible Prince Charming. Fate had other things in mind.

Her mind clicked back to Matt Cleary's comments. *Did* Nicholas have anything to do with that teenager's disappearance?

"Take all the photos you'd like. I'll lead you through the entire house, but then you are free to explore the rooms again if you're still curious. Ready?"

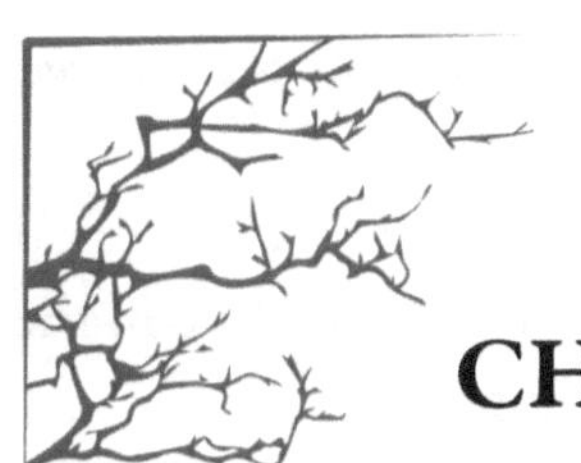

CHAPTER 2 - HUGH

The previous night, as the midnight hour approached, a figure dressed in black trudged around the three-story sandstone Tudor Revival mansion in the prairie city, lumbering from one tree shadow to the next as the moon inched across the starry sky. The moist fall air had been heavy with the scent of cedars, and the very last of the 17-year summer cicadas had droned from the old trees.

Hugh grinned—showing yellowed teeth through the mouth slit in the balaclava—as he watched for a twinkle of light at any of the dark windows. He sucked in the cool, moist autumn air, heavy with the scent of cedars and sycamores, and coughed as crickets played their violin legs. Blinking to clear his rheumy blue eyes, he peered into the darkness. No fireflies. An early first frost had taken care of them like it had birthed the pain in his arthritic knees and fingers.

Even in the cool air, sweat rolled from his armpits and smeared his forehead beneath the ski mask. He rounded a corner of the massive stone house, adjusted his backpack, and sidled to the back door.

Reaching for the keypad, he squinted, then punched in the numbers he'd memorized after inking them onto his wrist earlier. The lock clicked. He paused, strained to hear past the noisy crickets, and shoved the door open.

Aromas of floor polish and ammonia rose with the shifting air and tickled his nose. A professional-grade refrigerator hummed nearby.

He knew the layout. Thanks to the friendly woman, Zia, a staff member, he'd been in and out of the kitchen often in the past month. Recently, he'd enjoyed the glass of cool water she'd offered as he kept up his end of a friendly conversation, sipping like a gentleman as he followed her through the rooms on the north end of the main floor. Mudroom, two kitchens, two dining rooms, office. She'd pointed out the stairs that led down to the full basement or up to the second-story bedrooms, and then on to the attic. She had bragged about the size of the house. Who needed that many rooms, that kind of fanciness?

Tonight, he would climb up two flights of stairs to the attic. Then he'd be home free. By noon tomorrow, the others he had hired would be in the house. Another 24 hours and his revenge would be complete.

Nicholas Kamber and his wife expected their weekend party to be unforgettable.

What they weren't expecting was a nightmare.

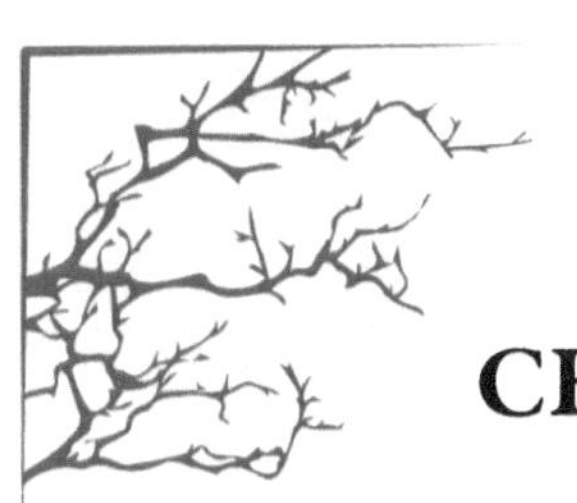

CHAPTER 3 - KYRA

Kyra and the others crowded around as Kamber stepped toward the living room. He pointed out the white marble fireplace. They progressed through the living room to the music room and its collection of instruments before Kamber passed through the family dining room and the kitchens. He led them into the formal dining room but abruptly left that room and marched down the hall again, motioning at a small office with a flick of his hand. He offered a brief history of his grandfather's company as he moved from room to room on the first floor, and then through the basement level and back up to the main floor.

Before long, they were all winded except for the shop owner. Whatever had caused the man's limp had not kept him from remaining strong and fit. Jerry brought up the rear of the group and didn't interact with anyone. Still, to Kyra, it seemed he listened to every word. They all did.

Kyra was fit enough, thanks to yoga classes and her work at the ranch, traipsing everywhere around their property with the dogs and riding the horses each morning and evening. She was grateful when they stopped to survey a new room. She could get her breath back and search her memory at the same time. Most of the rooms stirred nothing in her memories. Others left her with an uncomfortable feeling, some faint sensation just below the surface of her awareness.

Nicholas Kamber showed no personality as he led them through his family's home. At one point, when he paused to drink from his water bottle, she decided he was a stone-faced blue-eyed bully with a shaved head who had no regard for the comfort of his guests. Nicholas didn't want any of them here.

Did he not want to have this party tomorrow? Or was it that he didn't want his home open to strangers? Nothing in his face stirred warm memories. Most likely, it was figments of her imagination she'd been remembering all these years. She was glad for that realization, glad to put it all to rest.

At the north end of the house, Kamber lingered in the first-floor room he called The Salon. Kyra snapped a photo of the stone fireplace. A portrait above the mantel featured a family wearing clothing from the 1940s. The men carried rifles, and a large brown and white dog sat beside the boy. She took a closeup of the portrait and then rushed to catch up as Kamber led the group to the back stairs.

Up they went. They passed the second-floor landing and went through a door to another flight of stairs. With each step, Kyra's heart grew heavier. This part of the house seemed familiar. Too familiar.

Nicholas flicked the light switch before charging across the huge central attic room.

She paused, trembling when the dim light bulbs revealed the space. Closed doors led to small rooms tucked below the eaves on the east side of the attic. The large central room, divided only by thick roof support beams, stored not only discarded furniture but a partially constructed model train village on a huge platform table.

As the six of them milled around the space pointing out the various items of memorabilia that the family had collected, the gloom of the dim rooms diminished. Kyra's trembling stopped. Then when Kamber led them across the attic once again, icy fingers crawled up her back.

Kyra gazed around the dark attic; her foggy memory tickled again. She thought she'd put it to rest, but now she wondered once again, which of her memories were real and which were the product of an overactive imagination.

After her parents had died, she'd gone into one foster home, and then another. Her wild imagination had made it difficult to fit in anywhere, and difficult for her foster parents to believe she told the truth about anything.

If those dreams were only her imagination, why had those crazy, scary dreams persisted into adulthood? Those dreams were the reason she'd returned to this house. If they were only imaginings, she wanted to banish them forever. The only memory/dream she didn't want to banish was Shimmer.

Shimmer had been a real dog once. Now she was a guardian angel. Since the animal's death, she'd shown herself often to Kyra. The ghost dog's appearance had become a signal for Kyra to focus, to be aware of her surroundings. That hyper-awareness had saved her from injury more than once and given her insights into possibly dangerous situations. If she stopped having the dreams, would Shimmer disappear, too?

Her feet ached. She had worn the wrong shoes for their marathon tour, flats with inflexible soles. Her daughter, Skye, would be shaking her head at her if she was here. A no-nonsense girl who usually sounded wiser than her years, she didn't accept foolishness in anyone, and certainly not in her mother.

Kyra forced herself to listen to what Nicholas was saying. She already knew the Kamber story, although the history she'd been told was not as benign as Kamber's narrative. Kamber's look roamed the room as he talked. He repeatedly glanced at his watch.

The hair stood up on her arms as she eyed the huge attic space, and her stomach twisted. She pinched her eyes shut. Dreams. That's all those memories were. Nothing had happened here. She brushed at the bumps on her arms, and swallowed, hoping the unsettled sloshing in her stomach would subside.

Nicholas explained that the attic footprint was the same as the first and second floors, but it contained many side rooms and two large connected central spaces. Looking about, Kyra was sure that her ranch house, yard, and three sheds would fit into the central attic space with room to spare.

Kyra stood beside the model train track. Mostly completed, the track made a figure eight across the table. Several buildings had been placed, as well as the train station, miniature toy trees and fences, on a thin carpet of fake grass. Dust covered the roof of the station. She suspected that the track was a remnant from Nicholas' childhood, or perhaps his father's.

"Where are the engine and train cars?" Kim Spaeth asked.

Kamber ignored her question. He rushed them across the attic, stopping beside rooms with open doors and ignoring the others. When his phone rang, he pulled it out of his pocket and glanced at the screen, then whirled away. A minute later, he looked over at them, covered his phone, and said,

"That's it for the attic tour. I'll take the elevator down. Please exit the way you came and go down to the second floor. I'll meet you there."

Members of the group looked at one another as Kamber stepped to a paneled wood door off the central room. When the door opened, he stepped in and disappeared from view. The group muttered and headed to the stairway. Everyone was ready to leave the dimly lit, cavernous space. Even Jerry Newcomb's face was grim, his look pinned to the floor.

Kyra brought up the rear of the tour group and then paused to look over her shoulder at the wall of closed doors. Would anyone miss her if she stayed a bit longer? Nicholas Kamber was in the elevator on his phone, and the others were headed downstairs. It would only take a minute to fling open a door or two and look inside. Then maybe she'd rejoin the others on the second floor. A bathroom visit was a good excuse if anyone asked where she'd been.

She flicked the overhead light switch back on. Without other people and the stir they caused in the room, the air was stale and warmer than the rest of the house. She passed the big table covered by the model train village. Declan, her middle child, would love it. Give him any Lego kit or model car to put together and he would tackle it as soon as possible.

She pressed the camera function of her iPhone and snapped a picture. A chill ran up her spine. Her stomach clenched.

The feeling persisted that this was the room from her nightmare. She had an urge to bolt down the stairs after the group. Instead, she took a breath and focused on the wooden floors. Were there any scuff marks, any proof that something had been drug across the floor earlier? The floors were clean, with no dust or drag trails. But there was a throw rug piled up in front of one of the doors at the far end of the attic.

Kyra opened the door at the closest end of the huge attic and flicked on the light switch. Old chairs, gadgets, decorations, and knickknacks had been stored on shelves between twin windows covered with roller blinds.

She snapped pictures, turned off the light, and closed the door. Something rustled somewhere behind her in the dark spaces. Had one of the other winners come back upstairs to look for her? The hairs rose on the back of her neck. She examined the room slowly.

"Hello?" she called into the expansive attic. No answer. The air stirred as she moved, and an acrid smell of human perspiration drifted around her.

At the next door, Kyra turned the doorknob, pushed it open, and peered in. Old books lined shelves on all sides. A roller blind covered the single window. A brass reading lamp leaned awkwardly toward a faded overstuffed easy chair with a ripped maroon velour seat cushion. She felt a frisson of foggy memory. Or else it was her imagination, again.

The next few rooms were locked.

Kyra crossed to the far end of the central room, where the throw rug huddled near a doorway. She turned the doorknob and pushed. It stuck. She pushed again. When it gave way and opened, she wrinkled her nose at a faint, unpleasant smell.

In the shadowy interior, a bare lightbulb hung from the ceiling in the center of the room. Kyra stepped in. She pulled the cord that hung from the light fixture, and the bulb flickered on, offering a dim light that illuminated the floating dust particles her movements had kicked up. She turned on her phone's flashlight function and surveyed the room. Rusted filing cabinets and boxes covered with layers of dust lined the walls. A trunk in the corner caught her eye.

The Kamber monogram was imprinted on the leather below the trunk's lock. Earlier, during their tour, she'd fallen behind the group to open a similar trunk in a basement anteroom. It had been empty.

She pushed at the latch of the old steamer trunk. The lid didn't budge; it had been jammed down over the trunk's inner frame. She pushed and tugged until the lid lifted.

The empty eye sockets of a skull stared up at her.

CHAPTER 4 - NICHOLAS

Nicholas Kamber paced the salon, wishing he had put his foot down, and told Danielle she should not host this overnight or the party tomorrow. He had a bad feeling, and even though his grandfather had never trusted feelings, Nicholas sometimes did, and he believed this feeling was too strong to ignore. He ran his hand along the back of the leather sofa that had always been positioned in front of the fireplace. The room, his favorite space in the house, still carried the faint smell of his grandfather's pipe tobacco.

Nothing good would come of bringing these people into the house. It was impossible to keep an eye on all of them, and even though he had taken care to store valuable items in the vault at the bank, some of the family heirlooms were displayed. Anyone could take them.

One part of his brain argued that except for the lottery winners, the people they had invited were friends, people they had known for years. That didn't comfort him. Anyone could be tempted. No telling who in this crowd had gambling debts, had made a bad investment, or had an outstanding loan with creditors knocking on the door.

He was certainly familiar with what that sort of thing hanging over your head could do to a family. Wasn't that how it had all come down to him in the first place? He had never wanted any part of his grandfather's fortune.

The Old Man had been a tough businessman, willing to take risks, willing to do whatever it took so that his investments paid off. Nicholas wanted to believe that Grandfather had never resorted to murder, that his hands were clean. But he remembered seeing unsavory characters hanging around. One of the employees wore an eye patch. His working eye was constantly on the move, doing the job of two normal eyes. The boys had called the man Shifty.

Sometimes, Shifty stood in the corner of the study and watched the family. Listened. For Nicholas and his brother Stephen, it was like having Death hanging out beside them. They had speculated about how many people Shifty had killed, and whether he had done it on his own or at Grandfather's orders.

Neither boy had ever seen a body. Shifty was smart enough not to leave a blood trail or body parts behind.

He had always suspected that Shifty had something to do with the disappearance of Grandmama's dog. He remembered clearly. He and Stephen had been outside playing tennis on the court near the gardens one summer evening. Earlier that day, someone had dug up an old bush, planted a small tree, and added mulch around it. The next day, Grandmama moaned that her dog had gone missing.

Grandfather hated that dog. He'd claimed he was allergic, but the truth was, he didn't like dogs, especially Grandmama's brown-eyed spaniel. Anyone who paid it the slightest attention earned a scowl from Grandfather.

The boys at once cast suspicious eyes on Shifty, and ultimately Grandfather. He didn't mourn the dog. And Grandmama suddenly seemed to have an entirely new attitude towards Grandfather. She wouldn't eat with him. Instead, she invited the boys to eat in the kitchen with her an hour before Grandfather took his evening meal in the family dining room.

When summer vacation was over, Nicholas and Stephen left for the fall semester at boarding school in Connecticut. Nobody mentioned the dog again.

Nicholas thought about those long-ago summers as he stared at the family portrait. It included the dog; a Cavalier King Charles Spaniel Grandmama had raised from a puppy. She'd named him Basil Rathbone.

The following summer, his grandfather decided he should not only spend the summer with them but remain there for his last two years of high school. Looking back on it now, Nicholas saw it as the summer that changed his life. He'd learned every nook and cranny of this house, and every nook and cranny of his grandfather's personality. He learned things he shouldn't have known about the man, things he wished he could unlearn.

Grandfather would have hated the idea of both this sleepover and Saturday's pre-Halloween costume party. He wouldn't have let Danielle invite anyone to the house if he'd been alive.

But now, it had begun. The raffle winners were in the house, nosing around. And tomorrow, more visitors. As Danielle insisted, those people were all friends. Nothing bad could come from inviting them over.

He couldn't relax. Matt Cleary was also here, and nothing good would come from having that reporter in the house.

Outside the wide windows of the salon, a leaf tapped the glass, stirred by the autumn wind. Dusk had fallen, and long shadows darkened the yard outside. He turned off the table lamp and stepped over to the glass-paned atrium door. He checked to be sure that the lock was intact and had not been tampered with.

Leave it to the old man to include an exit on the north end of the house, close to his office. The door opened to the tree-covered north lawn, only a few steps around the building from the garages on the northwest side of the house. A speedy getaway, when needed.

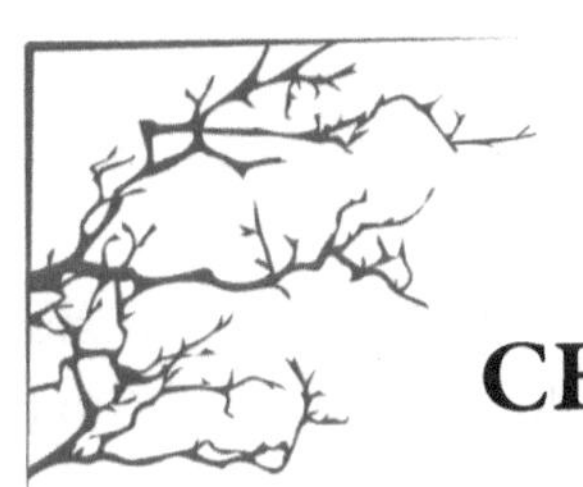

CHAPTER 5 - KYRA

Kyra stepped back and pulled in a breath. When the saliva in her mouth evaporated, she cleared her throat.

It couldn't be real. The skull and attached upper body had to be decorations for tomorrow's party. Where not covered by moth-eaten clothing, a tight parchment-like skin covered the bones of the neck, torso, and arms.

She touched the skull with one finger. The hard surface could be plastic. But she wondered about the tattered clothing. The motheaten rags would be hard to create. The strands of white hair, rooted in the patches of scalp-like paper that clung to the would-be bone, could be real.

Somewhere in the attic, something scuffed the floor. She looked over her shoulder toward the doorway. She was alone in the attic, wasn't she?

With shaking hands, Kyra turned on her iPhone camera. She snapped pictures of the skull and what she could see of the torso. Carefully, she attempted to shift the ribcage to look at the legs. There was nothing there. The hips and leg bones were absent.

Quickly, she photographed the old steamer trunk and took shots of the room. Then, Kyra backed across the floor and out of the room, leaving the door standing open and the dim overhead bulb burning. She whirled and dashed across the open attic toward the stairs at the far end. Grasping the stair rail with one hand as she went, she pounded down the steps. On the second floor, she took in the empty hallway. Every door was closed. No voices. She'd missed the rest of the tour.

She rushed down the next flight to the first floor where she stopped to catch her breath and reel in her imagination. Had she found a body? A BODY?

In the kitchen, two young women in black uniforms with white collars chatted as they towel-dried glass plates. One of them nodded at her when she paused in the doorway. Kyra rushed on to the study.

A man sat on the sofa sipping from a cocktail glass. The flat screen on the wall in front of him was on mute, but news footage rolled on silently. With a start, she recognized him. Taylor McDonald. Nicholas's high school friend.

Of medium height and build, his thin face and sharp nose made his face memorable. The scar on his chin from a high school basketball game was barely noticeable. Now, his wide green eyes were focused on the television. He glanced at her; his thick black eyebrows lifted.

"Can I help you? Um, is something wrong?" He uncrossed his legs and stood. She moved closer. His whiskey-scented breath reached her, and she took a step back.

"I need to talk to Mr. Kamber. Urgently. I found something in the attic." Kyra's heart thumped in her chest. "I'm Kyra Blackwood. One of the raffle winners."

Kyra knew what she'd seen. She'd once been to a museum with an Egyptian exhibit and recognized mummified remains when she saw them: stretched, leathery skin, strands of hair plugged into the scalp, scraps of clothing, faded and moth-eaten, covering arm bones and ribs.

"Mrs. Blackwood? You were up there with the tour, right? You saw all the things in storage. I'm sure it's nothing to be alarmed about. You didn't see any mice, did you? The exterminator came out to check things over last week." Taylor McDonald looked irritated.

Kyra pulled out her iPhone and punched the photo icon. "I took these pictures. In the attic." She handed her phone to him. "It's a mummified person."

"You found this ...where?" He frowned as he scrolled through the images on her phone.

"In a trunk in the attic. I stayed behind after our tour left the attic to check out the side rooms. That's when I found this."

"I'll notify Mr. Kamber," Taylor McDonald said. "He'll know what it is and why it's there. Could be something for tomorrow's event." He pulled his phone out of his jacket pocket, tapped in a text message, and then motioned for her to sit down. "You must have been very curious to stay up there alone."

He sat down on the sofa and crossed his legs. One foot jiggled up and down. He studied her.

Kyra tried not to squirm under his gaze. If Nicholas hadn't recognized her, Taylor wouldn't either. "We didn't spend much time in the attic. Mr. Kamber was rushed. He got a phone call. I wanted to check out the rooms under the eaves."

McDonald glanced back up at the television. "There's a lot of space for storage up there. Some rooms are in use. Others, not so much. I think that decades ago, when the family members were all living here, some of the rooms were servant's quarters."

Kyra's muscles were tight across her back; she tried to relax her shoulders. "Why are the rooms locked?" Her brain buzzed.

"Ms. Blackwood, valuables are stored upstairs. No need to tempt the servants or the guests this weekend by openly displaying expensive things throughout the house."

"In the past, could people have been locked in those rooms—imprisoned?" she blurted. And then immediately wished she hadn't spoken. "I'm sorry. I don't know why I said that, or even thought that. Surely no one was ever kept prisoner here, were they?" She swallowed the lump in her throat.

"You've been watching too many True Crime shows. That sort of thing would never have happened in the home of the founder of Kamber Company." Taylor's phone beeped. He read the message. "Mr. Kamber is on his way." His look moved back to the program on the flat screen.

McDonald's dismissive manner irritated Kyra. He was still friends with Nicholas Kamber, not a mere employee. An employee would not be watching the nightly news in the study and drinking whiskey. He could be a little nicer to guests of the Kambers or people in general. She seemed to remember that twenty years ago he had been.

Servants imprisoned in their rooms. Children locked away as punishment. Her thoughts buzzed. She looked up to find Taylor McDonald watching her. She turned away to study the volumes lining the bookshelves.

"There is an explanation for the 'mummified remains.' Mr. Kamber will clear that up as soon as he gets here." McDonald turned up the television volume as the weather forecast began. Clear skies, no rain, and a warmer-than-normal daytime temperature in the low 80s for the weekend.

This north-central region of the state was about as flat as it got in Oklahoma. Miles and miles of wheat fields in every direction, with a rare tree to block the wind outside of the cities and towns. Her ranch, northeast of here, was much the same. A creek that fed the Arkansas River meandered across their rangeland, and swaths of native oaks, ashes, and walnut trees hugged the streams and rivers that crossed the former tallgrass prairie. Any time of year, tornadoes could whip up and skip miles across the central US to Kansas, Arkansas, and Missouri.

If there was any sign of a coming tornado or hailstorm, she'd drive home immediately. She had to be there to help Dawson take care of the horses and other livestock. The three kids each had their assigned tasks in case of a storm, but something might fall through the cracks in her absence. She inspected the weather map again to assure herself that no inclement weather was likely.

Nicholas Kamber marched into the room; his gray eyes narrowed. "What is it, Mack?" He rubbed his right calf and muttered, "Damned charley-horse," then glanced at Kyra.

She saw no hint of a smile or any recognition.

Kyra let out her breath as she returned his look. Her stomach clenched.

"Ms. Blackwood found something in the attic that alarmed her. It's probably nothing, but I wanted to be sure you were aware of it immediately." Taylor McDonald stood.

Kamber turned toward her as she grabbed her iPhone, plugged in her code, and pulled the photos up again. "I was taking a few more pictures after our tour, checking out the attic rooms. I noticed an old trunk with your grandfather's monogram on it. I found this when I opened it." She held the phone out to him, the picture she'd taken of the skull visible on the screen.

"I'm sure that when I gave you all permission to explore, I did not mean you were allowed to open every box and trunk in this home. You won a ticket to stay here. Why would you assume you could open a storage trunk?" He snatched her phone out of her hand.

Kyra's face reddened. "Sorry if I overstepped. But it seems to me that a mummy in your attic is a little odd. Did you know it was there?"

Nicholas Kamber looked through the series of pictures, his finger hovering over each one as he swiped through them. He frowned at her. "I've never seen this before. It's a decoration or a prop, I'm sure. My grandfather loved Halloween."

"Let's go upstairs, and I'll show you." She would not argue with the man. In her childhood experiences, arguing never achieved anything except a slap or even a punch. She carried that lesson with her into adulthood, although Dawson had never abused her in any way. She wouldn't have stayed with him if he had.

Nicholas handed Kyra her phone and indicated the doorway. "After you."

She crossed the hall with the homeowner close behind, followed by Taylor McDonald.

Mr. Kamber stopped at the elevator. "I've taken the stairs often enough today." He punched the button in the wood paneling beside the elevator.

When the doors opened, he entered the tiny space and motioned for the others to enter. With barely enough room for the three of them to stand shoulder to shoulder in the padded leather chamber, Kamber shut the outer door and pulled the metal gate closed. The elevator moved slowly upward. The scent of his cologne, something woodsy and herbal, filled the small space.

He glared at her. "It's a dummy, a fabrication, or a joke," he said.

"Maybe," she said softly.

He shrugged. The elevator chugged upward and then shuddered to a stop. He slid open the grate and shoved open the outer door. "Where?"

She nodded toward the doorway a few steps away as she slipped around Kamber and out of the elevator.

"It's probably a prop, someone's idea of a Halloween joke from the past," Nicholas Kamber insisted.

She kept her thoughts to herself. They would see the corpse soon enough.

Kyra was certain that she had left the door open and the light on, but the door was now closed and the overhead light off. Kamber pulled the door open, letting out a blast of musty air. He reached inside the doorframe for the light switch. When he didn't find it, he stalked into the room to pull the light cord. The bulb flickered dimly, useless to make out anything in the dark, much less the contents of the trunk in the corner.

The scent of decay permeated her brain again, as well as the faint smell of sweat. Her stomach roiled. Taylor McDonald and Kyra both pulled out their cell phones and turned on the flashlight function. She led the small group across the room and shot her light beam onto the open trunk. The skull stared up.

Kamber blinked and then bent over the trunk to touch the skull and a clump of wispy hair with the tip of one finger.

McDonald snapped a picture on his cell phone. "What do you think?" he asked.

"I'll get a professional up here to look at this. It does appear to be human." Nicholas glanced at his watch. "I'll lock this room. We can't have anyone else snooping around up here."

"Do you think it's a good idea to have the party now, in light of what's been found?" Kyra asked. The suggestion clogged her dry throat.

Nicholas Kamber turned to her. "This has nothing to do with the party. My wife has devoted a great deal of time, not to mention the expense of setting up this event. I won't cancel."

"Won't that decision be up to the police?" she asked.

Taylor McDonald drew in a quick breath and plunged his hands into his pockets.

Kamber bristled and glared. "I've never seen this body, or whatever it is, before now. I'm certain that no one in my household had anything to do with it. What I'm not certain about is whether it was here before YOU arrived. Did you, or one of your fellow raffle winners, bring this thing into my house?" He glared at her as he waited for an answer.

"Of course not. I would never do something like that. I don't know the others well. Maybe you should ask each of them."

Nicholas Kamber crossed the room in two strides and stood at the door, where he dug in his pocket and pulled out a key ring full of keys. "Step out, and I'll lock the door. You say this door was not locked when you entered the room? Frankly, I don't believe that, Ms. Blackwood. I personally check these doors every night." He lifted his chin and stared at her. "I'm not sure I want you to stay in my home."

"I assure you, Mr. Kamber. I did not bring that into the house. Mr. Cleary saw me outside when I arrived. And Zia met me at the door. I have not gone out of the house since." Kyra met his look and did not back down.

"You can be sure that I will be talking with each member of my household staff. Please use the stairs to return to the lower floors."

"And you'll call the police immediately?" Kyra asked. Her voice sounded thin and uncertain to her ears. She cleared her throat.

"You'll be informed." He turned his back on her and punched at his phone.

"I'll check with you for an update when I get back from supper," she said.

Both men lowered their heads and spoke in low voices as if they'd already forgotten she was there. She'd been dismissed.

An electric emotion flooded her. She was a girl again, berated, discounted. She wasn't imagining it. Her past loomed in the dim corners of the attic.

There, near the attic stairway, Shimmer appeared. Her ghostly fluffy sheepdog shape with its unruly white and gray hair faded in and out of the background. The dog's tail wagged, and her tongue lolled as she watched Kyra.

Relief dropped over her. Kyra's footsteps pounded across the large expanse of the room, dodging the model train platform and scattered furniture pieces. Shimmer had not appeared for many months, but now that her guardian angel was here, calm enveloped Kyra. Had the ghost dog appeared because of the partial mummy in the trunk? Or was it because she was in this house, in the city of her childhood, where so many unresolved issues lingered?

Behind her, the men's voices droned on.

Would Kamber call the police? Should she speak with the authorities herself? She glanced at her watch. The other raffle winners had invited her to join them for dinner. They would be waiting in the back parking lot.

She hurried toward the doorway and the stairs, eager to see where Shimmer might lead her. The ghost dog's mouth hung open in what looked like a smile as she faded in and out. The ghost started down the stairs. Kyra followed, resisting the urge to hurry.

Her neck tingled, and unconsciously she reached up to rub it.

Shimmer was here. Shimmer would help her put an end to whatever mystery this house was hiding.

CHAPTER 6 - NICHOLAS

"What was she doing up here after the tour was over?" Nicholas Kamber whispered as he glared at his best friend.

"As she said, Nick, she was curious. You should have foreseen that someone would be curious. And you gave them *carte blanche* to tramp around the house." Taylor McDonald watched the woman hurry across the attic.

"Don't remind me. I hope no one else took that to heart."

McDonald shook his head. "I thought it would be the reporter we'd have to keep an eye on, but no, it's the ranch wife."

"Who is she? And who does she remind me of? Does she look like someone we know?" Nicholas squinted after her and shook his head.

"Nobody, Nick. Like I said, she's a ranch wife. Starstruck by the house, starstruck by everything in it. Don't you know the type? She's never had anything nice, never been anywhere the least bit classy. We all know the type; you can pull them out of any crowd. It's a look in the eye."

Nicholas Kamber shook his head. "No, it's more than that. It sounds crazy, but she seems familiar. I feel like I know her. She must remind me of someone, but I can't think who."

"She's from the area. Maybe you ran across her at a store, the movie, or a church function. She might have even gone to school with us. Our high school class was large, with over 500 people. You might have had a class together."

"I think I'd remember. She's pretty. Wouldn't she have reminded us of that if she was in school with us? Wouldn't she have said, 'We went to school together'?" Nicholas grimaced.

"Maybe. But the more important question you should consider is what that thing is in the trunk. And who the hell put it there?"

"I'm still thinking it has to have been one of those raffle winners. Cleary certainly wouldn't have done it." Nicholas ran his fingers across his scalp. "Blackwood or one of the others must have brought it in. Or maybe it's been there for decades. I seldom open those locked rooms and those windows are painted shut. When I lock up at night, I go up to the attic and look around. I don't check inside the small rooms."

"Your security team stays on top of that, Nick. Checking the windows and doors to be sure they are locked is not something you should worry about every night."

"Takes my mind off other things, Taylor. And helps me fall asleep, knowing I've done what I can to keep my family, and this house, safe."

"Far cry from the years you used to shout to me, 'I hate this house! I hate this place!'" McDonald smiled.

"You would remember that. We were teenagers. We hated anything if it wasn't our idea and didn't get our adrenaline pounding."

"Some people never outgrow that, do they? Always seeking out something that gets the blood pumping, even if it's dangerous as hell."

Nicholas nodded at his friend. "No, they don't outgrow it." He checked the doorknob to be sure it was locked. "Didn't she say the room was unlocked? I've got the keys. If it wasn't locked, who opened it? And how?"

Nicholas Kamber frowned at the door. His mind raced.

"You must call the police. Kyra Blackwood will do it if you don't," Taylor said.

"I'll call them after I've had Sarge come up here to check it out. Danielle is working with someone who is writing a pamphlet on the house's history. I'll ask her to join us after dinner. And I'll ask that mortician whose husband makes our foursome out at the country club. Someone will have to take charge of the remains, and I'd as soon it be someone who'll tell me the facts before the police. They'll all keep a lid on this if I ask them to."

"You don't think the police will want to have something to say about those remains?" Taylor stuffed his hands into his pockets and turned toward the elevator.

"Why? That thing is old. I'm not convinced it's real, anyway. I'll make some calls to set it up for 8 p.m. We'll know soon enough. Tomorrow's party will not be affected."

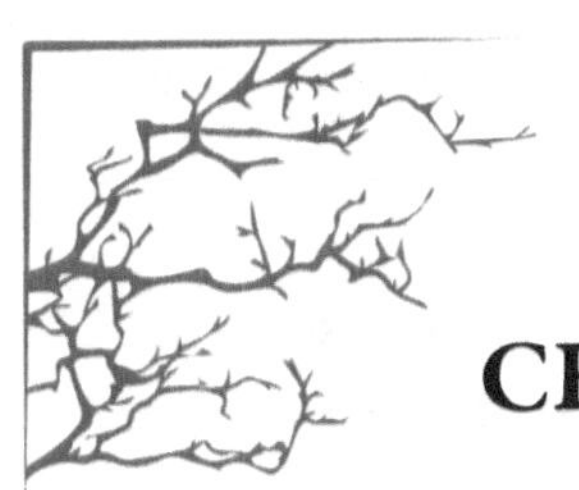

CHAPTER 7 - KYRA

Shimmer looked up at Kyra, her ghost eyes bright. Her tail waved back and forth. Kyra reached to pet her but stroked empty air. The dog had been her best friend. Those had been tough years, both before and after the animal had died. Now, she was a ghost, no matter how much Kyra wanted her to be real.

She descended the stairs slowly, nauseous from the musty, sweaty smell that permeated the attic. She pondered Shimmer's presence beside her. When was the last time she appeared? Was it last year when Skye 'ran away'? Her eight-year-old daughter had been hiding in the storm cellar. She was addicted to adventure stories and had decided to experience one of her own. Shimmer had led Kyra to the cellar the next morning after the search party had fanned out into the wheat fields and panic had truly set in.

Kyra reached the second-floor landing and stopped. She had hoped for the ghost dog to show up this weekend, to guide her to whatever she needed to find to finally stop those nightmares. A voice in her head had insisted she get the raffle ticket and had kept her from falling asleep until she had driven to the convenience store to buy the ticket at the display near the cash register. She'd never expected to win.

But she was here, like she was supposed to be. There was something she needed to do in this house, and unless she was mistaken, it had nothing whatsoever to do with that person whose partial skeleton had been stuffed into the trunk. Nothing had led her to that room in the attic but curiosity.

Kyra had to trust that Kamber would report the mummy to the police and that the police would come to the house and investigate. As the one who'd found the mummified remains, was she obligated to report it herself? Surely that was the homeowner's job. But what if he didn't follow through?

She glanced down at Shimmer. The phantom dog walked beside her, step after step, occasionally looking up at her.

Her mind clouded. Before they had started their afternoon tour, the local journalist had shared the story about a missing teenager. If she told the other winners about the remains she'd found, they would think she had located that body. She didn't think so. A leather vest? A brocade shirt? The clothes weren't something a teenager living twenty or so years ago would wear, certainly not a teen who bullied others because of their looks.

On the second-floor landing, she glanced down at Shimmer. The ghost dog was gone.

Kyra went to her bedroom where she collapsed into the soft cushions of the reading chair by the window. Her feet ached. She wasn't tired, and her brain buzzed. She flipped through the photos on her phone. They ran the gamut from ceiling detail to light fixtures, furniture, and moldings. She scrolled from one photo to the next, looking not only at the object she had photographed, but room decor, wall color, and carpets. She drank in the details.

The mansion deserved its status on the National Register of Historic Places. She was certain that the Kambers spent a lot of money each year on the upkeep of the house.

Kyra continued to scan her camera photos, including the shots she'd taken of the exterior when she had first arrived. She'd focused on the attic windows and the lightning rods on the slate roof. A shadow was clear beside the curtains of one window.

She clicked off her iPhone. She couldn't let her mind fill up with the scary possibility that someone had been lurking in the attic earlier when she had found the mummy. Maybe a sweaty person? She would be alone in her room tonight with a door she could not lock. The door had a keyhole, but she had not been given a key.

Kyra entered the bathroom and studied the small ceramic 'tub' across from the bathtub. She'd never seen anything like it. The fixture had a faucet, but at 20 inches square it was too small to sit in. Could it be a footbath? She'd read about them. In the wide cabinet next to the bathroom window, she found a packet of Epsom salts and a collection of fragranced soaps and lotions. Stacks of thick pastel-colored towels filled the lower shelves. She moved the vanity stool over beside the footbath, poured in a generous amount of the fragrant salt, and turned on the attached faucet.

As she soaked her feet, Kyra thought about the mummy in the attic. She could not imagine why it was there, or who it was. She'd been up there looking for clues to her nightmares, but she'd never expected to find something like that.

The board game, Clue, popped into her mind. The rectangular layout of this house, with one long central hallway on each floor, differed from the square layout of the mansion in the game.

She pictured the game board and compared the layout to this mansion. In this house, there was no billiard room, no true study (it was more of a den or office, with walls of bookshelves) and the closest thing to a ballroom was the large downstairs lounge. Kamber had not pointed out any secret passageways on his tour.

Would he have pointed them out? Probably not. To him, that would have seemed an open invitation to find and use them. Kamber would not want strangers exploring the house through wall passages. They would be excellent places to hide.

Kyra sucked in a quick breath. The passages were in her dreams. Were they real? Would she have a chance to find out this weekend? She suspected that Nicholas Kamber and Taylor McDonald would be watching her closely tonight and tomorrow. She wouldn't be free to check the house for passages.

She glanced over her shoulder into the bedroom. Could a secret passage be hidden behind the walls of her room?

Kyra got up from the foot bath, dried her feet with a plush aqua-colored towel, and padded into the bedroom. She circled the room, poking at the door moldings and pushing on the wall panels. At the bay window, she pulled up the velveteen cushions of the window seat and checked the cedar-lined chest beneath for a possible hidden compartment.

When she glanced up and out the window, stray leaves skipped across the yellowed lawn below. More leaves raced across the wide expanse of the park across the street beneath old trees.

Something scratched at her bedroom door.

"Who is it?" she called. When no one answered, she tiptoed across the room and opened the door to peek into the hallway.

Down the hall to her right, the end of a mostly white tail disappeared into the apartment Kamber had identified as the maid's quarters. Shimmer?

She rushed down the hall and pushed the partially open door wide. "Hello? Anyone in here?" When there was no answer, she stepped inside and looked for the dog.

The living room and kitchen of the apartment were both empty. She assumed the closed doors led to the bedroom and the bathroom. Feeling foolish, she stepped across the room, looking behind the furniture for the animal. In the apartment's kitchen, Kyra crossed to the window and glanced down at the greenhouse and the carport below. Her Bronco, and several other vehicles, were lined up in a row next to the carport. Flowerbeds bordered by hedges were scattered about the property. To the west of the greenhouse, she could see the tall fence surrounding what was probably a tennis court.

Behind her, a door opened. She whirled to face the kitchen doorway.

"Oh, didn't know I had company." Matt, the local journalist, stepped into the living room with wet hair and a towel around his waist. "I wasn't expecting anyone." He grinned at her and loosened his grip on the towel enough that it slipped a little, revealing more of his stomach. For an older man, he was in good physical shape.

She scurried across the kitchen and into the living room. "Sorry. I thought I saw a dog come in here. I shouldn't have barged in, but the door was open, and I didn't know you—"

"Stop apologizing. I'm glad you're here. I was hoping we'd have time together." He grinned at her and ran his fingers through his thick gray hair. He nodded toward the sofa. "Have a seat. Please? I won't bite."

"And I won't bite either, not even at your invitation to sit. I'm happily married. Have a good night." She rushed from the room and back down the hall to her bedroom. Happily married? Is that what she was? After fifteen years with Dawson, she was happy. Content. She didn't expect anything more. She'd lost any greater expectations long ago.

Kyra paused at the doorway to her room. There was a keyhole, but she had no key. Had any of them been given keys? If not, that meant that anyone's room could be entered from the hallway by anyone inside the house. She would block the door with the chair tonight and store her weekend bag in the car tomorrow while the party guests were here.

Why had Shimmer led her to Matt's room?

As she'd expected, two of the other winners, Kim, the mayor of Waukomis, and Jerry, a Medford store owner, were waiting for her in the back parking area, along with Kim's husband Richard.

"Andrea couldn't join us. Said she had plans with some college friends," the mayor said as Kyra walked up. The older woman studied Kyra's face. "What's up? You seem upset." Kim frowned at her. The motherly fifty-something mayor put her hands on her ample hips and tilted her head. Her curly red hair did not wiggle.

"Wasn't the local journalist going to join us?" Kyra asked, ignoring the question. As much as Kyra didn't relish seeing the man again after their encounter in his room, she hoped he would offer more information about the missing teenager he'd mentioned earlier.

"I haven't seen Matt since the tour. Have you?" She glanced at Richard and Richard shook his head. "Jerry knocked on his door a few minutes ago, didn't you, Mr. Newcomb?" Kim turned toward the middle-aged businessman. Kyra would have described him as handsome, except for the two scars that marred his face, one traveled down his cheek from his right eye to the corner of his mouth, and another dived through his eyebrow.

"I did. He didn't answer. Earlier today, he told me he wasn't staying here. But I think he changed his mind. Matt stayed on the second floor after we finished the tour. He went into the suite." The tall, well-built middle-aged man allowed the two women to pass in front of him. Kim's husband followed.

"I wanted to ask about that story he shared about the missing teenager. Why would he think the Kambers had anything to do with that?" Kyra tossed the words nonchalantly over her shoulder, hoping she didn't sound overly interested.

"I asked him that very question after the tour. Matt said the kid was a bully and a troublemaker like his father." Jerry Newcomb frowned and rubbed his eyebrow. "Figures, doesn't it?"

Kyra clenched her teeth and counted to ten. She doubted this man knew much about being bullied. Good-looking, apparently athletic, and smart. If he had been bullied, he'd brushed it off. But she'd noticed he had a way of ducking his chin and looking down after he spoke that didn't exude an air of self-confidence—probably related to whatever accident had ruined his face.

"So why did Matt think the Kambers had something to do with the disappearance?" she eventually asked.

"Cleary was a teacher at the time it happened. There was trouble at school between Nicholas and the kid. I guess Nicholas lived here with his grandparents during high school." Jerry pulled his cell phone out of his pocket and checked it as they crossed the asphalt parking area to Kim's car.

A faint hint of sycamore scent floated in the air and the setting sun glowed on the deep red leaves of the hydrangeas.

She needed to be careful. She wanted to keep the conversation going, but she didn't want to appear overly interested in that disappearance.

"Nicholas Kamber was friends with the missing kid?" Kim asked.

Kyra suppressed a smile. *Thank you, curious mayor.*

"Summer night escapades. And teenage pranks. His grandfather wanted to catch the kid defacing property and send him to jail before he corrupted his grandson. But the kid disappeared," Jerry explained, his look still focused on his phone.

"And no one ever knew what happened?" Kim's husband, Richard, asked.

Kyra watched a chimney swift flip and swerve above them, avoiding light poles and tree branches. The bird disappeared into the thick tree canopy. She was glad the others had picked up this conversation. Their perspective could be valuable.

"No." Jerry swiped his fingers through his thick prematurely gray hair. "Years later, according to Matt, the family left the city. No forwarding address." Wincing, he once again rubbed the deep scar above one eyebrow.

"Family? Other kids, no doubt. Sad. Wonder what happened to him." Kim unlocked her car and the four of them piled in.

Sad indeed. Kyra swallowed a clog in her throat as she looked back at the mansion. It was a beautiful house, made of brown sandstone with mullioned windows, many chimneys, and a slate roof. She could well imagine that the house held secrets. And secret passages and rooms. If she intended to uncover those secrets, she'd have to work fast. She didn't have much time.

Richard turned toward the back seat and peered at her. "I'm curious about you. Why did you enter this raffle? Something special about this house to you?"

Outwardly, she did not react; inwardly, ice crept into her chest. She took the opportunity to smile, using the feminine wiles that she could easily call up. Years ago, when she'd met Dawson, he'd called her a knockout, and at the time his face reflected his amazement that he'd gotten a date with the hottest woman to ever show up in his little town. Meanwhile, she'd considered Dawson perfect, too. No one would ever find her if she married this handsome and unassuming rancher.

"Who wouldn't jump at the chance to stay in this house?" Kyra said, her smile growing wider. "I've seen pictures in books of houses like this. Might not be as grand as someplace in New York City but when am I ever going to go there?" She flashed an even wider smile. "And spend the night? I feel like a princess in a fairy story."

Richard smiled a lopsided smile. "A little old for fairytales, aren't you?"

She let the smile wash off her face and lifted her eyebrows. "No one is ever too old, are they?"

Just once, she'd like to experience a fairy tale for real. She glanced at Jerry beside her in the back seat and saw his hazel eyes widen, and his look soften.

CHAPTER 8 - HUGH

Hugh huddled in one of the attic rooms, listening.

He hadn't counted on this. He knew that Nicholas planned to give a tour of the house to the sleepover winners—he'd seen it on Nicholas' day planner last night—but he hadn't expected the tour to include the attic, his preparation area, his safe place in the house. He'd thought through everything that might happen, every hitch, but he hadn't imagined people coming to the attic. On a tour. Crikey.

First, his plan had been to break into the house when the Kambers weren't home. But there was always someone staying there when the family was out of town. A car was parked in the carport, easily visible from the back drive. That meant that the time he could spend inside would be limited, and he might be seen. The police could be called. He would wind up in jail.

Then, he thought about getting into the house while the Kambers were home. He couldn't get up the nerve. It would be the same scenario. He could be seen, the police could be called, and he could be arrested.

Then he had a brainstorm. He could impersonate a gardener. He borrowed a rickety truck and a lowboy trailer from an old buddy that lived on the edge of town in a rundown farmhouse. The guy had given lawn care a go for a few months, but, as he'd told Hugh, that was hard work. Using his buddy's truck and trailer, as well as equipment from his garage, he'd looked legit enough to troll the neighborhood streets in early summer. Then he'd made sure the Kamber's current gardener was late to his scheduled appointment at their house. A flat tire (roofer's nails pounded in from the side), a dead battery (loose cables and corrosion), and empty gas tanks (siphoning is easy). Finally, he'd driven up the drive dressed in khaki pants and a blue denim work shirt, clean and shaven, rang the bell, and spoke with the woman who answered the door. She'd been happy to be offered an alternative to the unreliable lawn care company.

He'd hired two high school kids to help him care for the yard the rest of the whole damn summer. Hot and miserable. In the evenings he lay under the fan in his apartment's living room, treating his aching back to ice packs. But it had been worth it. He'd made friends with Zia, who often brought him and his crew glasses of water or iced tea while they were working. He started at 6 a.m. most days and finished by 2 before the blazing overhead sun made it too hot to work. And they kept the place looking nice, cleaning flower beds, and planting colorful annuals to brighten things up. He even supplied hanging baskets for the front porch, the porte-cochere, and the bay windows on both sides of the house. It was exhausting, and his aging body hated every minute of it, but he kept the end game in mind. Nothing could stop him.

A couple of weeks ago, he'd knocked at the back door and been invited into the kitchen. Zia wore a set of keys hooked to her belt. All he needed was a way to get her to unhook them so he could make duplicates.

But before he could figure out how to get her to unhook them, he overheard Zia talking on her cell phone about an upcoming party and everything that had to be done in preparation.

He offered to spend extra hours cleaning the flower beds and putting down fresh mulch. She also wanted him to remove the summer annuals and plant chrysanthemums everywhere. He was glad to do it. The two young bucks helped.

That's when the new plan appeared. A way to get in, and an event to cover his way in and his way out of the house. A way to wreak havoc in Kamber's world.

Hugh's plan came together. He found a few other people who needed the money he promised. He could trust them to do anything he needed. The money from Kamber's safe would more than cover any costs. And he would have his revenge.

All he had to do was wait for the weekend before Halloween.

Waiting wasn't that hard. Hadn't he been doing it for more than twenty years?

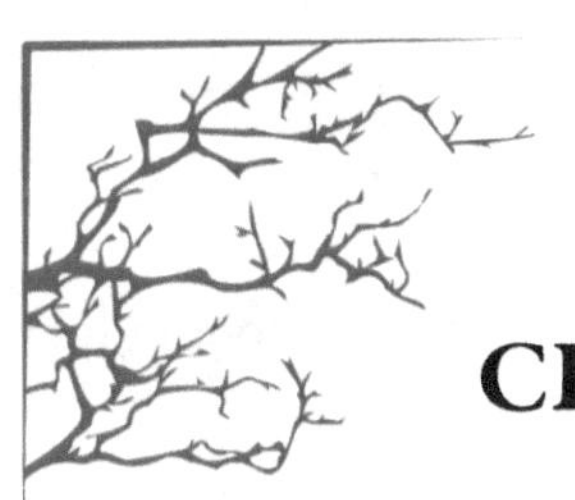

CHAPTER 9 - KYRA

When they returned from dinner, Kyra left the others in the salon at the north end of the main floor after promising to return soon to join them for a game of Scrabble. She needed to find out if Nicholas Kamber had kept his promise to contact the police.

Five people waited in the living room. Kamber and McDonald sat on the sofa while the others stood; a black-haired woman wearing a sedate navy-blue dress; Andrea Watts, the blond teacher who'd won her hometown raffle in Pond Creek; and another man who held himself erect as he looked intently at the others. A police officer?

Floral arrangements of sunflowers, babies' breath, variegated leaves, and chrysanthemums had been placed on the end tables and the grand piano. The sweet scent of the blossoms floated throughout the room. As she entered, everyone shifted their looks to her.

She shook hands first with the man standing closest to her.

"Sergeant Murray," he said. "Kamber security coordinator." Dressed in plain clothes with baggy slacks, his security badge was prominently displayed on his lapel. Murray, a fifty-ish man, not a pound overweight, with a full head of brown hair and blue eyes, nodded at her.

Then she smiled at Andrea. "And we've met. Back early from your dinner plans?"

Andrea frowned. "I'm a history teacher. Mr. Kamber thought I might be able to shed light on the identity of the ... mummified remains you found."

Murray frowned. "Let's continue the introductions. This is Olivia Rodrigues, the local mortician."

The woman, thin with her black hair cut in a chin-length bob with long bangs, stepped forward and extended her hand for a quick shake. "Nice to meet you." She smoothed the front of her knee-length dress.

Nicholas Kamber and Taylor McDonald got up from the sofa. "Now that we're all here, let's go up." Kamber led the way to the elevator. "Room for three, and even that's a tight squeeze. Taylor, can you take everyone else up the back stairs?" He motioned for Murray and the mortician to join him in the small elevator.

Kyra followed McDonald, along with Andrea, the history teacher. The group plodded in silence up the two flights of stairs to the attic and then she led the way across the large room, scanning the space. The hair rose on her arms. She peered into the shadows. Why did it smell like sweat up here? None of the people she'd seen during the day had been sweating profusely.

By the time they had crossed the central space, the elevator door had opened, and everyone assembled outside the room where she had found the mummy. Kamber unlocked the door and stepped inside, pulled the overhead light cord, and motioned toward the trunk.

"Is this how you left the room, Ms. Blackwood?" Sergeant Murray peered at her as he stepped inside.

"After I found the body, I left the door open and the light on. When I came back up with Mr. Kamber and Mr. McDonald a bit later, the door was closed and the light off. But nothing seemed to have been disturbed. I took pictures during that first visit." She reached into her crossbody bag for the phone, but Murray shook his head.

"We'll save the photos for later. But you're sure you left the lights on, and the door open that first visit?"

"Absolutely."

Murray turned to Kamber and McDonald. "And both of you are sure no one else came up here after Ms. Blackwood? Does anything look different to either of you now since you were all here?"

"No," Kamber said as his look crisscrossed the room. "Nothing has been altered. And I am unaware that anyone else came up to the attic after Ms. Blackwood's first visit. She was upset. Maybe her memory of what she did when she left the room was affected by her emotions. Most likely, she's confused."

McDonald agreed.

Kyra shook her head. She knew she'd left the light on and the door open. But she had no proof. Arguing with the two men would gain her nothing.

Murray and the mortician moved to the trunk in the corner, each carrying a small LED flashlight. The mortician slipped on latex gloves and quickly examined the torso and the skull.

Sergeant Murray stepped to one side, then turned to Nicholas Kamber. "We'll need to secure this scene. No one else goes in or out of this attic. Ms. Rodrigues, tell me if you believe this to be human. Is that possible without performing any testing? Looks like a Halloween decoration to me." Murray grinned at the mortician.

"The leathery skin, the teeth, the patchy hair on the remaining scalp, all of these are usually found in well-preserved or mummified bodies." Ms. Rodrigues pulled off her latex gloves.

"And also in well-made Halloween decorations," Kamber said.

The mortician shook her head. "It is human remains. There are ways to find out who it is," the mortician said. "DNA samples can be taken if hair follicles or teeth exist. The bones could tell us the age of the person when they died. As to how long it has been up here, that could be more difficult."

Murray scratched his head.

The mortician spoke up. "Through facial reconstruction, a likely resemblance of the corpse in life can be drawn. Comparisons with photos of missing persons can be made. The approximate age at death can be found by bone length, general health, and teeth wear. Genetic ancestry can also be detected by a DNA test."

"Such tests would require time, correct?" Murray focused his intense blue eyes on Rodrigues.

"Certainly. Extensive and complicated work."

Kamber pursed his lips. "Isn't it obvious to you that this body has been dead for a while? There's no telling how long it's been in this trunk or who put it here. Likely not by any of the people who are currently in the house."

"The coroner will make the final determination, but we appreciate your insight, Ms. Rodrigues," Murray said. "As a friend of Mr. Kamber, we also appreciate your willingness to step in for a primary consultation. Meanwhile, I'd like to hear what you have to say, Ms. Watts." Murray nodded at the history teacher and motioned toward the door. When he moved out of the room to the large central attic space, the others followed. "But I'm rushing. First, Ms. Blackwood, tell me how you discovered the body."

Briefly, Kyra explained how she had won the charitable raffle and then attended the tour with the other winners. When they left the attic, she'd stayed behind for a longer look upstairs. "I saw the trunk, recognized the monogram, and was curious about the interior. I opened the trunk and found the body." Her look skimmed the faces of the group. All eyes were focused on her, except for Nicholas Kamber, who was staring at the trunk.

"I'm sure the police will need all your fingerprints for comparison to any found on the trunk. And Nicholas, they'll need fingerprints from the other overnight guests, Danielle, your daughters, and any workers on the premises," Sergeant Murray said.

"Isn't that overkill? None of the people here today had anything to do with this body." Nicholas Kamber rubbed the back of his neck and grimaced.

"We don't know that for certain, sir. Have you seen the body up here before? Did you know it was in this trunk and stored in this space?" the security chief asked.

Kamber blinked. "Of course not."

Murray turned his attention to Andrea Watts. "What do you think you know?"

"It would help to have an idea, historically, who this might be, wouldn't it?" Andrea pushed her hair off her face and nodded at the group. "I also teach Oklahoma History at NOC."

"Northern Oklahoma College. Yes. You're the historian. Can you help?" Murray rocked back on his heels.

"I think so. At least I can tell you stories, unsubstantiated by any facts at this point, about historical mummies in the area. The Elmer McCurdy mummy is well documented. The bank robber came to Oklahoma, then died here in 1911 in a shootout after several robberies. His unclaimed remains, preserved with arsenic, ended up in a carnival, where he played the part of a funhouse dummy until one of his arms fell off 65 years later.

"Enid also has a legendary story about a resident who was mummified by a local doctor. The name he was known by locally was David E. George. He died here before statehood." Angela combed her fingers through her blond hair and cleared her throat.

"Was mummification practiced before statehood in Oklahoma Territory?" Murray asked.

"Not usually. The doctor used mummification because he needed time to prove the man's claim that his true identity was John Wilkes Booth."

Kyra pulled in a quick breath, as did Kamber and McDonald. She'd never heard this story, at least she didn't remember it from her years in Enid schools. Such a story would have stuck with an impressionable child. If any of her children heard it, they would be bursting with the news at the dinner table. And Declan would research Booth until he became an expert.

"I know this story," Murray scoffed. "Mr. George had a poorly healed broken leg. But this man's legs are missing." Murray frowned. "Besides, the man's claim was never proven."

"Mr. George had a scar from surgery on the back of his neck, another similarity he shared with Booth. An examination could reveal that." Andrea Watts peered back into the room toward the mummy.

Rodrigues smiled.

"George had twice before confessed his identity when he believed he was dying, once to a doctor in Granbury, Texas, in 1872, and once, decades later, in El Reno to the wife of an undertaker," Andrea continued. "The doctor confirmed that the man had suffered a broken leg, which caused him to limp. It was an injury of the type that someone would receive if they jumped from a height like Booth did when jumping from Lincoln's theater box to the stage in 1865."

"This man, George, was theatrical, well-educated, and could recite Shakespeare from memory. All lending credence to his story," Andrea added, nodding at the others.

A shiver shook its way up Kyra's back. John Wilkes Booth. Who would ever believe this?

"So how do you suppose the withered body ended up here?" Murray asked.

"After the man known as David George died, it is said the local doctor wanted to preserve the body in case it could be proven to be Booth. Years later, after keeping the body on display at his funeral home, he sold it to Jay Gould's Million Dollar Spectacle, a traveling circus. The last known advertised site of that circus was Hutchinson, Minnesota. In 1938."

"You know an awful lot about this." McDonald frowned.

"It's the nature of my profession as well as my avocation. Earlier this evening, Mr. Kamber called me. He knew I was a history teacher. Danielle Kamber and I talked earlier this year. Our phone conversation about the house was one reason I entered the raffle, other than my desire to contribute to the charity offering after-school care for the kids in my town. Danielle wondered what improvements could be made in the house since it's on the National Historic Register."

"My wife wants to take down the greenhouse and build a swimming pool." Kamber sighed. "Not that she swims now. Guess she plans on getting serious about it."

A swimming pool? Kyra could picture a huge pool deck in the backyard somewhere, but not necessarily at the current location of the greenhouse, right next to the carport.

"I don't think there will be a problem as long as the greenhouse is not part of the Historic Register listing." Andrea looked around the group, but no one else spoke. "One final thing, I find it an interesting coincidence that the last known appearance of the mummified remains was in 1938. Is there a possibility the mummy has been here in this trunk since the carnival disbanded and was brought to your attic in 1939 when the house was finished?"

"You think my grandfather bought the corpse and brought it here? I can't think of any reason he would have done that. He wasn't a history buff. He knew nothing of the area before he moved here."

Murray scowled. "Too bad the body has no legs. The legs are where the proof lies."

"So, you'd have us believe that what we have here is the long-lost remains of David E. George, a.k.a. John Wilkes Booth?" Kamber asked.

"It's a possibility. You can believe what you want. That's all I know." Andrea Watts shrugged and then glanced around the shadowy central attic room.

Kyra glanced at the other members of the group. Kamber shook his head, McDonald smirked, and Murray smiled. The mortician looked back at the room where the partial mummy lay in the trunk, her face an emotionless mask.

"Whoever that may have been, it's obvious we need to contact the police. It doesn't matter how long it's been here," Rodrigues said.

"But there's no urgency. I don't see any reason we need to call them tonight," Kamber insisted. "It's after nine."

"I disagree, Mr. Kamber. The police will need to follow procedures." Murray glanced at his watch. "I'll wait until morning, but no later. The police will decide whether your party plans should continue and the urgency of the situation. Determining whose body this is and who put it here could take days."

Kamber frowned at his chief of security, and then his look moved to Kyra.

She met that look. Whoever she'd found deserved an investigation. A horrific thought struck her. If it was John Wilkes Booth, there was no way she could escape media attention.

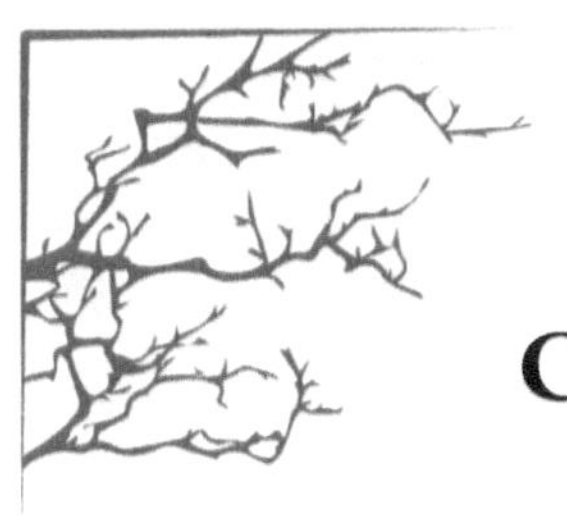

CHAPTER 10 - TY

Ty Harper, a.k.a. Jerry for the weekend, sat in the dark on a park bench across the street from the Kamber Mansion. He zipped his jacket closed against the cooling night as he watched a large man leave the house, saw Nicholas Kamber in the doorway, and noticed the porch light flick off. He sat a few minutes longer.

He had not expected his brain's response to being in the house. He'd seen flashes of blackness and felt closed in, afraid. He'd been on the verge of a PTSD episode several times, but he gritted his teeth and then focused on the nearest window and the autumn world outside. The park across the street drew him. Then he climbed the stairs to the attic with the others. Resisting PTSD had only been possible because he kept his eyes either on the back of Kyra Blackwood's head or on the floor. In his head, Willie Nelson's song "On the Road Again" looped.

He looked around the park. Where the streetlights didn't shine, shadows covered the grass, creating long pool-like expanses. How many hours had he spent playing in this park?

It was a neighborhood gathering place when he was growing up. Located blocks from his elementary school and from his house, it was the biggest nearby open space, providing room for a game of tag, touch football, and even war battles, using the scattered bushes and trees for cover.

Paintball was forbidden, but that hadn't kept him and his friends from trying it. At the insistence of his mother and their parents, as punishment, he and three of his gang spent several weekends removing the paint from their war game, dabbing water on tree bark, and spraying it on the grass using hoses screwed together and drug across the street from one of his friend's houses. It had cured him of any desire to ever play war with paintball guns again.

He remembered summer nights in the park, too. In particular, he and Shelley Meers had met there and kissed for the first time. It was before he could drive, before they could park somewhere and make out for hours. They'd sat on a bench under a tree instead.

The house had loomed over everything, seen everything. It was before his life had taken a turn.

Today, Nicholas Kamber had been uptight. Pretentious. He seemed to be hiding something. Certainly, he was not being entirely honest with them. And he wasn't the only one.

The woman, Kyra Blackwood.

Like his best friend, Jerry, whom he was standing in for, she'd won a ticket to spend the night and attend the party. But something had happened between their tour and when the four of them met for dinner. She'd seemed upset, and preoccupied.

He'd sensed that she didn't care much for the journalist during their tour, but then she'd wondered if the journalist was going to join them for dinner. She'd wanted to learn more about the teenager who went missing. But the Spaeths took over the conversation, and Kyra seemed to lose interest. She stared out the car window during the drive to dinner and hardly spoke while they were eating, except to make comments about her children, and her life on the ranch.

When they got back to the mansion, there were more vehicles jammed into the parking area. Voices sounded from the living room, and instead of coming with the three of them to the salon to play Scrabble, Blackwood had met with that group. From what he saw, he guessed that one of the visitors was a police officer.

Something wasn't right.

Ty studied the house. Imposing was the word that came to mind. What would it be like to live there, to have all those rooms to spend time in? The entry hall and the adjacent living room alone were impressive. And an elevator? What did that cost to build back in the 30s?

He crossed the shadows to the swing set, remembering those football games and that sweet kiss once again. When he glanced back up at the house, a small twinkle of light in an attic window caught his eye. It had to be a reflection from the four-lane highway that bordered the park's east side behind him. No one would be in the attic now.

A sharp pain shot down Ty's leg. He limped the rest of the way to the swing and settled in the flexible plastic strap.

He hadn't thought this through when he'd agreed to pretend to be Jerry for the weekend.

"It'll be good for you, Ty," Jerry had encouraged. "You have issues with that town, and don't tell me that you don't. You wince every time I mention going over there for any reason. And I'm not saying this to get you to tell me your secrets. Lord knows we've all got things in our past we'd rather forget. I'm not wanting anyone from here to go down to Florida and dig up my past. Like as not they'd get bit by a gator during the investigation. I'm a swamp rat, but don't tell anyone, okay?" Jerry had chuckled.

Remembering, Ty smiled, his mind whirring. What Jerry didn't know was that there was a lot Ty didn't remember. The bomb had blown it straight out of his mind. All he had left was bits of memories. Combined, they didn't make sense, and each of them by themselves ... Well, trying to decipher those memories would make anyone question their sanity. He wasn't even sure they were memories. Might as well be scenes from movies or television shows he'd watched years and years ago.

At this moment, he hoped he could get through the weekend without something setting off his PTSD. The way he figured it, if he interacted as little as possible and spoke when spoken to, he could get through the next 18 hours. Then, he'd have completed his favor to Jerry. He wouldn't 'owe' him anything. He'd drive back to his little cabin out at Lake McMurtry with new memories to cushion his crazy ones. And hopefully, his dread of this town—and especially the house across the street—would have disappeared.

CHAPTER 11 - KYRA

Kyra rushed back to her room after the group in the attic separated. She didn't want to run into any of the other raffle winners. They would be full of questions. Where had she gone in such a hurry? Had she met up with someone? Kyra wasn't sure she could prevent them from becoming suspicious of her if she evaded their questions. And she didn't want to tell them about what she'd found.

Finding that mummy had complicated things, brought her under the watchful eyes of Nicholas and Taylor. The others would wonder why she'd gone snooping and why she hadn't told them about it at dinner. She couldn't begin to answer that or any related question. She'd not allowed anyone to get close enough to ask any question about her past for twenty years, except for Dawson. Thank goodness he valued his own privacy just as much as she valued hers. Now she wasn't sure she could make it through tomorrow without being found out.

Kyra slumped in the comfy reading chair by the bedroom's bay window and propped her feet on the ottoman. She was tired. The day had been both physically and mentally exhausting. Shimmer vanished soon after appearing, then reappeared at her door minutes later only to lead her down the hall to Matt Cleary's room. There was no obvious reason as to why the ghost dog was here. Surely something would become apparent tomorrow.

Get your head on straight, her brain urged.

She glanced out the window at the fall evening. Even under the streetlights, she could see leaves jumping off tree branches and running along the yellowing grass lawn. Above the trees, puffy turtle clouds trudged across the moonlit sky.

If she had been at home today, she and her family would have spent it outside. Robbie and Declan would try to catch the breeze to fly a kite, and Skye would run around the yard, pretending to be a horse, or at least to be riding one. Kyra would sit on the porch and read, then go inside to make cookies, or to work on the Halloween costumes the kids had asked for.

Robbie wanted to be a surgeon for Halloween this year. One of her old bathrobes would do, with a COVID mask over his face and hair. Dawson's worn-out green t-shirt from a box in the attic, stuffed and stitched to define 'muscles,' would turn Declan into the Incredible Hulk. And Skye, usually a horse, twisted a unicorn horn out of a cardboard roll, painted it silver, and attached it to a headband. She'd found an inexpensive long white wig to wear as a mane. White makeup from the Halloween kit completed the equine look.

Their big worry about her being gone Friday night and Saturday was that she would not be able to get their costumes finished by Halloween next week if she didn't work all weekend on them.

Kyra wasn't worried. There was plenty of time to do the basic sewing, with extra time for any needed alterations. She'd promised them she'd be home early enough Saturday night to work on the costumes for an hour or so and expected the party would conclude in the late afternoon, surely not past seven p.m. Unless more was planned for the guests than she'd been told.

She pulled her look away from the window and glanced around the bedroom. Shimmer. What had the ghost dog wanted to show her? What was she missing in this house? It wasn't the mummy. She'd not even seen Shimmer before the animal appeared. What was she missing? She had no clue.

Maybe if she went over everything that had happened and everything that she'd seen since she arrived, she'd come up with something. She'd been hyper-vigilant during the afternoon tour, trying to remember everything. She'd shoved the home details into her memory and taken no notes. And as far as her picture-taking was concerned, she would share those with her family but only if Dawson and the kids would express interest when she got back home.

Finding the mummy had startled her. Then, Shimmer appeared. Why? The ghost dog was her link to the past. And her past was here, in this town. Was it also in this house? Shimmer always helped her find answers. This time would be no different.

She couldn't explore this late in the day. If someone saw her roaming around, they would want to know why. Her only excuse was curiosity. She was already under suspicion because she'd found that mummy. Maybe she shouldn't have said anything about it. But she'd been shocked, and part of her wondered if the mummy was the teenager from the story. She shivered and hoped with all her heart that it was not.

Instead of roaming about the house like a burglar, she would stay in her room and solidify her memories. She needed to make sure she didn't forget anything that she'd already seen or heard.

Kyra pulled her knees up and settled into the pillows, remembering the minutes when the raffle winners had gathered in the front hall that afternoon and the first part of the tour.

After touring the first floor, Kamber led them up the front stairway to the second floor. When he stopped to wait for them just past the stairway, he stuffed his hands in his pockets and frowned.

He'd identified the master suite behind him as his grandmother's bedroom and said that the other rooms on either side of the hall had been occupied at various times by family members. His only personal comment was that he and his wife had the house to themselves now; their daughters were away at school.

He'd led them along the hallway, opening the door of each bedroom and gesturing inside. Each room had a private bath and featured tile and paint of different colors. Most had fireplaces, cedar-lined closets, and wide windows overlooking the lawns. At the north end of the hall, he paused and pointed out steps that led into a small living room and adjacent apartment. "This suite is for the governess. It includes a kitchen and a small bedroom. All the comforts of home."

As she'd followed the group back toward the front stairway, she'd overheard Kamber ask Matt, "Aren't you staying here tonight? In the apartment?"

"Who could resist the opportunity?" The journalist chuckled.

Back on the first floor, Kamber had led the way around a corner to an iron gate that prevented entry to a narrow stairway leading downstairs. He unlocked the gate and took them down to an anteroom at the basement level.

"Here's the catering kitchen," he said as he pointed into a full kitchen with a wide serving window. "And this is the lounge, the largest room in the house."

The group followed Kamber into the huge room, where he pointed out the teak floor and the massive fireplace. Kyra snapped pictures, focusing on the stone fireplace and the window wells that allowed light into the below-ground room.

Kamber stepped out to the anteroom and led them down a central hallway. He opened doors to a mechanical room, an exercise room, and a large laundry before pausing in front of two thick metal doors. He identified those as wine and whiskey cellars before moving into a large room at the end of the hall. After flicking on the light, he called it his wife's craft room.

Seconds later, they followed him up the backstairs and emerged into the first-floor hallway. Then they climbed the stairs to the attic. She didn't need to review her memories about what had happened next. Kyra would never forget it.

Why had Kamber seemed so distracted during the tour? Because of the party? He didn't seem to care about the tour or the people that had won the raffle. He'd certainly taken no special notice of her. Why had she expected anything different? Over twenty years had passed.

As she sat in the upholstered reading chair, her body began to relax, and her thoughts slowed. Eventually, she yawned. Time to get ready for bed. She checked the door where she had placed the desk chair, hooking the back of it under the doorknob so that the door couldn't open inward as it was designed to do. She'd balanced her car keys on the edge of the seat so that any movement would cause them to fall to the floor. The noise would surely wake her.

Kyra crawled into the comfortable bed after going through her nightly routine. She thought of her kids, wondered what they had done all day, wondered if Dawson had made them take their baths and put them to bed at their scheduled bedtimes. A smile broke across her face. She loved her family. She had made a good life with Dawson. Had she been wrong to come here? Was she stirring up things she should have left buried?

Too late for regrets now.

Shimmer's presence told her she needed to be here. For years, she'd had nightmares, possibly about this house, and she wasn't sure if the dreams were based in reality, or if they were all the imaginings of a teenager in crisis, which she certainly had been.

Kyra would never get over her past if she didn't face it. Now, she had no choice.

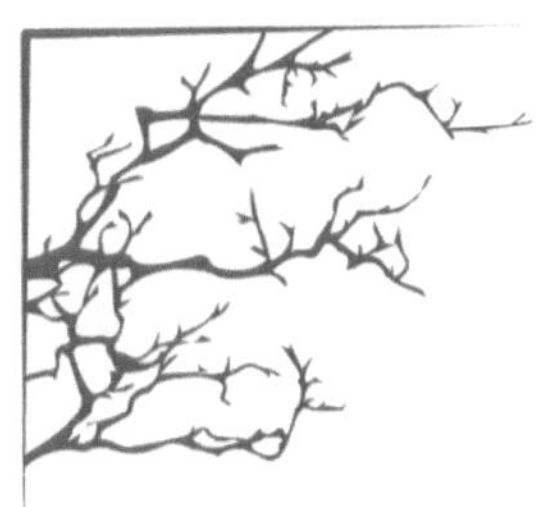

CHAPTER 12 - NICHOLAS

Nicholas Kamber sat at his desk in the downstairs office of the dark house, two fingers of Maker's Mark bourbon in the crystal tumbler on the table in front of him. He'd left Danielle lying on her side in their enormous bed upstairs, a pillow tucked against her back to make sure space separated them when he came to bed. She had another of her headaches and couldn't stand to be touched.

He rubbed his forehead. This party was a bad idea. He hadn't slept well since they'd started talking about it. But he had no reason to feel this way. Feelings can't always be justified. They were what they were. And could not be prevented.

His grandfather had never given any credence to feelings. Grandfather had called them 'Pansy feelings.' He led a life void of emotions. And he did what needed to be done, regardless of the emotional cost to anyone involved. Nicholas had decided years ago, after the old man was gone, that Grandfather's philosophy of doing business and of running the family was the real reason his father had stayed away from here for so many years, had left his older brother Robert and Grandmama to run the company without him after Grandfather died. Then, after Uncle Robert had died, his father had no choice but to return despite his 'pansy feelings.' Eventually, they'd eaten him up. Stomach cancer. Since returning here, Nicholas had done his best not to let his feelings prevent him from doing what needed to be done, both for his business and for his family.

A noise somewhere in the house brought him out of the chair. Was Danielle up? He stepped into the hallway and listened to the old mansion whisper. It had stood eighty years against the prairie winds, swaying with them, making minuscule movements, slight twists and turns, enough so that the shifting walls whispered like dancing slippers on a wooden floor, enough so that the stones of the outer walls hissed in protest.

Nicholas heard the house sighing in the prairie wind and felt certain it was something more. There was something here. Or someone? But he'd turned on the alarm system, he'd checked the locks, even the locks on the windows in every single room, basement, ground floor, second floor. Not quite a hundred windows on all those floors. Maybe he should have checked the attic.

But why should he? Those attic windows had been locked and painted shut long ago. The doors to most all the rooms on the outer attic walls were locked and would stay locked after that woman had opened the trunk. No reason to add them to his long list of 'before bed' duties.

The feeling persisted. He would not sleep tonight, and probably not tomorrow night even after the party was finished and the guests were gone. He would not sleep until Danielle had accomplished her dream of successfully hosting a party in this house. He'd given up trying to figure out why it was so important to her, or why she couldn't find peace in other pursuits, like local charities. And she wouldn't talk to him about it.

Nicholas stepped quietly down the hallway to the salon, where he paused in the doorway. The wall of windows in front of him provided a minimal barrier to the trees next to the house and the lawn beyond. Moonlight and streetlights from the corner illuminated exterior plantings but cast no shadows inside the room. He could sit here, unseen by anyone outside, and unexpected by anyone in the house. Anyone? There was Danielle, Matt—the journalist she had requested to cover the party—and those four people who had won their local raffles and chosen to spend the night and attend the party. Surely, that one woman had learned to keep her nose out of things that didn't concern her.

None of them should be wandering around at this hour. He sipped his drink, let his tongue savor the flavor of the liquor, and then swallowed. The liquor burned as it slid down his throat, fanning the embers of memory.

He'd found the note that afternoon, tucked inside his day planner on his office desk. At first, he'd not understood the meaning, thought it was a biblical reference he'd written down during a conference call, something he needed to look up. But tonight, with the unexpected October wind whistling around the house, he thought there might be another meaning to the words: 'The Beast Has Risen.' If that were true, and the meaning of the words lay in his past, who had written the note and left it for him to find in his planner?

The Beast. He'd known several men who fit that description in his life. His grandfather for one, but he was long dead and unable to rise in any fashion that made sense in today's world. And others. He could think of no reason they would take revenge on him. He tried to be fair and strove for equity in his dealings with employees, contracts with landowners, and owners of mineral rights. Had someone slipped through the cracks and decided retribution was in order?

He took another sip, let the liquid roll around his tongue, and swallowed.

No one came to mind.

But there was that incident when he was in high school with the kid they had nicknamed The Beast. It flashed to the forefront of his churning thoughts in vivid color.

What happened afterward had not been his fault. Truth was, he didn't even know for sure what had happened. He only knew that Warren had disappeared after that almost-fight at school, years ago. He would never forget it, or the aftermath. He let the memory tape roll.

Warren Switzer strutted down the high school hallway. He tossed his head so that his greasy long hair flipped and fell over his zit-covered forehead. His hazel eyes narrowed as he looked at the group of boys who stood in front of old Mr. Gates' algebra class, blocking his way.

"S'up?" he asked as he neared them. He lifted his chin. Taller than any of them by inches, he was always looking down his nose at people.

"You gotta stop, Beast. Everyone's sick of you," Nick said gruffly.

The teenager smiled. His head wobbled back and forth. "So, as if. You and your home skillet here gonna stop me?" He sneered at 'Mack' McDonald. "Whatever."

"We mean it, and everyone here agrees." Nick glanced around the group and the boys nodded. Others were suddenly interested in their feet.

A dozen kids stepped in to surround Warren. The hefty boy, tall and muscular at seventeen, scanned the crowd and snorted.

"Bring it." He fisted his hands and moved one foot over and back, widening his stance.

They all knew that Mr. Gates would barge out of his class before anyone threw a punch. But Warren had to put on a show.

"You're a bully. We've had enough. Katie was seriously upset. You need to stop teasing her." Nick frowned at Warren.

The Beast nodded. "Oh yeah? That girl is a 'Monet.' Looks better from far away. Up close, her eyes are uneven, she's got lots of zits, and her hair is like straw. You all know it's true."

"You're a scrub!" someone shouted.

Warren lunged toward Nick, but before he could swing at him, the teacher stepped up and grabbed his arm.

"Cut it out, Switzer. No fighting. To the principal's office," Mr. Gates announced. He grabbed the teenager's shirt sleeve and pulled him down the hallway. Off balance, Warren "The Beast" Switzer stumbled.

Behind him, the crowd of kids snickered. Nick sighed, relieved. But keeping Warren under control at school was only half the battle. He lived in their neighborhood. The kids were all on their own there, with no grownups to count on to intervene. His beastly bullying was sometimes ten times worse outside of school. When they played football in the park across the street from his house, everyone wanted Warren on their team. But they didn't want what happened when one of his teammates fumbled the ball or made a bad play.

Even now, years later, Nicholas felt the tightening in his stomach as he thought of Switzer. He wished he could forget about the kid and everything that had happened. It had been so long ago. But it could be that someone besides him remembered. 'The Beast has risen.' What the hell did that mean? And how did that note get inside his day planner?

Someone in the house had left it there.

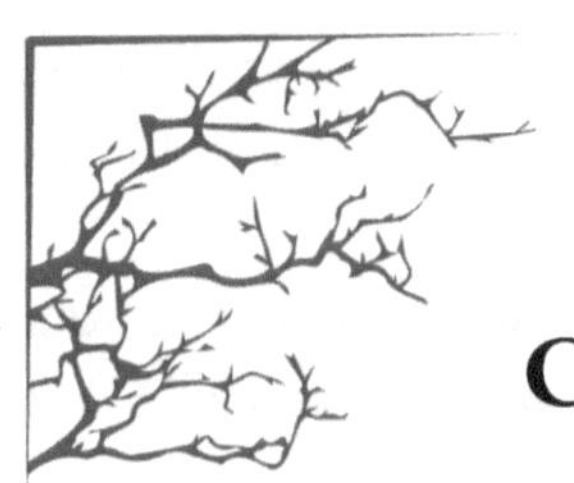

CHAPTER 13 - TY

Ty Harper closed his eyes and adjusted his position in the desk chair of his bedroom, stretching and refolding his long legs so that his knees didn't bump into the bottom of the desk. After a moment, he refocused on his laptop screen and the old newspaper story he'd pulled up about the teenager who'd gone missing twenty years ago. A person can find anything on the internet these days.

He'd been brainstorming about why the police had been here tonight. He was certain something had happened, and certain that Kyra Blackwood had something to do with it. A sensible explanation existed, and it was his nature to want to solve the riddle.

This house intrigued him. He had vague memories of playing in the park across the street as a boy. It would have been natural to wonder what life was like in the house. Back then, he'd thrived on adventure stories. Funny how he could remember reading Hardy Boys' mysteries. The books, hidden on a shelf in the closet, belonged to his much older brother Will. Why did he remember that when he remembered nothing about other potentially important things?

He was certain that he wasn't the only person here intrigued with the house. All the winners had an interest, or they wouldn't have bought a ticket, and they certainly wouldn't have accepted the offered night in the mansion.

The place was a little on the spooky side, although he hated to admit it. During the tour, he'd had chills in certain hallways and rooms. Vertigo had struck him at one point, and he'd had to stop and reorient himself as he leaned against one wall. How much of his response was triggered by his PTSD? And why? The house had nothing to do with the bomb blast he'd experienced.

He could leave at any time. Maybe he should go before the party started. What had made him decide to accept Jerry's offer and pretend to be the Medford winner? Nostalgia?

He couldn't imagine only two people living in this place. An entire floor of empty bedrooms, not to mention two kitchens, two dining rooms, and a full basement. He'd have rather gone camping, alone, than be here.

Curiosity was the best reason he could come up with. A chance to return to those days when he'd read books, days when he could allow his imagination to race with the story. Before nightmares had haunted him day and night. Now, he didn't need anyone to place a frightening scenario in his mind. They appeared regularly without prompting.

The psychiatrists had all told him that the PTSD wasn't his fault, and neither was the bomb blast. He'd simply been in the wrong place at the wrong time. His question was, how could you keep such a tragedy from happening again if something similar could happen to anyone at any time? It could even happen this weekend in this house.

An unpleasant sensation buzzed in his lower back.

Once Jerry had convinced him to come, he'd been determined to do it. His past experiences would not prevent him from living. No amount of exercising, no amount of running, no amount of forcing himself to attend meets and gatherings would ever get rid of this feeling in the back of his mind, this creepy, crawly tingling that warned him 24/7. He had to live with it.

Ty turned back to his laptop and the newspaper archives: interesting family, interesting house, interesting history.

He'd read all about Old Man Kamber, and then the sons, and then Nicholas himself. He'd read business reports and society page events. None of them indicated anything odd about the business or the family.

As a final thought, he made another request to the computer, and something new popped up.

Local Teenager Last Seen at Kamber Park

He read a brief news article, noting that the last known location of a missing teen, Warren Switzer, 17, had been Kamber Park at dusk, two nights before he had been reported missing by his mother and stepfather. The news brief included a plea for anyone who saw him or might know anything about his whereabouts to contact the police. His forehead began to pound.

Ty cradled his head in his hands and rubbed his eyes. He pulled his thoughts away from Kamber Park and the nearby mansion. Of course, they flicked to Sydney.

His engagement was over. He'd given it his all, but for every step forward he made with Sydney, she shoved him back two. For a time, he'd thought it might work anyway.

History had repeated itself. Did that mean he had not learned his lesson with Darcy?

"Sydney was different from Darcy and that was a long time ago," he said aloud. He'd hoped to keep the anger out of his voice but didn't manage it.

Ty felt his face redden. He'd waited too long to tell Sydney about his first wife, and when he finally did Sydney snapped. He relived the scene in his brain and heard the 'bink' of the engagement ring as it hit the hallway mirror. 'What other secrets have you been keeping from me? I can't DO this anymore,' she'd shouted. The sound of the door slamming reverberated in his head.

Ty shoved back from the desk and took one long step to the bedroom's bay window. Maybe he should call Darcy. But he didn't want to admit what had happened with Sydney. He could imagine her 'I told you so' look, and the snarkiness in her voice. She might tone it down if he explained what had happened, how the nightmares had taken over his life. But he couldn't do that. He'd tried to get the therapists to understand, but that meant digging into the terrifying holes of his past, and he wouldn't do that either.

Ty Harper turned back to the desk. He swiveled his chair around so that he could lift his legs and prop them up on the bed before he settled in. He closed his eyes. Despite the intriguing information his brain had just consumed, a hole opened, and a face appeared.

Sydney.

What was she doing this weekend? He shouldn't care. It was over. Why couldn't he get it through his thick skull?

Ty checked his phone messages. Nothing. He tapped the end of his mechanical pencil on the edge of the slick black desktop.

He had to pull his head back in the game. And get past Sydney.

He touched his phone and navigated to messages. He scrolled through Sydney's un-erased messages, written when they were engaged and before the big Darcy blow-up.

"*Thinking of you, love you. Can't wait to see you when you get home. Love, Syd.*"

He hit *erase all messages.*

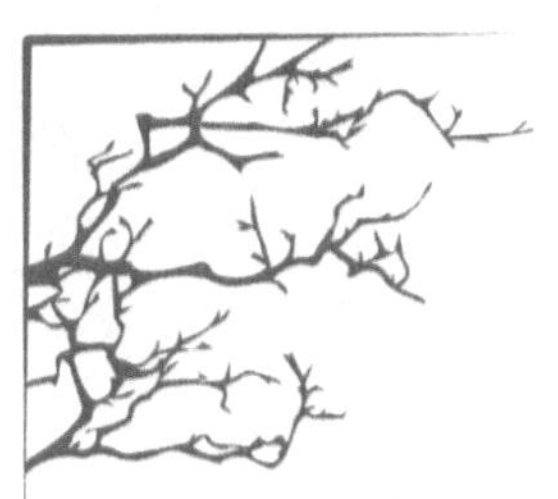

CHAPTER 14 - NICHOLAS

Nicholas poured another two fingers of Makers Mark and settled back into the old leather chair in the salon. He detected the faint scent of Grandfather's pipe tobacco. Even after all these years, the sofa cushions were saturated with it, still exuding the fragrance in damp air.

Outside the window, an owl hooted. The sky was a muddy gray, sunrise was coming. The memory swooped in, as clear as if it had happened yesterday.

"I had a call from your school today." The tall muscular man leaned back in the desk chair as he returned the desk telephone to its cradle and looked at the teenager standing before him. "You've been back here exactly one week. What's this about your involvement in a fight with another boy?"

Nicholas straightened, peering at his father. He rarely talked to him about anything, much less something that had happened at school. But he'd been called into the home office that was Grandfather's sanctum, and Grandfather was watching from the leather wingback in the corner.

"I didn't get in trouble. Why did they call you?" Nicholas addressed his father.

"That youngster needs a good talking to," growled the elderly man across the room. "Boys like that need punishing. Nip that behavior in the bud. Don't suppose the school is going to do anything?"

"The principal said the boy has been suspended for three days. They've been unable to speak to his parents." His father frowned. "You know it doesn't look proper to the community for you to be involved in petty arguments. You have an image to maintain."

Nicholas chose his words carefully. "He was bullying a friend. I couldn't just stand by."

"My guess is, this isn't the first incident with that boy, Adam. My grandson, your son, has a strong sense of right and wrong." The old man sat up, puffing his pipe. "Never the one who starts something, but trouble finds him anyway. You can't get ahead in life without taking charge. Your boy knows it. Not sure you do, Adam."

Nicholas's father pursed his lips and Nicholas turned toward his grandfather. Taking charge. Another way to say it was to bully your way to the top. *He thought the words but kept his mouth shut. He'd watched his father be the focus of his grandfather's bullying nature his entire life, but especially since his recent arrival. Spending his high school junior and senior years in his grandfather's city instead of at Phillips Academy would do him good, his father had said.*

"What was the kid's name?" The old man sucked in the pipe smoke and puffed it back out into the room. His blue eyes narrowed as he studied Nicholas.

"Warren Switzer."

"Switzer? His father wouldn't happen to be Hugh Switzer?" When Adam nodded, the old man cursed. "Should have known. The apple doesn't fall far from the tree. Fired his dad twice myself. After the first time, he came begging for a second chance. I never should have relented. He took me for all he could get within a month. Tools and supplies disappeared. Who knows how many things or how many times? Security finally caught him. S.O.B still tried to deny it."

"Did he threaten you, Grandfather?" Nicholas asked.

"Of course, but he didn't show up at work with a gun and blow everybody away. Wouldn't have put it past him, though. Haven't thought about that man in years. He was a bad one. I'm surprised he's still in the area."

"The principal said the boy's mother and stepfather were unavailable to come and get him. He spent the afternoon in a corner of the school office. I don't think the father is in the picture anymore." Adam steepled his fingers and sat back.

"Doesn't surprise me. He'd be one to watch out for." The old man tapped his pipe bowl on the ashtray in front of him, reamed out the remaining tobacco, and filled the bowl again from the wooden humidor on the table. The scent of fragrant tobacco rose into the air. The elder Mr. Kamber shoved the pipe stem into his mouth and huffed as he lit the tobacco with a match. Smoke billowed from the pipe.

Nicholas Kamber sat up. He'd dozed off. From the look of the rosy clouds visible in the east windows, the sun would soon rise. He had no time for remembering the old man, or Warren Switzer. Thanks to that woman, the police were coming to take away the desiccated corpse in the attic and interview everyone.

Who the hell did it belong to? And what was it doing in his attic?

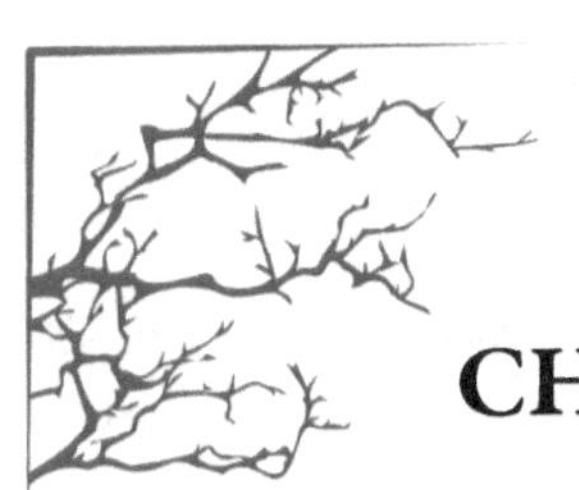

CHAPTER 15 - KYRA

Before dawn on Saturday morning, as the sky behind the sheer draperies brightened, the celadon green walls of her large bedroom glimmered. Kyra got up and dressed. She moved the chair from in front of the door, peeked out into an empty hall, then went down to the kitchen where she poured herself a glass of iced tea and wandered through the downstairs rooms.

House cleaners were sweeping and dusting, and others had begun to set out trays and serving ware for the afternoon event. It appeared that the party would happen in this part of the house. She wasn't certain if or when the guests would move downstairs and into the ballroom-like room Kamber had called the lounge.

Kyra returned her tea glass to the kitchen and slipped out the back door.

Why had she bought into the raffle, and why had she acknowledged to anyone that she had the winning ticket? It was a mistake, just as Dawson had said. And he didn't know half of it. At the ranch, chores crowded every minute of the day. Animals to feed and gardens to hoe, meals to prepare, and floors to sweep. Kids to corral and transport. Never-ending. She'd often yearned to get away. Now she wasn't so sure that getting away for the weekend had been a good idea.

Disjointed memory fragments had kept her awake all night, and now a headache niggled in her skull. She needed to get out of the house and out of her head. She unlocked her car, slipped in, and drove down the back driveway and into the neighborhood.

Straight ahead for three blocks, her brain remembered. Turn the corner. A brick wall of memories stood dead ahead. Her foot punched the brake and the car jolted to a stop. Her heart pounded in her throat. She closed her eyes.

No. No. No.

She opened her eyes slowly. The house sat dead in front of her, its Dutch Colonial lines clear in the curved eaves and wide front porch. It looked better than it did in her memories. Someone had painted the siding blue and added black shutters beside the front windows. Her look was drawn to the second-story window on the left front of the house. The white curtains were pulled to the sides. No one stood there, peering out. And Shimmer was not reclining on the long front porch as she had loved to do during her life. A fall wreath of red, orange, and yellow leaves hung on the black front door.

She turned her car around in the nearest driveway, but then pulled to the side of the street, staring at the house in the rearview mirror. She saw herself, climbing out of the window, balancing on the sloped roof as she made her way to the drainpipe. Saw herself clambering down and landing on the soft earth, where rainwater had puddled the night before. Mud squished beneath her shoes as she stepped away from the flower bed to the grassy lawn inches away.

What if she hadn't snuck out that night? What if she had instead stayed tucked in her bed, tossing from the scenarios that ran through her brain, her mouth dry and her heart pounding?

Kyra punched the accelerator and drove back to the corner. Then she turned the corner and let her Bronco roll away from that street. In minutes she had reached the neighborhood elementary school. Her fingers gripped the steering wheel with white knuckles. She pulled up to the curb in front of the wide double-entry doors that led into the school and her memories.

Those memories flooded her mind. Not all of them were bad. She had a few friends, other girls who had played tag and hopscotch with her at recess, climbed the jungle gyms with her after school before she walked home, and giggled at the boys.

Life at her second foster home hadn't been bad until 7th grade. She was clear in her head about that but couldn't pinpoint the exact moment when her young life had turned into a horrible nightmare. She couldn't distinguish one nightmare memory from the nightmare reality that became her life

Those memories whirled. One of them took over her mind.

Kids filed outside to the school playground for recess. Behind them, a man swaggered his way out of the school. He was a teacher. He was also her foster father. Playground duty. Once in place as the sole guardian of the playground, he sneered and laughed as he strolled around, knowing exactly what to say to vanquish the kids, freeze their hearts, and eat their dreams.

She should have had an advantage and should have been excluded from the caustic torrent of words. They lived in the same house. She knew him. That day, Kyra had shivered and moved far, far away from the other children to hide under one of the six-foot boxwoods that rimmed the sandy playground. There was no escape, either at home or at school. Not anymore. She would pay for her actions on the playground tonight when the lights went off and she was locked into her attic room.

Now, parked in front of the school, she buried her head in her hands and hunched over the steering wheel. This whole weekend had been a bad idea. She'd been wrong about needing to remember. But she couldn't stop it now. The memories were coming. She was in the middle of it all again.

She accelerated away from the school, wishing she could accelerate away from the memories, too, wishing she could push them to the back of her brain again, let them lay there, untouched for the rest of her life.

What had she released by coming here?

Kyra pulled her car into an open space on the back side of the mansion. She climbed out stiffly, stretched, and peered up at the tall chimneys and their chimney pots. Intricate metal trim accented the roof. Above the bay windows, the roofing was aged copper.

Although the house was very different from the one she'd just driven by, both houses haunted her nightmares. She wanted to put an end to those bad dreams. The only way was for her to face the past. Maybe that was why Shimmer was here, to help her put the past to rest.

Dawson would be astounded if he knew the real reason why she had accepted the ticket.

Her thoughts and her heart softened. One of the ladies at church had repeatedly told her she was a lucky woman. Kyra had turned away from the comment, scoffing, but the woman was right. She'd found a good man, had a family, and a purpose for her life. She loved her children, and as tiring as it all was, she loved the daily routine, the work that supplied a home for all of them. She was proud of Dawson, and each of her children held a special place in her heart. They were all unique, and she intended to be sure that they left high school confident and ready to tackle the world.

That had not been her experience. Building self-confidence had been an impossible struggle. After running away, she'd educated herself at the small local library in the town where she lived. When she wasn't working at the diner, she was studying to get her GED. Later, after she met Dawson, she'd lied to everyone about having a high school diploma, but no one had ever checked.

She'd also lied about having six semesters of college classes to her credit. No one had verified that either. If anyone had ever asked her to account for her classes or ever evaluated her on any of those subjects, she felt sure she would have passed the test. She was smart and capable. Hadn't she been able to keep her secrets for nearly twenty years?

She smiled, thinking about her children.

Robbie, their firstborn, an alpha male like his father, smart, athletic, and an extrovert, was always the first to make a new friend on the first day of school, camp, or training. Quick to laugh, slow to anger.

Declan, second born. The opposite of his brother. An introvert, happy to be at home, in his room, where he had created a display case full of model airplanes, LEGO villages, and also filled shelves with hundreds of books. She never knew what he was thinking; his face hid his emotions.

Skye, third born, only daughter. At 8, full of mischief, but always the center of attention. The perfect likeness to her mother, Kyra dreaded Skye's approaching teenage years. What in the world would she do if this child ever found out she'd been lying to them all, forever? All Skye's trust in her mother could be lost.

Everyone's trust in her would be lost.

Happily married. The phrase she used yesterday with Matt, the journalist, burst into her brain. How could she say she was happily married when her husband didn't know her past? Granted, he didn't seem to mind. But something lingered there in the back of her brain, twisting and turning: the possibility that if he knew her past, he would think less of her, and maybe even decide he didn't love her.

It would devastate her if Dawson stopped loving her. He'd kick her out. Where would she go? What would she do? He wouldn't let the kids go with her. She didn't deserve to have them. When your marriage—no, your whole adult life—was built on lies, how could anyone ever trust you again once they knew the truth?

A flash of white in the bushes drew her attention. Shimmer watched her with those big, bright eyes. The tears that had hung in her eyes cascaded down her cheeks. Shimmer. Thank God. The ghost dog was her only hope to get through the coming day.

Kyra remembered the first time Shimmer had appeared as a ghost. It was hours after the dog had been buried in the backyard. Her foster brother had dug the grave, all the while growling at her while she sobbed.

"Dumb animal," the teenager had muttered. "Should have known this would happen. Joe lost it, didn't he? But YOU caused it. What were you thinking? Sneaking the dog into your room."

"It was cold outside. She was shivering. She wasn't doing anything. Not making a sound." Kyra pinched her lip between her top and bottom teeth. It WAS her fault. But she'd been so lonely and needed the dog's warmth so much.

She shook her head, remembering her foster dad's temper and how she'd cowered, her arms shielding her head, afraid that the tempest that had turned itself on the dog would turn on her. Instead, it had blown out as quickly as it began. He'd turned away and taken his quart of beer out to the garage.

It had been up to them to get the dog's body out of the house and into the ground. Then she scrubbed the carpet in her room, trying to clean up the blood stains.

Shimmer had come to her that night, jumped up on her bed, and slept beside her. The dog was weightless and bodyless, but she was there, and her ephemeral presence was a comfort that Kyra had not known since her birth mother had died years before.

Standing there in the parking lot beside her SUV, Kyra rubbed her arms, blinked away the tears, and took a step to follow Shimmer. The dog had disappeared. She sighed. Her heart slowed and her sadness eased. She could get through the next ten hours knowing that Shimmer would appear if she needed her. Kyra grabbed her hanging clothes bag from the back seat and locked the car doors.

Yesterday, when she'd arrived, she had rung the front doorbell and studied the stained-glass windows in the gleaming oak door. This morning, on the back side of the house, a glass storm door protected a solid wood door. She punched a button and a buzzer sounded inside the house.

When the door swung open, Zia motioned her inside. Her cautious brown eyes flicked over Kyra quickly before her lips curved into a smile. "You've been out shopping? So early?"

A brief nod was her answer. No need to correct Zia about the clothes bag.

"Didn't think the stores that are in business out at the mall opened this early," Zia added.

Kyra stepped past the woman and into the kitchen where the stainless-steel countertops gleamed beneath LED lights.

"It was nice to have all four of you winners come to spend the night before the party. Are you having fun?"

Kyra nodded and ignored the pinch in her stomach. Fun? Was that what she was having? Sleep had been impossible last night. In between bouts of dreams, she'd listened intently for footsteps in the hallway, a dragging noise in the attic, or the creak of her door opening and her keys clanking to the floor.

Someone else knocked at the back door, and Zia let two people into the house, a young man dressed in white and black, and a young woman, wearing a black shirtwaist dress and a frilly white apron.

"Maybe we can talk later," Zia whispered to her as she pushed the door closed again. Kyra hurried out of the kitchen and turned toward the back stairs. Her thoughts turned back to the dream of the night before.

In the dream, she had arrived as she had the previous day, had come into the dim, wood-paneled front hall with its multi-colored slate floor. An open doorway on the far side of the hall led to the study with wall-to-wall bookshelves and an oriental rug. The wide oak stairway led up to a landing featuring a stained-glass window. To her left, a carpeted living room painted a light blue held two seating areas, a grand piano, and an elegant fireplace.

In the dream, Zia grasped the banister and climbed the front stairs. Kyra followed, captivated by the stained-glass window on the landing. A purplish light radiated over the stairs. In her dream, the entire house swirled with prisms of light from the window. A cacophony of voices rose and surrounded her. Someone screamed. The light behind the window went out, and the glass shattered.

When Kyra woke from the dream, she had tossed and turned, wrapping herself in the bedclothes, trying to decipher *the voice*s in her dream. What had they said? What did the dream mean?

As she climbed the backstairs to her room, Kyra asked herself those questions again. Her conscience sometimes badgered her to do something, like buy the raffle ticket. But dreams were different, harder to interpret. What did this dream want her to do? Or was it foretelling something? Had something like that happened in the house before or was it going to happen?

She hurried upstairs to her room and hung the clothes bag in the cedar closet. Kyra hoped that the outfit she had selected would be passable and wouldn't call any undue attention to her.

Her room was bright with morning light, so she went back down the stairs she'd just climbed, wandered through the front hall, peeked into the study, and then the living room. Where were Kim and the others?

She stepped out the front door and onto the driveway. A riding lawnmower chugged across the wide expanse of the Kamber's front lawn. In the park, a family had taken over the tall swing set. The children clutched the chains attached to the black rubber seats of the swings as the adults pushed them high. Laughter rippled in the air.

Keeping to the grass but out of the lawnmower's way, she crossed the lawn around the south end of the house and entered the rear gardens. Although neatly trimmed, the bushes and the gardens in general were not flourishing. Most of the flower beds held mulch instead of flowering plants, but the large ceramic pots that were placed randomly around the garden were overflowing with multi-colored chrysanthemums.

A black Challenger rumbled up the back drive and Jerry, the Medford shop owner, exited the car. He ran his fingers through his thick, curly silver hair, creating a disheveled look, and then peered sideways at her. "Morning, Mrs. Blackwood. You're up early."

"So are you. And call me Kyra, please."

It occurred to her that he wasn't necessarily up early. He could have been out all night. Was that the same shirt he'd had on last night at dinner?

"Going for a walk?" He lifted his eyebrows with a question. Well-toned muscles bulged beneath his t-shirt as he moved his arms. He was in great shape, physically. But something had happened to him. His face bore scars.

He probably had some horrific memories. Yesterday, he'd seemed reticent, unwilling to say much as they toured the house. He'd opened up as the four of them shared dinner. But she didn't want to encourage conversation. The last thing she needed was Jerry following her around like a puppy.

She nodded absently as she glanced at the trimmed lawns and forty-foot-high trees that surrounded the stately brick homes of the area.

"So, was the party the reason you entered the raffle, or was it the chance to spend the night before the party in here? Do you think all of the winners entered the raffle for the same reason?" Jerry smiled at her and then surveyed the yard.

"I have wanted a glimpse inside the mansion for a long time. My husband is excited to see my pictures when I get home. I've been taking so many."

"I noticed that yesterday. You know, I wish we'd had longer to talk last night. You never showed up to play Scrabble with us. You met up with Kamber after we had dinner, didn't you?" Jerry peered at her, then glanced up at the second-story rooms.

"Andrea came back from her dinner date early. She had some history questions and asked me to go with her after dinner to talk with Mr. Kamber." The lie slipped easily out of her mouth. That's what decades of lying taught you.

"Then that explains it. We weren't up very long playing Scrabble. Richard thinks he's an expert, and I was tired. How was your 'night in the mansion'? The bedrooms are spacious, but it bothered me that I couldn't lock my door."

"I know. I put a chair in front of mine. Still, I didn't sleep very well. Weird dreams."

"Tell me about it. I'll be heading home as soon as I can this afternoon. Probably won't wait until the party is over." He smiled at her, and she felt a pinch in her stomach.

Her brain said, *don't fall for it. He's not who he seems.* Kyra knew what her brain meant. A one-nighter. A 'go for the gusto' type. Not to be messed with. She took a step back from him. What did he want from her?

"Not me. I want to enjoy every minute. It's a beautiful home."

Jerry tilted his head. "Beautiful?" He frowned. "Not the word I would use, but then I'm not glamorizing the family or the house. We're both observers, having an experience. I'm trying to figure out how this experience fits into my life."

Her brain buzzed. This experience? Even as attractive as he was, she didn't intend for their acquaintance to be anything more than that. Her anonymity and solitude were crucial to her survival.

"I suppose so. See you later, Jerry." She started across the driveway.

He reached out to stop her. "Look, I hope I didn't offend you. I would have enjoyed talking more, that's all. I hope you enjoy the party."

Kyra backed away and turned to study a dried hydrangea bloom. She shrugged. "I'm married and have a family at home. I'm not offended by anything you said."

"Good. We can both leave here with clear consciences. No hidden bodies and no skeletons." He grinned.

Kyra dropped her look to the asphalt. Why, of all things, had he referenced skeletons and bodies? Did he know what she'd found in the attic? She continued down the driveway, moving away from him and toward the greenhouse.

"See you later, Kyra. Enjoy the day."

Her head buzzed, and then Shimmer was in front of her, sniffing the soil of the empty flower bed outside the greenhouse. A large vacant dog kennel was attached to the greenhouse. She moved toward the ghost dog, but as she came closer, the dog faded into nothingness.

Kyra lingered, studying the kennel and the greenhouse. Both were empty and looked completely abandoned. Apparently, the Kambers weren't currently into gardening or dogs. But the original owners of the house must have been. Interests change as decades pass.

Nothing she'd learned yet explained why Shimmer had appeared here. What would the rest of the day bring?

Kyra pulled out her cell phone and typed in a message to her family, then sent it to Dawson and each of the kids.

"Hey, guys. The mansion is beautiful. Lots of pictures to show you. Hoping the party this afternoon is fun. I know the food will be great. See you in a few hours. Love you. Mom"

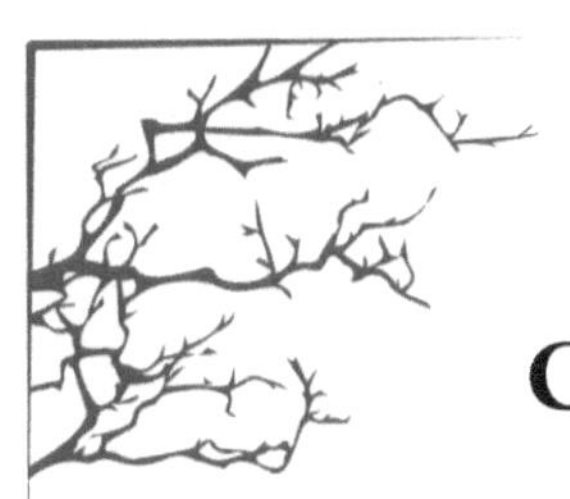

CHAPTER 16 - TY

Ty Harper glanced at his watch as Kyra Blackwood walked away from him. 8 a.m. She wasn't interested in getting to know him, and that was okay. Kyra was pretty. Even if he did feel drawn to her, he had never dated a married woman and she seemed committed.

He didn't need a woman right now anyway; he was a mess mentally. Sydney had wounded his heart, but he still dreamed about his ex-wife Darcy.

The morning sun illuminated the still-green leaves of the tall oaks that surrounded the mansion. He wandered down the driveway and over to Kamber Park.

Forget Kyra. He needed a distraction, something positive to focus on. The PTSD he suffered from often surfaced in an unknown situation, where he had no control over the circumstances or the people around him.

Ty had stayed up most of the night working on his laptop, investigating the other people in the house. He needed to know more about them to assure himself that they would not act in unexpected ways.

When he closed his eyes, he could picture the list as he'd assembled it:

- Matt Cleary – 62, a local man, OU graduate, 30-year career in local news after a brief career in coaching/teaching at Enid High. The business editor. Currently single. Ex-wife in California, another in Memphis. Grown children in Arizona and Florida. No prior arrests, three speeding tickets. Active on social media.
- Kim Spaeth – 48, mayor, OSU graduate, 25-year career and residence in Waukomis. Married to Richard (63) – his third marriage, her first. Three stepchildren, all living in California. Birth record: Dallas. Active on social media.
- Andrea Watts – 34, teacher (6 years). Pond Creek and the Enid NOC campus. From Bentonville, AR. Single. Never married. No

children. Birth: Tampa, FL. Active on social media.
- Kyra Blackwood – 38, Garber area ranch wife. Married to Dawson Blackwood for 15 years. Three children, Robbie (12), Declan (10) and Skye (8). No social media.

(That caught his attention. What woman in her 30s was not active on social media, especially when she had children to spout off about?)

He hadn't listed his friend Jerry. No need; he wasn't here. But in the description, he would have said, best friend of a former army buddy/recluse. Franchise owner of Dollar General, Medford. Birth: Martinsville, LA.

He glanced at the names of the two staff employed at the Kamber's house; Zia Anderson was the house manager, 40, and a lifelong friend of Mrs. Kamber. Taylor McDonald was Mr. Kamber's assistant, 42, a long-time friend/associate.

Sometime early this morning, Ty had read about the Kamber family online. While young, Nicholas and his older brother Stephen had spent the summers here with their grandparents. That changed the summer before his junior year in high school. Nicholas spent not only the next two summers but his junior and senior years, under the old man's eye. His prep school years were over. Nicholas Kamber had come to Enid permanently when his father, Adam, moved the family so he could help run the company after his grandfather passed away a few years later.

Ty scratched his head and sat on a picnic table, resting his feet on the bench. His body tingled with nervous energy. A sniper could be up in the trees, or someone could drive by shooting out of a car window. Highways bordered the park on the east and north sides. Sweat broke out on his forehead. He swiped it away, fighting the urge to go hide in his room. He stared at the mansion Kamber's grandfather had built and forced himself to think about what he'd learned in the previous hours.

The Kamber family made their money in oil and dabbled in technology but hit it big in real estate. Nicholas' father, Adam, delayed his entry into the family business but bought real estate for the right price in the right place before prices went sky high, adding to the family fortune. His son, Nicholas, took over the family business following the death of his father and then his grandmother.

Danielle was Nicholas Kamber's wife. They attended the same college, and then the same law school, where they started dating. They now have daughters attending out-of-state universities. Mrs. Kamber practices family law specializing in adoptions and engages in philanthropic endeavors.

Kamber had done much for the city in addition to running Kamber Company, including occupying his family mansion and keeping its listing on the historic register, a state and local treasure.

Ty's skin crawled, as if bugs were scampering over him. He surveyed the surrounding park. He was too exposed. He propelled himself off the picnic table, jogged across the park to the street, and then across the street to the mansion. He resisted the urge to look over his shoulder.

Once he'd passed through the front door and stood in the large front room they called The Hall, he began to relax. At least here he was sheltered. Tables were being erected in the living room and hall by a crew of uniformed helpers.

He took the front stairs up to the second floor and hurried to his bedroom.

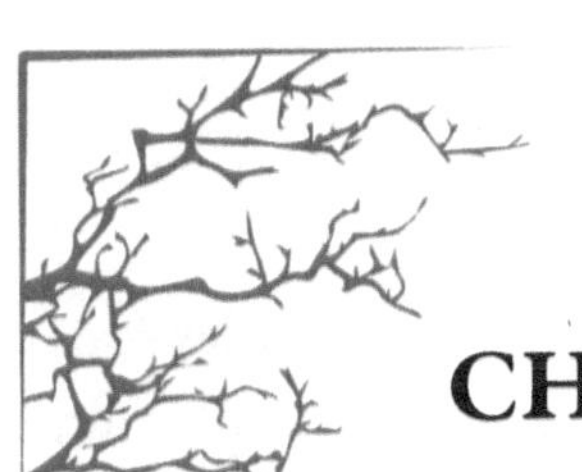

CHAPTER 17 - KYRA

Kyra had time on her hands. The house was bustling with party preparations. She'd taken plenty of pictures, and she didn't want to get cornered by Matt Cleary and forced to talk about herself so he could put it in a news article. And she didn't want to encounter Jerry again. He was good-looking, but something seemed 'off' about him. Uncannily, a glint in his hazel eyes tweaked her memories. Better to get outside and enjoy the park-like neighborhood.

She jogged across the street and then ran toward the far end of the park before looping back and turning into the neighborhood. This time, she avoided the street she knew so well, running past the intersecting corner without a sideways glance.

The long ranch-style homes were well-kept, the streets paved and curbed, and most lawn edges neatly trimmed. Tall pin oaks and evergreens studded the lawns, and flowerbeds full of lingering summer blooms and assorted colors of chrysanthemums spilled over brick borders. Painted shutters hung beside large windows, decorating the front facades of the homes.

The area was very different from the graveled 'street' that had meandered through the trailer park she'd called home for five years before she met Dawson.

As she ran past, a garage door went up at one home and a car backed out. At another, a kid on a bicycle wobbled down the driveway and into the street. A jogger turned the corner a half-block ahead and ran toward her. She raised a hand in greeting and ran past a woman kneeling beside a flower bed, pulling out weeds and adding them to a growing pile in a bucket.

Thirty minutes later, after running the grid of streets around Taft Elementary School, she turned back toward the mansion. She passed more homes that qualified as mansions in her mind before she saw the peaked roof and chimneys of the Kamber mansion a block away.

As she neared the mansion, she focused on architectural details, noting the roofline, the multitude of windows, chimneys, and the lightning rods on the roof of the big house. She noticed the stained-glass bay window on the second story, something she was sure she hadn't seen during yesterday's tour. It must be in the Kamber's bedroom at the south end of the second floor, a room Nicholas had not included on the tour.

Movement on the edge of her vision drew her attention. A large fluffy white dog sniffed the lawn. Shimmer again. When Kyra stopped, the animal wagged a plumed tail and lifted her head. Kyra offered her open palm and eased toward the dog, but the ghost trotted away.

"Shimmer," she called softly. The spirit animal ignored her.

She glanced at the nearby houses and yards. No one was outside in the immediate area. She looked down the street, then glanced over her shoulder at the house.

Why did she keep seeing the ghost dog here? What did that mean?

Turning back to the house, she inhaled deeply, closed her eyes, and felt the cool morning breeze on her face. She sensed autumn in the October day. Was it a smell, or something in the air? A lone crow cawed from a tree. Seconds later, another flew, cawing, from a tree in the park and landed on a gable of the house.

Kyra shielded her eyes with one hand and gazed up at the attic windows. As a child, she'd imagined living in a mansion like the girls in the books she read. Endless rooms to play in. Secret passages and hiding places everywhere.

Her adult mind took her to the realities. The house had to be cleaned and kept in order. Repair people had to be called to fix things. The electric bill, the gas bill, the phone bill, and the cable bill all had to be paid. Her grown-up self knew that living in a house like this was no fairytale, but full of responsibilities for the adults in charge even if a staff of servants was available to help with the actual housework.

On top of that, she knew all too well that no matter where people lived, or how they earned money, they still had problems. They dealt with disappointment, they got mad, discouraged, lonely, and jealous. Life was no picnic. Hers certainly had not been.

Kyra saw the ghost dog again, disappearing around the corner of the house. She started up the back drive at a slow pace, studying the landscape plantings. She wouldn't chase Shimmer. The dog would lead her where she needed to be, and for now, that place must be here.

To her left, a woman stood hidden behind big oak hydrangeas with leaves larger than her hand. Andrea Watts bent to capture the right angle while photographing a statue. A marble nymph frozen in time held a giant fish. Water poured from its mouth into an oversized clamshell.

"Andrea?" Kyra pushed through the bushes toward the fountain.

The woman jerked the camera away from her face and whirled, her surprised expression quickly changed to recognition. She exhaled deeply. "Morning." Andrea tucked her straight blond hair behind her ears, let the camera fall loose on its strap, and smoothed the front of her cream-colored blouse. "Taking more pictures. With a little work, this garden could be so lovely."

"Hard work." Kyra scrutinized the flower beds. Most of the soil surface was covered by fresh pine bark mulch.

"I agree. But the greenhouse is empty. They should have a staff of gardeners." Andrea glanced around the yard before shifting her look to Kyra. "Yesterday afternoon after the tour, you found the mummy. I was surprised when Danielle Kamber asked me to return to confer about 'something' that had been found. And there's no mistake. It's a dead body. Part of one anyway. And the party is still on. That car over there looks like an unmarked police car. It's probably Sergeant Murray's. Seems like there should be more police here."

"Do you know Murray?"

"I've heard of him. He was with the Enid Police years ago and heads a security firm now. Might be providing security for the party."

Kyra followed Andrea's gaze to a black sedan parked near the garage. Although unmarked, the vehicle had the appearance of a police vehicle. She shrugged, unwilling to vocalize a guess as to whether the car belonged to Murray or not. She was more concerned about whether Andrea would tell the others what Kyra had discovered in the attic. Would she also share her theory as to the possible identity of the mummy?

The Kambers did not want people to know about the attic mummy or have it mentioned in articles written about the weekend party. She would keep her mouth shut and keep her thoughts to herself, as she always did. She hoped that Andrea would do the same.

Andrea positioned her camera again and snapped more pictures. "I like being here. It's nice. Quiet. No disruptions. In the apartment where I live, the walls are thin. I never feel like I'm alone. I even wonder sometimes if the neighbors can hear my thoughts."

Kyra nodded. At home, she spent many weeknights and weekends alone. The kids were involved with their friends, school sports and organizations, and their electronics. Dawson always had ranch chores to do. He came to the house mostly to eat and sleep. Any conversation the two of them had was about trivial things. She'd like to have a conversation with an adult sometime. It was a consequence of keeping her privacy. No close friends.

Recently, it was hard to talk to normal people after days of having conversations with herself. When she did get away from the ranch to attend a meeting or church event, she was always glad to get home afterward to a place where she could hear herself think.

"It's quiet at my ranch, too. But I like it that way. Peaceful." Kyra could commiserate with Andrea. When she had lived at the trailer park, her world was seldom quiet. People zipped through on their motorcycles or peeled out in the gravel street. Music of all kinds blared, vibrating the fiberglass walls of her trailer. "Maybe you could find another apartment?" She had often made that suggestion to herself during those years, but in the small town where she had lived before she married Dawson, cozy apartments or small houses were hard to come by.

The women crossed the driveway together and stepped up to the side portico and doorway of the mansion.

"My landlord probably wouldn't return my deposit. I signed a two-year lease, and that was three months ago. If I'd known then what I know now ..." Andrea's voice had become soft and whiny. She shook her head suddenly, and her hair flew about her head. "Why did you enter this raffle? I just wondered if I could win, and thought it'd be fun if I did. Thought maybe I'd meet someone new. And I'll never turn down the chance to spend the night in a nice place."

"I entered on a dare. The rancher's wife wants a peek into a mansion. That's all."

Andrea stepped ahead of her and into the house. "You ought to talk to Matt. I'm sure he'd be willing to give you your ten minutes of fame in his news piece."

Kyra didn't respond. She'd just as soon stay under the radar, where she'd been her whole life.

CHAPTER 18 - HUGH

In the attic, Hugh cast aside his black hoodie. He moved to the side of the small window and peered down at the women in the garden below. The dark-haired one was looking everywhere, checking out the gardens. Since she had spent the night, she was probably one of the three women who'd paid good money to enter a stupid lottery for the chance to stay in the f'ing mansion and go to today's shindig. The rancher's wife most likely. Confident, curious.

He squinted down at the women. Different in size and shape. The brown-haired one was older, but, more than the blonde, she caught his attention. Shapely, taller, bigger boobs. The newspaper he'd read last weekend said the winners were from nearby towns. The fifty bucks they paid for the ticket had gone to a local charity. A hospital, a library, a children's daycare. Someplace the rugrats could go when Mom and Dad were not home. Doing community service for a DWI, he bet.

Hugh stepped back from the window and swayed, off balance in the blackness. DWI. Useless parents. Not his problem. And he'd never let it be. A smile started to erupt on his cautious face, but he squelched it, then blinked until his eyes adjusted to the darkness again.

He'd found the guest roster Thursday night on top of the desk in Kamber's office. Then he'd dug through all the drawers, picked the lock on the filing cabinet, and located the safe behind a section of the bookshelf. He hadn't found the code for the safe. No problem. Safecracking was his specialty. Unless Kamber had a safe equipped with a biometric lock, he could crack it open, no problem.

He was sweating like a pig, stink rolling down his flanks from his armpits, beading on his forehead. He was burning up. Yesterday, the attic had been a freakin' oven all afternoon and hadn't cooled overnight. No air moved. No windows to open. He'd stripped to his skivvies and emptied a water bottle over his head and made it through the second night. This morning, he could count the hours yet to pass on his hands. And then ...

Despite his aches and pains, he was ready for the party. Bring on the mayhem.

His crew was in place. Each of them knew what he wanted them to do, and knew they'd be paid after it was all over.

Hugh pulled back from the window and stretched, lacing his fingers as he reached his arms overhead. His joints cracked. He'd slept like crap last night, and not only because he'd been hot and uncomfortable on his makeshift pallet. Heart pounding, he'd been jumpy with excitement.

"Everything will go right," he whispered to the room even though he knew overconfidence was dangerous. In prison, he'd learned that if anything could go wrong, it would.

He'd made the plans. He'd checked and double-checked each detail. There would be no missteps. He and his team were ready.

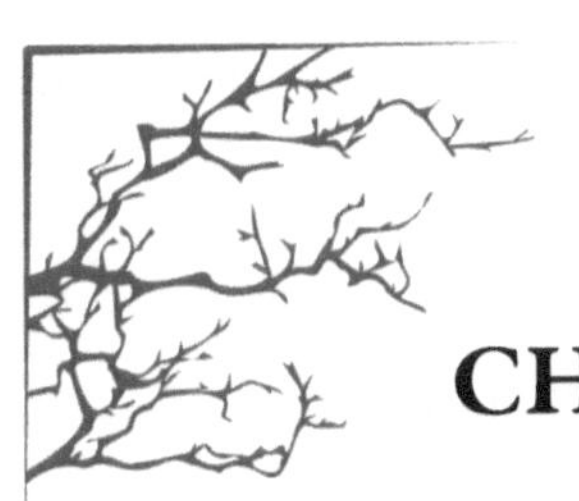

CHAPTER 19 - KYRA

As Kyra moved out of the kitchen and away from Andrea, heading toward the back stairs and the upstairs bedrooms, an attractive blond woman in slacks and a matching sweater/cardigan set sauntered out of the office. Their eyes met. The woman tilted her head.

"I don't believe we've been introduced. I'm Danielle Kamber. And you are one of the lucky winners. Right?" She smiled, revealing straight white teeth.

"Yes, I'm Kyra Blackwood. My husband and I own a ranch northeast of here."

"Oh." Danielle's smile faded and her lips thinned. "Well, I hope you're enjoying the house. I heard you've been exploring our attic."

The Kambers had probably talked at length about what she'd found yesterday. The woman had already judged her. Kyra forced a smile. "I've taken lots of pictures and I'm looking forward to the party you've planned." She wouldn't admit to any wrongdoing. If they had wanted the contents of the trunk safe from prying eyes, they should have either locked it or kept it stowed away. She wouldn't be badgered about it.

"I'm glad." Danielle Kamber appraised Kyra's athletic wear.

"Thank you for sponsoring the raffles. Your home is lovely." Kyra smoothed her hair. She didn't want to show that she was self-conscious in front of this put-together woman. At least her exercise clothes were fairly new, Christmas presents from her kids last year.

Mrs. Kamber tilted her head and studied her face. "I hope you had a good night's sleep. After finding that frightening thing in the attic, it must have been hard to settle in." She looked over her shoulder and down the hallway toward the salon. "It's a big house. Creaking floors and walls. Strange sounds that old houses make. Nothing to worry about." A smile flitted across her face. She straightened her shoulders.

"Have you wondered if there are ghosts in the house? Did any family members or any of the staff die here?" Kyra voiced the question that had been lingering in her head since finding the mummy in the attic. Not to mention the story of the missing teenager.

Danielle swallowed hard. "No ghosts. And nothing sinister. Just the walls and the floor, contracting and expanding with moisture and airflow. Or with the wind and outside elements."

She nodded but kept her eyes on Mrs. Kamber's face. "About what I found in the attic. Any idea who that might be?"

"Of course not. A decoration, I'm sure. I doubt it's even real." Danielle Kamber brushed at the front of her sweater, but Kyra saw nothing there to brush off. "No one here had anything to do with that thing in the attic."

But Kyra wasn't so sure. The house belonged to the Kambers, and someone had put that body upstairs. She thought again about the story that Andrea had told them last night. "Has anyone ever mentioned a possible ghost in the house, maybe related to the land or the regional history?" she persisted.

Danielle opened and closed her mouth. "David George. Some people continue to bring up that story. As I said, no ghosts here. I've opened a rabbit hole, and you have a wild imagination. I don't believe in such things." She stepped away and started down the hall. "I've so much to do to get ready for my guests. Enjoy the party, Kyra."

"Can I ask you one more question? About the dog?"

Danielle frowned. "Dog?"

"I noticed the kennels outside, and the dog in the family portrait in the lounge. Beautiful animal. A Spaniel? My cousin had one. Always wanted to play, especially to chase a ball. What was the dog's name?"

Danielle Kamber frowned and then her smile turned to a grimace. "It's been a long time since we've had a dog in the house." She turned away again. "No name comes to mind."

"But you keep the kennels?"

Danielle stopped. "They've been empty since Grandmama died. She was the one who loved animals." Her voice dropped. She cleared her throat. "No dogs here since."

Kyra sensed that Danielle Kamber was lying. But about what? And why?

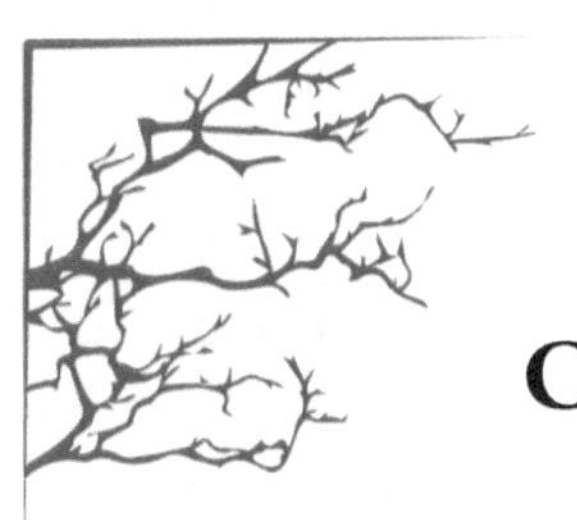

CHAPTER 20 - TY

In his room, Ty Harper settled into the desk chair and turned on his computer again. He scrolled through the news stories, scanning them until he found one of interest. It was about a gang working in the southcentral region of the United States, robbing wealthy people during dinner parties and group gatherings.

According to the online article, the gang included 4-6 criminals, and so far only a few minor injuries had been reported during the heists. Ty was well aware that things could escalate quickly if the victims resisted while being robbed. The crimes could become much more serious—deadly even—with the gang's next job.

Ty ran his fingers through his hair. His mind raced. This shouldn't concern him. He was no longer in law enforcement. But he couldn't keep his eyes, or his mind, off the article on his computer screen. He knew how things like this worked.

The gang had already targeted Dallas, Oklahoma City, Kansas City, and Tulsa and might be planning heists in smaller regional cities.

Although the article did not reveal anything about the investigation, he could see the authorities trying to get ahead of the criminals by focusing on social media, news sources, and event calendars. They'd zero in on upcoming parties or fundraising events. Work would include combing through arrest records, accidents, and accusations—anything that might link the families or hosts of an event to a scandal or perceived injustice. Strong emotions were always involved. Hate. Fear. Jealousy. Anger. Various scenarios, endless possibilities. Anything could set off an unstable person.

The Kamber family had a history here. Stories had circulated about what it was like to work for Kamber's company.

STOP! His mind screamed. Why was he imagining that a crime could be taking place at this party? He was a guest. He'd be back at his cabin tonight.

There was no gang working this party, and nothing suspicious happening. Why couldn't he turn off this part of his brain that was always on alert, always suspicious, always seeing problems where none were likely to exist?

For about the tenth time, Ty considered pulling out his phone and sending his ex-fiancée Sydney a text to let her know where he was this weekend. But did she care? They hadn't spoken in two weeks. And he couldn't sleep.

He should let her go. He'd been fighting this fight for months. It was time to accept that a relationship with Sydney was not possible.

Ty swore under his breath as he trudged across the room to the bathroom and a shower.

He traced their relationship history through his memories as he stood under the hot water spray of the shower.

He'd joined the FBI and started dating Darcy who was also with law enforcement. Now, so long after the fact, he could acknowledge that they'd gotten married because their relationship was convenient, and their chemistry was intense. She understood the pressures and dangers of his work even though her office job wasn't as demanding or as exciting as his. In his twenties, he'd been addicted to the unknown, to the excitement of adventure, even to the possibility that injury or death might wait around the next corner. Their sex life was one more addiction neither of them could break. Even now, he woke up in a sweat after dreaming about it.

Ty wiped the beads of sweat off his forehead and pinched his eyes closed, not wanting to see the scenes that swept across his inner eyelids.

Darcy had wanted him to settle down. Wanted kids. He couldn't do it. The thought gave him cold chills. Still did. No kids.

After five years of marriage, his aversion to a family caused constant bickering. Without the commitment of children to tie them together, they grew apart despite their fantastic sex life. Without asking him, she applied for and accepted a position in the field and left the office duties behind. For a time, the shared danger drew them closer. Then, their assignments took them to different places. They were constantly stressed. He worried about her; she worried about him. Neither of them was willing to compromise on what they wanted.

The lump in his throat made it hard to swallow. His thoughts raced. If only ... He couldn't go there.

After six months of being assigned to different countries, they divorced. A year later, he'd started dating Sydney. She had nothing to do with the law enforcement world and was fascinated by the excitement of his daily life. They'd become engaged, and then he had joined Special Forces and gone overseas. The bomb exploded.

He'd been chasing the ultimate adrenaline rush.

For Sydney, the ultimate consequences of his need for danger finally struck home after his injury. At that moment, what he needed was someone to hold onto, someone to offer him a sense of security until he could heal and work again. But that wasn't what Sydney wanted. She told him she missed hearing about the excitement of his former life.

He'd eventually discovered that wasn't all there was to it. In reality, she missed his out-of-country assignments, missed having him gone so that she could live a life very much like the one she'd lived as a single woman. Meet-ups at bars, one-night stands. Once he knew the truth, everything that had bound her to him unraveled.

There was no way he could make their relationship work. It was a real possibility that he couldn't make any relationship work. He would spend the rest of his life alone.

At one time, Ty had made fun of people like Darcy who talked about soul mates. Darcy had believed there was a special person out there for everyone, a person who would not need excuses or apologies. Yeah, the *Love Story* analogy, 'love means never having to say you're sorry,' even when you've been an s.o.b. He didn't think that apologies were overrated but he did believe that if someone knew you, they would understand when you messed up, accept your apology, and not make a big fuss.

If he ever fell in love again, he promised himself that he'd share much more about his work with that person than he should. She would keep his confidence and would understand that his safety as well as the success of his work depended on her, too. In his mind, he would think of her as a member of his team. Did such a person exist? Would he ever find her? If they'd tried harder, could Darcy have been that person?

Of course, that all meant that he had to heal, had to get well so that he could go back to work again. He had healed physically, but mentally, he was a mess. He kept reliving what had happened and at the same time, he was recalling more of his youth. Nightmarish memories from the years before the FBI had begun to surface at odd moments. He had no idea how to make them stop. This weekend wasn't helping.

CHAPTER 21 - KYRA

Kyra threw down the *People* magazine she'd been thumbing through. Why had she picked that up at the convenience store? She didn't care about those 'people,' especially the ones who made a living off posting their personal opinions and seeing how many 'likes' they could generate. Who were they, really?

She'd fixed a sandwich downstairs and brought it up to her room to eat, even though there would be plenty of food to eat later after the party started this afternoon. Kim and her husband were roaming around the house; she'd heard their voices when she was downstairs. She'd gone the opposite way to avoid them.

Their conversation would be a repeat of last night, she felt sure. She'd managed to divert many of the probing questions they'd asked about her life and her past by talking about her kids and her work on the ranch. Jerry Newcomb had not responded to personal questions either. He had managed to make it through last night's dinner adventure by making observations about Enid and swapping fishing stories with Richard.

Kim had willingly talked about how Kim and Richard met, about Richard's four children, and about how Kim became interested in local politics after ten years of teaching and administration at the local high school. Kyra had tried to focus on what she was saying and comment now and then. But she did not join in with anecdotes about her past.

It had been an exercise in killing time, and she excelled at that. How to hold a conversation and not reveal a thing about yourself. Her specialty. And apparently, it was Jerry Newcomb's specialty as well.

She had another hour until it was time to dress for the party, and she'd seen all of the mansion that she needed to see. As beautiful as it all was, she couldn't concentrate.

She had not noticed any police presence, so she assumed neither Nicholas Kamber nor Sergeant Murray had called the police about the mummy in the trunk. They could be waiting until the party was over. By then, she would be headed home. If the Kambers lied about the mummy's discovery, no one would seek her out. No one would ever know who that body had been or what had happened to it.

Did it matter? She'd be off the hook, and they wouldn't dig into her past. Could be a good thing.

She tried to convince herself that was true. It wasn't working. She wanted to know whose body that was and how it had gotten to the Kamber mansion.

And as much as she wanted to know that, Kyra wanted to know even more why Shimmer was appearing here at this house. It meant something.

Kyra lay down on the bed, but her thoughts kept her tossing and turning on the plush bedspread. Repeatedly, she thought she heard something in the attic above her. A stealthy footstep, a low cough. She wasn't going up there again to find out what it was.

She wrestled with why she was here. If there was nothing in this house for her to find why was Shimmer here, and why had her mind insisted she buy a raffle ticket? Why had she won the raffle? Why had she agreed to come? She didn't have to use the ticket. She could have stayed at home. But her brain had persuaded her easily.

She had wanted to come here. She had wanted to come inside the house.

The walls of the mansion loomed around her. The ceiling pressed down.

She wanted Shimmer to appear here, in her room. Without the dog, she felt completely alone. It was doubtful she would discover anything more than the half-skeleton she'd found last night. And that skeleton was not the missing teenager's. Whose was it?

Kyra pulled herself back to the present and got up from the bed, then slipped her feet back into her athletic shoes. She pounded down the front stairs and across the hall where a flurry of pre-party activities was underway. Then, she ran out the front door, and across the street to the park. The fast pace made her heart pound. She gasped for air; her vision was sharp and focused.

Her earlier anxiety at being here in this city and in this mansion ballooned. This place had lingered for years in her memories. It was a black hole, an unknown menace that haunted her. Fear kept her on edge.

Kyra peered up at the attic windows. Was someone up there? Had someone been moving around up there minutes ago, or had she imagined it? She wanted to know the answers, but she was too terrified to seek them.

From the distance of the park across the street, she watched a dark sedan pull into the front driveway. A woman wearing slacks and a blazer got out. Immediately, Taylor McDonald appeared at the front door; Sergeant Murray stood beside him. Were the police finally here?

They would want to talk with her. Kyra had to keep her composure. She couldn't say too much, couldn't let them consider that she was here for any other reason than that she'd won that raffle.

Taylor McDonald stepped onto the driveway, walked to the woman, and shook hands with her. The scar on his chin was not visible from here. Last night, the vivid line of the injury added something unexpected to his persona. Without it, he was still as handsome as ever.

Her thoughts shifted to Dawson. Tall and tanned from the sun, it was his grin and the sparkle in his eyes that had drawn her initially. They had met in the feed store. She'd been shopping for birdseed. In the scrap of a yard outside her trailer, she'd nailed a feeder to a tree. At certain times of the year, she fed more squirrels than birds, but the feeder gave her something to watch and something to care about.

Dawson had followed her around the store but had never asked a single question about her past, or where she was from. He wanted to know what she liked to do, what she thought about, and whether she knew anything about farming and ranching. He'd invited her to his parents' ranch, which he had begun to oversee as the foreman.

Kyra had tired of the loneliness she'd protected for so many years. She'd been young, 23. Wide-eyed, yes, but not exactly innocent. Dawson had disarmed her.

She pulled out her cell phone and punched the 'favorite' button for home. She needed to hear his voice. Then, as the answering machine came on, she remembered that Robbie had a soccer game this afternoon. They would be at the field.

She left a message for Dawson: "Checking in. I'm having a good time looking at all the rooms and furnishings. And I had a good run around the neighborhood earlier. The party starts in another hour or so. Guess I'd better go get ready. I'll see you tonight! Hope Robbie scored goals at the soccer match! I love you."

Kyra punched off the phone. She was going to go home tonight knowing nothing more than she had before, with no clue about the crazy memory/dreams.

Something twisted in her heart. When she decided to marry Dawson, she willingly gave up any ambition of her own. She'd never had any, except to be free of her foster parents, and be free to live her own life. She'd gotten a college degree after Robbie was born and finally developed dreams beyond having a family. She wanted to develop a work program for foster kids and set up counseling for foster parents in her area of the state, both programs designed to prevent the abuses she'd experienced. But it would be hard to make those dreams a reality when her own family had no idea about her experiences. How could she explain her compassion and determination to help?

Kyra stared across the street at Taylor McDonald. She might have lived another life if the circumstances of her early years had been different.

As if he could sense her watching him, McDonald glanced over, then waved. The others looked her way. She smoothed her hair.

Kyra jogged over to the group waiting on the driveway, heart hammering. She had to play it cool; she could not lose her focus. Nobody here knew who she really was, no one knew she was here to dispel nightmares and dreams and answer questions from her youth.

Then it occurred to her as she crossed the street, could she accomplish that mission if she didn't reveal who she was and why she was here? That would be the trick. So far, her only intentional step toward that mission had been to linger in the attic and nose around after the tour. Doing so had unintentional consequences. The discovery of the mummy.

Shimmer had appeared several times. Wasn't that significant—a sign she was where she should be and doing the right thing? A sign that she could accomplish her mission?

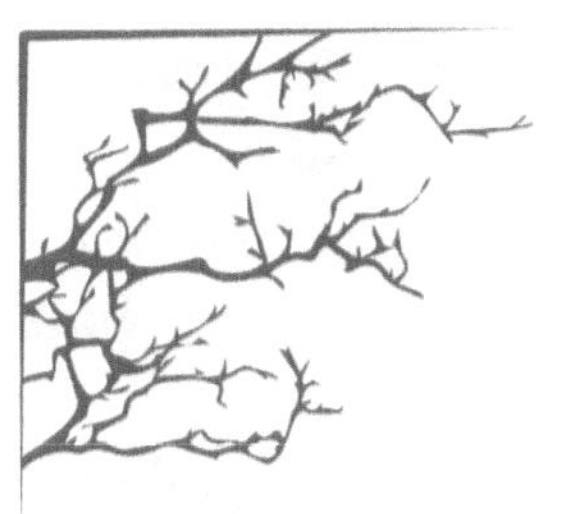

CHAPTER 22 - NICHOLAS

Nicholas Kamber burst into the bedroom, looking for his wife.

"Danielle, where are you? The wait staff is downstairs, and they need your direction."

"I'm here," his wife called from the bathroom. "I've been downstairs instructing them already. Now I'm touching up my makeup."

He stopped in the doorway of the glistening white bathroom and eyed his wife where she sat on the overstuffed bench in front of her makeup table.

"You look stressed, darling. Not a good look for the host of a party." She continued to blacken her eyelashes with a mascara wand.

"It's your party, not mine. And with this business of the mummy up in the attic ..." Nicholas ran his fingers through his hair and then rubbed his eyes. She was right, he was stressed. He didn't need this. He couldn't get that note about The Beast out of his head. "Did you leave a note in my day planner?" He'd thought it unlikely, but he needed to ask.

"A note? About what? You know that I keep all my paperwork up here, at the desk in the alcove. I have no reason to go into your office except to see your face a few times a day. Even then, you are often not there."

"I am taking care of the business, as you well know. But about that note ... Have you seen anyone going in or out of the office?"

She tilted her head and adjusted a short, black wig. "Mack, on several occasions. Could it be something he left there? A reminder, or a note taken following a phone call?"

Nicholas visualized the scrawled message. The icy dread he'd felt upon first seeing those written words dropped over him. "Not likely. Maybe I should ask him about it." He was certain that Mack had nothing to do with the note. However, he was likely the one person in the house who knew about the Beast. They had lived through that ordeal together.

"Is there a possibility it has something to do with that ghastly thing in the attic?" She put down her mascara wand and turned to face him.

Nicholas frowned at his wife. "What a strange thing to say. Of course not. That mummy has likely been up there way too long to be—" He stopped himself.

Danielle got up from the vanity and scrutinized his face. "What do you mean? What are you not telling me?"

"Nothing, Danielle." He shook his head. "I'm tired, and I'm concerned. I've been doing all I can to be sure we can continue with the party. And it hasn't been easy. If the police had their way, they'd cordon off the house, fingerprint us all, and administer lie detector tests. I think that skeleton is something my grandfather stored away. God knows why."

"Your Grandfather, or Grandmama? From what I've gleaned about her over the years, she would never stand for having something like that in the house. Your grandfather, on the other hand ... The bigger question is 'why.'"

"We may never know. A detective will be here soon to consider if an investigation is warranted. Would it be too much to hope that will be the end of it?"

"At least we won't have to deal with that while the party is taking place." Danielle gave herself one last look in the mirror and then strutted away from Nicholas and out of the bedroom.

Nicholas dropped onto the edge of the bed. He rubbed his forehead. That had been close. After all this time, he'd nearly told her. Mack had warned him that this day would come, that he couldn't keep a secret from Danielle forever. He'd assured himself that she didn't need to know, that it was one of those things that had happened long before they met. It had nothing to do with her, and nothing to do with the life he had built.

But, he conceded, she had astutely brought up a possible connection between the mummified remains and The Beast. Now he wondered, was there a connection?

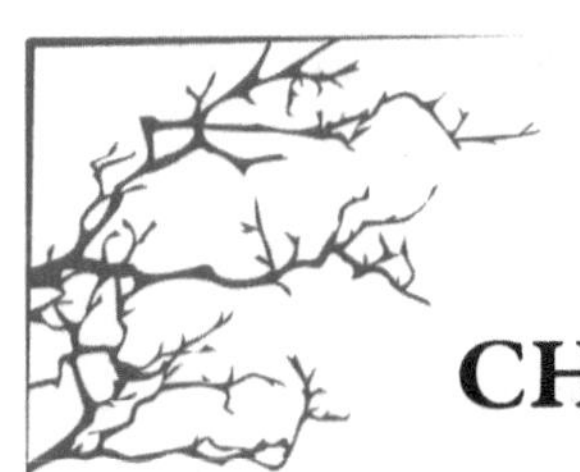

CHAPTER 23 - KYRA

Taylor McDonald and Sergeant Murray w their hands in greeting, while the woman simply smiled as Kyra joined them on the driveway.

"Ms. Blackwood, this is Nikki Wright with our local police department," McDonald said. "Detective Wright has questions about what you found last night."

Kyra focused on the woman with smooth coffee-colored skin who studied her with sharp brown eyes and a no-nonsense look. Kyra pushed her shoulders back and let out her breath. She would say what had to be said to answer their questions and nothing more.

"Sure. Inside somewhere?" Kyra asked. No telling what questions Detective Wright had for her. In her experience, women detected lies more easily than men. She'd be on her guard, using all the tricks she'd learned over time about what body language can reveal.

"After you. I'm guessing you know this house better than I do," Wright said.

Kyra shrugged. "Yesterday was my first time here, but Mr. Kamber gave us a great tour. Maybe we can talk in the salon. That's a nice room."

Taylor McDonald led the group into the house. In the hall, Seargent Murray motioned for Detective Wright to continue on with Kyra; he and McDonald stopped to speak with two other uniformed officers who had crossed the room to meet them.

"McDonald, may we use the study as home base?" Kyra heard Murray ask as she and Detective Wright crossed the hall.

"Of course. I'll have signage made so the guests know the room is off limits."

Kyra exhaled as she and Wright headed for the salon. She could surely keep it together to manage one detective on her own.

In the salon, Wright at once crossed to the wall of windows to look at the front yard and the park beyond. "Great layout here. Had you been to the mansion before, Mrs. Blackwood?" The detective turned her back to the view and peered at Kyra.

"No. That's why I entered the drawing; I hoped to spend the night and attend the party. Too good of an opportunity to pass up."

"You and your husband own a ranch?"

"Northeast of here. Cattle. We have a quarter section in wheat."

"Lots of uncertainties in ranching and farming. That must be stressful." Wright smoothed the sides of her head. She was wearing her abundant curly black hair in a puffy ponytail.

"We're at the mercy of the weather, and economics. But it's a great way to live. Fresh air, and independence." How often had she heard her husband mumbling about his chosen profession? But he had never talked about doing anything different or learning a new trade. She doubted he'd ever thought about it. At 45, he wasn't going to make a change now. He'd continue until he was too old to run the place. Both hoped one of the kids would want to take over at that point. None of them seemed to be leaning in that direction. But, they weren't even talking about college, yet.

"Did you know of the Kambers before you entered the raffle?"

"You can't live around here without hearing of them. Most people in the area come to Enid for shopping or medical reasons. The mansion isn't exactly hidden."

"True. There are a couple of mansions to the north on the highway, and some homes in the newer housing additions of the city that sure look like mansions. Agreed?"

Kyra shrugged. Wright was stalling. She suspected the detective wanted to ask about more than ranching. Had she looked for info about Kyra's life before her marriage and her family west of Billings? Thanks to her name change, there were no records of her childhood. But those missing years would make the police very curious.

"What was your first reaction upon seeing the mummy in the attic? Were you familiar with the story about David George?" Detective Wright circled the room, glancing at wall photographs and items on display.

Kyra pulled herself out of her thoughts and smiled at the pretty detective. "I was startled when I opened that chest. I probably shouldn't have done it, but I saw a chest like it downstairs, and I was curious. I didn't recall that story about David George until after Andrea mentioned it. I think I heard it in high school from a history teacher."

"You grew up and went to school around here? Tell me about your family."

Her heart raced. She'd opened the door to this line of questioning, and Detective Wright was moving through it. Kyra blinked and looked straight at her as she told the partial lie she'd been using for years when people asked about her past. "I spent years in foster care after my parents died. Too many schools to remember exactly where I was or when. Not a lot of happy memories." She rubbed her forehead and turned her look to the north windows and the evergreens that pressed in on the house.

"That's too bad. I grew up here in Enid myself." Wright cocked her head, no doubt expecting the usual follow-up questions from Kyra: what year did you graduate? What elementary school did you attend? Kyra said nothing.

She felt the detective's look on her. She wasn't going to respond to her questions or ask any of her own. Instead, she shrugged. Then she looked up with a sigh and let her gaze sweep the salon and the interior décor of leather and autumn-colored fabrics.

"This house is so grand. I can't imagine living here, having the whole place to play in as a child. All the rooms and closets. That immense attic. There were several rooms in the basement that we didn't get to see, including a wine cellar and a whiskey cellar. I'd still like to look inside those, but I haven't gone downstairs since Mr. Kamber's tour yesterday afternoon."

The detective smiled. "Curious even after all you've seen, and even after what you found? You are on a mission."

Kyra stepped away from her and moved to the window. The slight smile she'd pasted on her face disappeared. How had the detective guessed she had a mission? "Oh, you know. TV shows glamorize those types of wine cellars. Some are equipped with a tasting table, televisions, and sound systems. Do you think the Kambers have that kind of a room?"

Behind her, Wright cleared her throat. "A whiskey cellar sounds interesting to me. Wine cellar, I get, but the Kamber family must be whiskey aficionados to have a second cellar for whiskey. I agree with you about that. I'd like to see it too."

She turned back to the detective and pulled in a deep breath to settle the jitters that Wright's questions had set off in her stomach. "There isn't anything else I have to see. I've been trying to take pictures of it all to show my husband and my kids."

The detective nodded. "They will enjoy seeing those pictures. It's quite a house." Wright looked around the room again and then glanced at her watch. "You know, I bet no one would mind if you peeked downstairs. After all, the house will be open in less than an hour for the party, and people will be wandering around."

Kyra smiled. "No more questions? I'm always willing to tell you about my husband or my children, Robbie, Declan, and Skye." Anything but her childhood.

"I think you've clarified your interest in the house and explained the accidental discovery of the mummy. Anything else related to that you'd like to tell me?"

Kyra shook her head and looked at the picture above the fireplace. "Just lucky to win the ticket and get to come here. Nothing more to add."

Glancing outside, she noticed the yard crew using leaf blowers around the north end of the house, close to the large windows. Yellow leaves fluttered down from the big ash tree nearby. "Must be a lot of work to keep this place in tip-top shape, inside and out." She said in case the detective was thinking about asking her any more questions.

Wright looked out the window, nodding. "I can't imagine. The yard around my house is enough for my husband and me to take care of. I'll be glad when my son is old enough to take over the mowing. They've got several acres here, including the gardens in the back and the greenhouse. Lots to take care of."

"Beautiful back in the early years, I bet. Do Nicholas and Danielle Kamber plan to return the grounds to their original beauty?"

"Haven't heard anything about that. It would be expensive. I think most residents are happy to have him living here, using the house, and making it available for events." The detective stared out the window for another few seconds before she turned back to Kyra. "Why don't you go down and check out that whiskey cellar? I need to check in with Murray and the others."

When the detective tossed her a broad smile, Kyra relaxed. It didn't seem like Ms. Wright was out to get her after all. But that didn't mean she wouldn't continue to be on her guard.

CHAPTER 24 - HUGH

Hugh shuffled around the attic, kicking up dust.

Time passed so slow in this f'ing attic. And it was f'ing hot. A few more hours. No choice but to wait. Timing. Can't jump the gun.

If the damn thing fell apart, he'd be to blame. His plan, his timeline.

The note had been f'ing brilliant. Wish he could have seen Kamber's face when he found it.

The Beast. That's what the kids had called his son. Stupid idjits.

He'd taught his boy what was right. Stand up for yourself. No one else would.

He'd planned it all in prison. Lived each day for this. Kamber would finally get his due. This was justice.

Get in and get out, he'd told his crew. They'd get on with their jobs after, like nothing had happened. No one would question them. They'd been hired for the party. But they'd also do what he'd pay them for. After, they'd have extra dough in their pockets. And he'd have had his revenge.

Hugh scratched his shoulder and turned his head from left to right, rolling it on his neck. His neck joints popped. Last night he'd been too hot and too keyed up to sleep. His mind relived the past.

He'd been tough on the boy. Let his anger get the best of him. But the kid had to be taught, and his simpering wife wasn't going to do it. Bitch. Divorced him, and tried to take the boy away from him when he was in jail and couldn't do nothin' about it. She married that sob. Piece of work he was.

And Kamber sittin' high and mighty in his cushy mansion. The Old Man had his way with the boy and that s.o.b. and his once-wife let it happen, didn't even try to save Warren.

He could have told them they were dealing with the Devil. Did they ask?

Hugh scowled at the books that lined the shelves of the small room. He'd never been much of a reader. Nancy had been, but he beat it out of her. He'd been out of control, he knew that. Maybe he wouldn't have lost Nancy if he'd held his temper. Maybe he'd have been a better father to the kids. Maybe he'd still have had a family waitin' after prison. Maybe he wouldn't be alone.

His arm darted to the bookshelf and swiped at the row of books. They crashed into the end of the shelf, and two of them fell to the floor. Had anyone heard? He didn't need another snoop up here. The door to this room was locked, and it would stay that way unless Nicholas himself with his set of keys came up to unlock it.

Wouldn't be such a bad thing if he came alone.

The shelf creaked, and Hugh stepped back and watched the floor-to-ceiling bookshelf crack and split in two. One side swung toward him; an opening revealed a dark space. He grabbed a flashlight from the pocket of his windbreaker and flicked it on. He aimed it at the dark passageway crisscrossed by sticky spider webs that had opened along the inner wall.

So, it was true. There were tunnels in the walls. Dread dropped over him. He had to go through those passages. What if he found Warren's body? It would have wasted away, most likely be only bones, covered by the clothes he'd had on his back when he disappeared.

Hugh stared into the darkness of the passage. Anger bubbled inside him. His poor boy. If he found him ... if Warren had died here in this house at the old man's hand.... He'd kill them all, kill their friends... and burn the house to the ground. They deserved it. He'd be an avenging angel, and he'd never look back. If he died while conducting this mission, that was the cost of it. He was ready.

Maybe the truth would be found after all. Right here, in these passages.

Hugh growled at the darkness before he stepped through the opening.

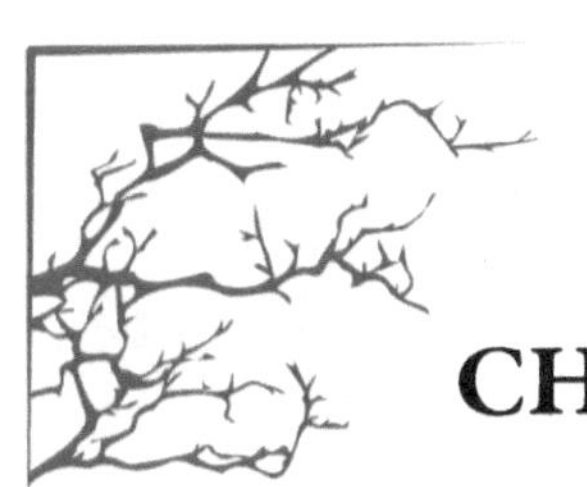

CHAPTER 25 - KYRA

Kyra walked out of the homey salon and around the corner to the stairs leading down to the basement level. She descended the steps slowly. At the bottom of the stairs, bright lights lit the hallway. The cream-colored linoleum floor tiles glowed with recent polishing.

Kyra glanced ahead. The door to the whiskey cellar was ajar. Kyra grasped the metal latch and pulled the heavy door slightly open. An automatic ceiling light clicked on. Ceiling-to-floor shelves lined the walls. Most likely made for storing wine bottles, the shelves were mostly empty. A small step stool had been shoved to the side of the room near the door. As she pulled the heavy vault-like door completely open, an acrid scent rushed out.

She gasped.

A body curled in a fetal position lay in a pool of blood on the far side of the room.

Kyra stepped back and lost her balance. She reached out to the door frame and steadied herself, then moved back into the hallway.

Kyra covered her mouth with her hands. She peeked inside the room again.

The gray face was turned toward the doorway. Open eyes stared at nothing.

Although the side of the head was beaten and bloody, she recognized the victim. She gagged and fought the urge to vomit.

She closed her eyes, hoping that when she opened them again the whiskey cellar would be empty of everything except shelves covered with bottles of assorted shapes and sizes, each filled with brown liquid.

Finding an old mummy in the attic was one thing, but this was entirely something else.

She opened her eyes again. The empty eyes still stared out from the gray face. Kyra shoved the door partly closed and dashed up the stairs.

Her mind churned as she pounded up the steps. Why had this happened?

This death had nothing to do with her, but she had been in the house all night, and she had found the body. She would be interviewed and fingerprinted. She would have to comply.

She would have to admit who she had been.

Surely the investigation would go no further than that. No one outside of the local police needed to know who she was. She would be lectured about her deceit, but, most likely, she would still be safe. Her life would not be placed in danger.

They wouldn't have to involve Dawson or her family.

Upstairs, in the study, Sgt. Murray, Detective Wright, and the two uniformed officers were talking in low voices. When Kyra opened the door, their conversation stopped. Murray frowned at the interruption. Kyra stepped quickly across the room.

"There's a dead body in the whiskey cellar," Kyra blurted. She wiped her sweaty hands on her leggings.

All four people stared at her. Sgt. Murray signaled for silence. "Show us."

The four of them followed Kyra into the hallway and then descended the stairs quickly in single file.

When they reached the basement hallway, Detective Wright slipped on a pair of latex gloves. The whiskey cellar door was slightly ajar as Kyra had left it moments ago. Wright grabbed the handle and pulled the door completely open. All five of them stared into the small narrow room.

"Any idea who this might be?" Wright asked. She looked at Kyra before she stepped into the room and then to the body.

"I think it's Matt Cleary, the Enid news reporter. He was here yesterday for Mr. Kamber's tour. He was supposed to spend the night."

Detective Wright felt for a pulse in the man's neck and then straightened. She scanned the small room.

"Is he dead?" Kyra asked in a low voice.

"I'm afraid so." Detective Wright lifted one of the man's arms a few inches off the ground and then let it drop to the floor beside the body. "He hasn't been dead long, a few hours. Rigor has begun but isn't complete."

Wright looked at Sgt. Murray and the other officers as she crossed the room to the door and pulled off her gloves. "I interviewed Ms. Blackwood upstairs just moments ago," Wright explained. "When the interview was over, Kyra mentioned that Mr. Kamber had told them about a whiskey and a wine cellar in the basement but didn't show them the rooms. She wanted to see inside the whiskey cellar. I suggested she come down here to do that before the party started." She shifted her attention to Kyra. "Tell me what you saw when you came downstairs a few minutes ago after our interview."

"That. I saw that. The door was not latched. Just slightly ajar. I pulled it open, and the light came on. That's when I saw him." Kyra cleared her throat. "I ran upstairs to tell you. I didn't go inside the room. I didn't touch anything." Something was clogging her throat. She coughed. "You'll cancel the party, won't you?" She could picture it now, the police rushing everyone out, locking the door to the mansion before the party had even begun.

"That's not for me to say. Normally that would be protocol. It's important to maintain the scene and to investigate everyone currently in the home." Detective Wright looked at Sergeant Murray and tilted her head.

Murray frowned and scratched his ear. "The Kambers aren't going to like this."

Wright pulled her cell phone from her pocket and turned on the camera/video function. "Stanton, would you record?" She handed her phone to one of the other police officers and looked down at the body.

"Male, late 50s or early 60s," she said. "Kyra Blackwood observed the body from the hallway after opening the whiskey cellar door. Mrs. Blackwood has tentatively identified the man as Matt Cleary, a news reporter with the local media outlet. Significant head wound, possible means of death. No obvious weapon, but many possibilities on these shelves."

From the doorway where they all stood, Sergeant Murray scanned the shelves and the blood-covered floor around Matt. Why did you come down here, Mrs. Blackwood?" he asked, frowning.

Kyra didn't like the look Sergeant Murray gave her. "Mr. Kamber didn't show us the whiskey or wine cellars during the tour yesterday. I wanted to see them. Detective Wright suggested I do it before the party started, just like she said."

Murray glared at Wright. Kyra hugged her arms close around her body. "When I got down here, the door was ajar. I pulled it open and saw Mr. Cleary," she repeated.

Kamber's security chief sighed as he looked at Kyra. "How is it that you've managed to find another body when you haven't even been in this house twenty-four hours?"

She glanced again into the small room where Matt Cleary's body lay. The side of his head was a bloody mess. The world began to spin. She reached for something to keep her from falling. Someone grabbed her arm and steadied her.

"Are you okay?" a voice in her ear asked.

She looked up at Detective Wright. "Give me a minute. Thanks."

"It's a little close down here with all these people," Wright said softly as she nudged Kyra away from the group in the hallway.

"Did you know the victim?" The Sergeant's voice boomed at her. Murray stepped away from the cellar door to join Wright.

"We met yesterday. We were all trying to keep up with Nicholas Kamber as he gave the tour, so we didn't talk much. Then I saw him upstairs yesterday evening before dinner. We spoke briefly." No need to tell them she had gone into his room uninvited as he was showering.

"Was that the last time you saw him? Did you have dinner together?" Detective Wright asked.

"I went out for dinner with two of the other guests. Cleary didn't go with us, and I didn't see him again last night, or at all today."

Detective Wright jotted something into a small notebook.

Behind them, heavy footsteps descended the back stairway. Nicholas Kamber rushed over to the whiskey cellar door. "What's going on here?" He glanced into the whiskey cellar and then took a step back. "My God. Is that .... Matt?"

"Sorry to say it is, sir," Murray said. "Mrs. Blackwood found him."

Kamber stared. "This is horrible. Our guests will be arriving soon. Danielle will be extremely upset. I've got to let Mack know." He shook his head slowly

Detective Wright grimaced. "About the party... Someone in this house murdered this man today. This party can't happen."

"What? Danielle will be devastated." He glanced at his watch." It's nearly 2 p.m., too late to cancel. The caterers have set out the food. Everything's on the tables. The bars are all ready. Everyone will be coming soon. What will we do when they arrive?" Kamber's look flashed from the body on the floor of the wine cellar to Detective Wright, his security chief, and each of the police officers.

Kyra turned away from the conversation in the hallway. The details didn't matter. They'd all go home. Someone had killed Matt Cleary. Emotions warred within her. She was sorry the man was dead, but, like Kamber, she wanted to party to do on. She hadn't accomplished her mission. She'd learned nothing that would help dispel the nightmares or answer the questions she had about her past.

Kamber continued to rant, arguing with Wright and with Murray. Kyra looked the opposite way, down the hallway toward the lounge.

In the anteroom by the narrow stairway, Shimmer stood, tongue lolling, tail wagging. Kyra started down the hallway, her heart galloping.

She glanced back at the group. No one was watching. She moved on.

When she reached the anteroom outside the lounge, the dog was climbing the narrow front stairway toward the iron gate on the main floor. As Kyra followed the ghost up the stairs, it passed through the bars of the gate and disappeared. The dog was trying to get her attention.

She still didn't think it had anything to do with the murder of Matt Cleary.

CHAPTER 26 - HUGH

Hugh followed the dark, narrow, passageway, alert to any turns or changes in the wall material. So far, he thought he was passing between two of the small attic rooms. Then the passage turned right.

He stepped slowly, putting his foot down carefully. Damn floorboards, he could just see them giving away beneath him, rotten. The fall would have him crashing down into a room below. Good that they weren't creaking. But, by the size of the spider webs, no one had been in this passage for years.

Another turn to the left, and then a blank wall. The passage ended. He squinted at the wall, then pointed his flashlight at it and ran his hand over the wood surface. Had to be a door. He felt around for a lever or a handle. Twice, he jerked his hand back when sticky strands of spider web stuck to his fingers. There had to be something that would open a door, or a hatch. Seconds later, he found the lever, pulled it, and the door swung open.

He was in a room at the end of the attic. His light showed seasonal decorations, garlands of fake pine needles and piles of red bows had been piled on the shelves. Wreath-making materials rested on a table in the center of the room. The door to the central attic space stood open.

Hugh stepped inside the small room. Behind him, the wall panel started to close. He watched. There would be another release on this side. He had to figure out where that was before the passage entry closed. If he didn't, he couldn't get back to his supplies in the room he'd just left; he'd locked the door from the inside and had left his set of keys inside it when he explored the passageway. As the door continued to close, a small piece of the shelf next to the passage door moved half an inch and clicked. He pushed it. The door reopened, then closed again.

This room felt cooler, and the air felt fresher than the room he'd spent the last two nights in. With the door open, he could hear if someone came up the stairs and entered the attic. With the lights off, even with the door open, it was a good hiding place. No one could surprise him. He had the upper hand, just like he liked it.

Hugh needed his bag from the other room to complete the first part of his plan. Everything else depended on it. He pressed the release on the hidden door to the passage and returned to his original room through the tunnel.

So, he was right, the mansion was riddled with secret passageways. Old Man Kamber had used them, sneaking around the house, hiding things, probably even hiding people–people like his son. The Old Man had been capable of anything. The family must pay for the father's sins.

His body shivered again with the dread of finding his son's body in another passageway. Warren had to be dead. If he was alive, he would have contacted his dad. He wouldn't have stayed away all these years on purpose.

If Warren's body was here, it would prove what he'd thought all those years ago. Old Man Kamber was the devil himself. His mission of revenge against the Kamber's was overdue. Warren's body had to be here, somewhere. He needed to find it.

His conscience poked at him. He felt a little sorry about what had happened last night. But that too had been justified. Nothing would prevent his mission from succeeding. Nothing and no one.

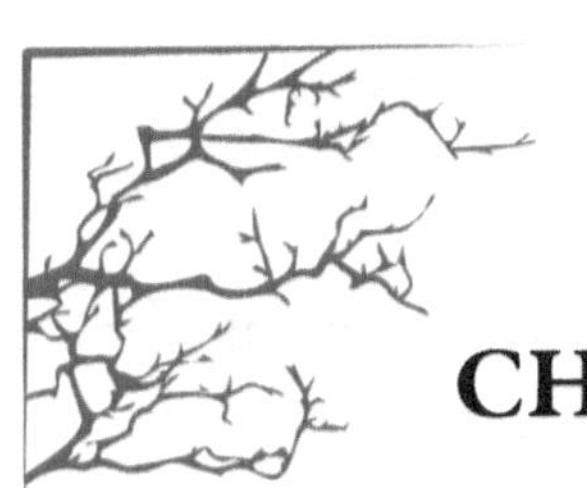

CHAPTER 27 - KYRA

By the time Kyra reached the main floor, Shimmer had disappeared. She glanced into the hall. The other three winners and Kim's husband Richard stood together in a corner of the room. Food tables were being set up, and the four of them were eying the steaming dishes as they arrived. Kim and Richard laughed, apparently ready to dive in and taste whatever wonderful hors d'oeuvres the Kambers provided. Ceiling fans circulated the aromas around the room.

She felt a brief hunger pang, but it disappeared when she remembered what she had just seen. The others were oblivious to what she'd found in the attic and what she had just discovered in the basement. She stood near the side door that led to the porte-cochere to compose herself. What should she say to them? Should she tell them about Matt?

"Kyra!" Kim called from across the room as she paused. The mayor hurried through the caterers and the food tables, followed by her husband, Andrea, and Jerry. Kim put a hand on her arm and peered into her face. "I think the police are here. I can tell by their somber expressions and their clothing that they are law officers. Do you know what's going on?" Without waiting for Kyra's answer, Kim stepped back and looked at her clothes. "You're not dressed for the party. Guests will be arriving soon. I think some are here already." She nodded toward a couple standing in the front hall, staring up at the crystal chandelier.

Kyra glanced down at the athletic gear she had been wearing all morning. Was there any need to change clothes? Like them, she would be packing up and heading home. The party was not going to happen.

Don't be so sure. Her brain whispered.

How well had any of these people known Matt? She'd spent little time with any of them, except during their dinner together last night. Kim had mentioned that Cleary was single for the third time. When Richard had called him a notorious flirt, Kim's face had turned a shade of pink. Her husband had coughed and held a napkin over his mouth.

"Well? Do you know anything?" Kim asked again.

She met Kim's look. "I think Mr. Kamber will make an announcement soon. The party may have to be canceled."

"What's happened?!" Kim's eyes widened. Jerry frowned. Andrea glared at her and then smoothed her hair.

Kyra cleared her throat. She had to tell them. It was all going to come out soon. She might as well start at the beginning.

"The police came to the house this morning. They are investigating something I found in the attic yesterday. I was snooping. I shouldn't have, but I was curious. I opened a trunk in one of the rooms under the eaves. There was part of a mummified body inside."

Kim's mouth dropped open. "And you didn't think to mention it at dinner!" She rolled her eyes.

"I was asked not to tell anyone. A detective was here this morning asking questions. The Kambers don't know who the mummy is or how long it's been in the attic. And something else. Matt Cleary—."

"Mrs. Blackwood, could I speak to you for a minute?" Detective Nikki Wright put her hand on Kyra's shoulder and turned her away from the group.

"What? What were you going to say about Matt?" Kim blurted.

Wright smiled soothingly. "You'll have to ask her later, ma'am. Kyra, could you step over here for a minute, please?" The detective touched Kyra's elbow and nudged her across the room.

"I was going to tell them about—," Kyra began.

Wright put herself between Kyra and the group. They were still watching the pair. "I know what you were going to tell them. Police Chief Casey has asked that we allow the party to go on as planned and that we observe. If the perpetrator thinks no one has discovered the body, they may return to the scene hoping to conceal or dispose of the body, or to remove the murder weapon."

"You found the weapon? It must have been something heavy. And with all those bottles sitting around ..."

Wright grabbed her arms and peered into her eyes. "Don't say anything more. An item has been taken in for forensic testing. We'll know more after the lab completes the assessment."

Kyra clasped her hands. "Someone in the house did this."

"We are investigating all possibilities. It's been several hours since his death. Lots of people on the premises. Lots of suspects."

"Including me, I'm guessing."

Wright tilted her head and peered at her. "You can start by telling me where you were all night."

"Seriously?"

But Wright's frown and intense look told Kyra the detective was serious.

"I was in my room all night. I woke at about dawn and went for a drive around the area. I came back here, and then I went for a run. I was at the park when you arrived, remember?"

"I'll make a note of that. If anyone asks any questions about Matt's whereabouts, don't reveal what's happened." Wright shrugged. "Maybe suggest that he's helping with details on the party? You'll come up with something. Meanwhile, you better change your clothes and come back down to the party. Cars are arriving. Act as normal as you can. And say nothing about the body."

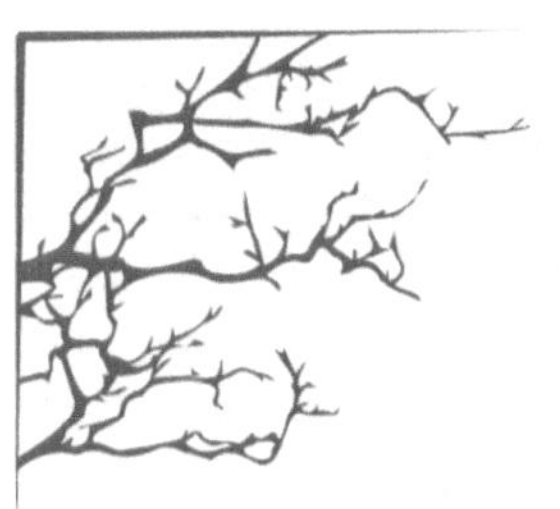

CHAPTER 28 - NICHOLAS

Nicholas Kamber abruptly dropped into the chair behind the walnut desk in the study. "You're telling me that Matt was murdered in my house? This morning?" Kamber swiveled the chair away from the desk, bent over, and put his head in his hands. This was unbelievable.

"You knew Mr. Cleary well, then. What can you tell me about him?" Detective Wright asked.

"I don't know him well. But he covers city events for the local news. You know that. He was going to write an article about our party." Nicholas rubbed his palms together. Where was Mack? He needed to be here.

"Married? Children? Any idea who should be notified?"

"Not married. Divorced. Several times. Not sure about children. I've no idea where he lived or whom he lived with."

"Have you recently had any problems with Cleary?" Wright probed. "Did you like him?"

Sweat beads appeared on Nicholas Kamber's forehead. "I hadn't seen him for several months. A year, maybe. I'll have to check my engagement calendar to be exact. He was nice enough. An acquaintance." Should he tell her he didn't trust the man? He was always after a good news item, even if it was only gossip. Nicholas couldn't risk a friendship with Matt even though they had known each other for nearly thirty years. There was too much at stake.

The detective nodded. "Where were you early this morning? Between the hours of, say 4 and 8 a.m.?"

"You're not suggesting that I—" Kamber looked her squarely in the eye. "Who do you think you are?"

"You know who she is." Sergeant Murray broke in. He'd been standing by the hall door to the study, hands folded in front of him like a policeman.

Only he wasn't, anymore. "And as your chief of security, I recommend that you cooperate fully. Let's contain this thing and help the police. I'm trying to protect you. Trust me. And tell her the truth." The Sergeant held Kamber's gaze. Finally, Nicholas looked away, shaking his head.

"I had trouble falling asleep last night, but I awoke at about 6 a.m., as usual. I got dressed, came downstairs, poured a cup of coffee, and went into my office. Read the news online. Did today's Sudoku. Taylor came in and we talked about the day's schedule. Party details." He stared toward the bookshelves, his brow furrowed. "I went upstairs to talk to Danielle. I don't know what else. It was a regular morning for me. I didn't see or hear anything unusual." Kamber sat back in his chair. His breathing had calmed, and the sweat beads had disappeared. He rubbed his shaved head with one hand. "Why did this happen in my house?"

Detective Wright sighed. "My department is trying to figure that out. For the time being, I ask you not to mention to anyone that Mr. Cleary is deceased, certainly not that he's been murdered. Can you think of anyone in your household who might have wanted to do him harm?"

"He was an assistant coach at my high school my senior year. Fresh out of college. But I don't know him well enough to know who might want to do him harm. He writes—wrote— for the local news. Online and print. Maybe someone didn't like one of his articles. I can't even tell you if the man plays golf." Kamber pushed away from his desk and got up to come around and stand in front of it.

"If you think of anything else that might be helpful, please let me know," the detective said. "I've called this in. More officers will be here momentarily. We'll interview everyone. Take prints. Possibly DNA swabs."

"Other members of my security team are already here. They'll be circulating too." Sergeant Murray rubbed his chin and crossed the room.

"That rancher wife found the body. Have you talked to her?" Nicholas stared at the detective.

"Detective Wright came here this morning as a favor to me, before notifying the Enid Police about that mummy," Murray said. "Her father was my partner in the force twenty years ago. She interviewed Ms. Blackwood about the mummy just after she arrived. Before Blackwood found Cleary."

Kamber rubbed his forehead. "Can I speak to my wife about Matt, about what's happened? And to McDonald? They should be told. Surely you can't suspect either of them."

"Don't speak to anyone about what's happened," Detective Wright instructed. "If, for any reason, someone asks about Matt, say you haven't seen him today. It's not a lie. You haven't. At least not alive."

"Can you ... can you tell me what happened? How was he killed?"

Wright shook her head. "The cellar is now locked. I examined the body and will file my report. The forensic team will arrive soon. Meanwhile, don't touch anything. I've told Kyra to keep it quiet, too."

Nicholas Kamber took a step back. "Kyra Blackwood." He shook his head. "Offering that raffle was a bad idea. I don't trust her. She should be your prime suspect."

"Did you know Ms. Blackwood personally before she came here yesterday?" Wright asked.

"No. And she apparently never learned to mind her own business. The minute she breezed through the door yesterday she had her nose in everything. The sooner she is out of this house, the better. I know that she was with Cleary yesterday afternoon, in his room. He told me himself."

"When did he tell you this?" Wright asked.

"Last night. He and I went to dinner. As I said, he was going to write about the party for the local news."

"What exactly did he say about Kyra?"

"He said that she came to his room. He implied that she was interested in him. Before yesterday's afternoon tour, Cleary told all the winners that ridiculous story about the teenager who disappeared decades ago. The kid's father blamed my grandfather for his disappearance. Of course, there was no substance to it."

"And Kyra wanted to talk to him about it?" Wright pushed.

"He didn't say. But he made sure I knew that he'd dressed for dinner after she left his room."

The detective made some notes on her notepad. "Okay. Any idea where I can find Taylor McDonald? I should speak with him." Detective Wright stood beside the leather sofa as she returned the small notebook to her pocket.

"He's around here somewhere. Supervising the caterers or something." Nicholas ran his hand over his bald head again..

"What time are the partygoers expected?" Wright asked.

"Any time. They were invited for an afternoon party." He glanced at his watch. "It's nearly 2." Damn. They'd all be arriving. Danielle needed to know what happened.

Wright and Murray left the study. Nicholas sank into the soft leather cushions.

Kyra Blackwood. He wasn't a fan. She had stirred up his world, first by finding that partial mummy, and now by finding Matt Cleary's body. And she had met with Cleary and probably did him yesterday afternoon. She was a rancher's wife, but she was more. He could see it in her eyes, as much as she tried to hide it. Was she something besides a winner? Was she here in this house for something besides a tour, an overnight, and the party? Did she know Cleary before yesterday? He should have pried into it and asked Matt the details of what had happened between them. His thoughts raced.

Had Kyra's background been thoroughly checked? Murray's favorite detective, Nikki Wright, had interviewed her. What had she found out before Kyra went down to the basement and found the body? The woman could easily have committed the murder hours ago and then pretended to find the body.

Nicholas left the study and marched down the hallway to his office. His grandfather's old chair creaked with his shifting weight as he sat down and leaned back. Creaked. Like the old man. "Thank God the man is dead." Nicholas freely spoke aloud, even though the old man could probably curse him from his grave.

What had he left him, after all? Inheriting a company worth several hundred million dollars was one big headache, and he'd realized it long before Danielle insisted that they 'finally' throw a party and let people into the house. Show off their wealth a bit. Share their lifestyle with friends.

He picked up a notepad and pitched it across the room.

So far, in a mere two days, all the party had gotten him was a note from The Beast, memories better off forgotten, and the discovery of a mummy someone had thoughtlessly stored in his attic. Who had done it? Grandfather? His uncle? A servant?

And that wasn't the worst of it. Now an acquaintance had been murdered in his whiskey cellar.

An acquaintance. That's how he'd characterized Matt Cleary. They were acquaintances now. They'd been a little more than that thirty years ago. Cleary had been a just-out-of-college assistant coach at the high school and had known most of the crowd Nicholas had run with, if you called it 'running.' A bystander in the restaurant where they'd eaten last night might tell the police the two men had argued at dinner.

Truth be told, he'd wondered if it was Cleary who had left the note about the Beast. They'd all taken a pledge of silence back then, never to be spoken of, never to be broken. As far as he knew, it hadn't been broken by any of them.

Last night he'd asked Cleary point blank if he'd left the note, and the man had denied it. Nicholas had pushed, asked repeatedly, trying to wear him down and get the truth, but Cleary had insisted he hadn't left the note, hadn't even thought about what happened back then for many years. After all, a promise was a promise. He was true to his word.

Cleary was now dead. If he hadn't sent the note as a stupid threat, who had?

Nicholas shot to his feet and paced around the desk, his footsteps following the familiar trail in the floor carpet, around and around.

Cleary. Beast. Grandfather. Mummy. Cleary. Beast...

He rubbed his temple. Then two new faces were added to the mix. Kyra and Matt. His mantra began again. Mummy. Kyra. Mummy. Danielle. Grandfather. Matt. Kyra. Mummy. Grandfather. Matt. Kyra. Mummy...

Why was he obsessed with the rancher's wife? She was an added element, true, but other than finding the old skeleton in his attic, she had nothing to do with his life, did she?

He wasn't sure about that anymore. Matt had said she was asking questions about that boy's disappearance. Why? Damn Matt for telling that story to them. Why had he done that? And why had Kyra been so interested?

Something buzzed in his head. The first time he'd met Kyra downstairs before he'd given the tour, he saw something in her eyes. Something that seemed familiar. The way she'd looked at him.

She was pretty, but not in the way that Danielle was. Not in the way of a woman well-bred and cared for, a woman with self-esteem and the funds to allow her to look good as she aged. It was in the way she held her head. Kyra seemed confident. The look in her eye made it very clear that she was curious and willing to take risks.

Maybe that's what he recognized in her, she was a risk-taker like he was. And Danielle.

But there was something else. It was like she *knew* him. But that wasn't so. He'd never seen Kyra Blackwood before in his life. He blew out his breath and turned his mind to other things.

The mummy should have been removed by now. The forensics team had come this morning, and they should have finished hours ago. That thing was surely out of his house.

Nicholas stepped into the empty hallway. No security staff, but he glimpsed activity in the front hall, people setting up the buffet, and others working on the beverage bar in the living room.

He slipped across the hallway to the backstairs, climbed to the second floor, and then to the third. He opened the attic doorway and waited, listening for any bit of activity. All was quiet. The lights were off.

He walked into the first of the two large rooms—pitch black—and reached for the light switch. No reason not to. No one else was there. He'd find out what he needed to know and return to his office. He flipped the switch. Light from bare bulbs suspended from the ceiling cast halos on the floor. The usual musty, dusty smell and the scent of human sweat floated in the stagnant air.

Nicholas studied the room, searching every shadowy corner for movement, for something unfamiliar. Nothing. He strode across the first half of the attic and then paused before the remaining portion of the central room. The old train set. A pain speared his gut.

He should have torn it down long ago, thrown the track away as well as the buildings he and Stephen had built. He had good memories of them working together, but they were eclipsed by one winter afternoon. They'd been up there hard at work, and suddenly the Old Man had strode off the elevator and intruded into the space the boys had claimed as their own.

In hindsight, Nicholas suspected the Old Man might have been drinking. That day and many days. He'd kicked them out of the attic. And when Nicholas eventually made it back up there, the train engine, the coal car, boxcars, and caboose, were gone.

Nicholas pulled his look away from the track, seeking something to take his mind off the tightness in his throat. A pile of boxes, a rocking horse, a child-sized plastic kitchen. The detritus of his family.

He crossed the attic. When he reached the door to the room that had held the chest and the partial mummy, he pulled out his keyring and sought the blue key that would open the door. He inserted it in the lock, turned the knob, ducked beneath the crime scene tape, and stepped into the room. The ambient light from the outer room revealed the trunk, its domed lid standing open, the interior empty. The mummy was gone. As he crossed the room, he reached up for the light bulb hanging from the ceiling and pulled the cord. Nothing happened.

The bulb had been dim yesterday, hardly offering adequate light when they were all up there to view the trunk. The light from the bulbs in the larger nearby room was not bright enough for any further investigation. He had left his iPhone, with its flashlight function, downstairs in the office. He stepped farther into the room and waited, allowing his eyes to adjust to the dimness.

Nicholas did not remember seeing the trunk in the attic before yesterday. Yes, there was one downstairs in the anteroom outside the lounge, and it too bore his grandfather's initials. That trunk was in much better shape, less scuffed, and the interior lining was intact. This one seemed older, dirtier, more battered.

The forensics team had been here. The area around the trunk had been cleaned, and the items stored around it shifted out of place. Why hadn't the police taken the trunk itself?

He heard a scuffing sound somewhere in the attic. Then, the overhead lights in the main rooms blinked out, leaving him in total darkness.

"Hey, I'm up here. Turn the lights back on." He listened and waited, trying to quiet his rapid breathing, hoping the lights would come on again, or someone would respond to his call.

Footsteps trudged across the attic.

"Hello? Turn the lights on, please. This is ridiculous."

He sensed air movement and stared into the blackness toward the doorway but was unable to even make out a pinprick of light from the central room. He sensed something darker than the background of the attic moving his way.

Nicholas Kamber could think of no one who would wish him harm, and no one who would play a joke like this on him. But someone was. Any moment now, a flashlight would flick on, and someone would cry, "Boo!"

Grandfather would have played such a joke.

A breath of air moved. The blow came out of nowhere. Nicholas Kamber fell to the floor in a heap.

Sometime later, Nicholas woke up. His head felt as if it had been split in two. Not even the pounding headache he'd had yesterday compared to this.

He forced his eyes open. Blackness. But he sensed another presence, and gooseflesh rose on his arms. He was not alone. His mind filled with thoughts of his grandfather. Damn the man.

Whoever was with him in the room did not speak, and he could not hear them breathing. Yet, he sensed them. And he smelled the lingering acrid scent of human perspiration.

When he turned his head to see who was with him in the room, a quiet voice said, "*The Beast Returns.*"

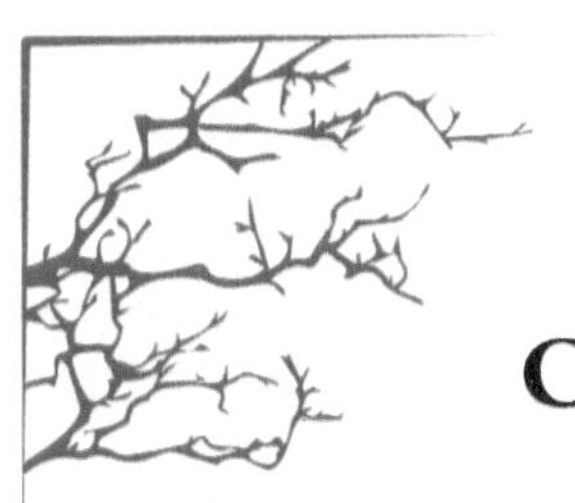

CHAPTER 29 - TY

Ty Harper watched a woman he didn't know move away from Kyra Blackwood and the other people in the living room and hurry toward the kitchen. She had the purposeful look and walk of a police officer. A detective? No doubt she was here to interview the catering staff and to ask if anyone knew anything about what Kyra had found in the attic last night.

He wished he knew what that was, wished he'd seen it. But then, probably better that he had not. It might have been a trigger, and he didn't need to have one of his episodes this weekend. No one here had any idea what he suffered from. No idea that he was NOT a raffle winner, that he was a substitute, a stand-in for a buddy who knew that Ty had an interest in this mansion and knew the history of the family and the house.

Jerry knew Ty's history, and so did Ty's ex-wife, Darcy. He'd not told anyone else. But then, he didn't talk much to anyone anymore. He wouldn't speak of that history to anyone ever again. There was no need.

The craziest thing about this weekend was his interest in Kyra. There was something about her. She had secrets like he did, and she had an intensity about her, a purpose. He saw it in her eyes. But he doubted either of them would ever know the other's secret. He wouldn't talk, and she wouldn't talk. Surface banter was all he'd get from Kyra. That was all he'd given and gotten from just about everybody but Jerry, and years ago, Darcy.

So much of his memory was mush. The army shrink had tried to help him retrieve his memories when he returned from the Middle East, but after a little bit of prodding, he'd stopped going to the sessions. He did his best not to put himself in certain situations that would trigger his PTSD. He usually succeeded. The attic had almost triggered an episode yesterday afternoon. He didn't intend to go up there again.

Viewing a body or a brutal crime might also be a trigger. He kept his eyes open and scanned the living room. Nothing scary here. Nice furniture, pleasing walls painted blue. Heavy fringed drapes on wide sparkling windows, a beautiful fireplace with a white marble mantle. Expensive. Beautiful. Calming.

Zia had let him into the house after his arrival yesterday without even checking his ID. He and Jerry Newcomb resembled one another in height, weight, and coloring. Jerry had even lent him his driver's license in case there was any kind of formal process of identification.

No one had checked for Jerry's name on the winners' roster.

He thought about insinuating himself into the investigation into what Kyra had found, but he no longer had his credentials. He wasn't police and never would be again if he couldn't get his head on straight.

Ty wandered over to the bar and ordered a cola. The bartender smiled at him. He'd changed clothes into a new golf shirt, sports jacket, and slacks. He'd shaved close, his cheeks looked smooth and a little sunken due to the weight he'd lost recently. The scars from the bomb blast were vivid on his cheeks and forehead.

He patted his jacket, feeling the set of small tools he always carried in his inner pocket. It was a reflex to have them with him. He could no longer carry a gun, but the tools were the next best thing. They'd gotten him out of many predicaments. But they hadn't helped him with Darcy, or with Sydney.

It hadn't mattered to Sydney at first that he was going through a tough time after the bomb blast. She stuck by him as he healed physically. Then, when he kept freaking out when they were together—on the street, at restaurants, at the movies—he guessed that she had just had enough. Period.

Darcy had been a different story altogether. A different time. But he still thought he saw her everywhere in Tulsa. Hardly a week went by that he didn't think he saw his ex-wife sitting at a table in a restaurant on Cherry Street, getting into a car on a busy street like Yale, stepping into an elevator in a downtown office building, or staring out the window of a passing car. So, he stayed on his acre by the lake. And he spent a lot of time with Jerry.

Ty limped across the room with his cola. The woman detective had gone into the kitchen. He stepped into the hallway and paused outside the kitchen doorway. Her conversation was easy to overhear.

"Detective Nikki Wright. I'd like to ask you a few questions."

Startled, the young woman, her streaked hair pulled into a tight ponytail at the top of her head and her brown eyes thickly lined with black, wiped her hands on a white apron. "Sure."

"Your name, please?

"Sissy Patel. I'm here to help with the party."

"Did you work yesterday?"

"Yes. Pretty much all day. 8-4 anyway."

"So, you were working. What did that involve?"

"I spent most of it in the dining room, polishing silver and then here, rinsing, and drying glasses. Would have been better if they'd rented the stuff from my boss. Less work for us. Cheaper, too." The young woman shook her head and grinned slyly.

"And what time did you get here today?"

"Too early. 8, I guess. Been here ever since. Probably time for a break." She looked around the kitchen, presumably for signs of the person from whom she took orders.

"Did you notice anything when you arrived? See anybody outside or inside who wasn't here yesterday?" Wright asked.

The young woman thought for a minute. Then she pouted her lips and shook her head. "Nope. An old lady met me at the door. The other older worker was already here. Didn't see anyone else." She nodded toward the other woman in the room, whose back was toward the hallway where Ty Harper stood listening.

"Did you hear anyone else? Any conversations going on in the hall or maybe in the dining room?"

"Nope. Like I said, nobody else was around."

"And nobody went downstairs or came up from downstairs after you arrived?"

"Didn't I tell you nobody else was around?" She crossed her arms and glared at Detective Wright.

"All right, Ms. Patel. You can get back to work."

That woman returned to the sink and the other woman glanced at Wright.

"A moment of your time, please?" Nikki asked.

The woman folded her towel, laid it next to the sink, and stepped over to the detective. He listened from outside the room as Wright repeated her questions for the second woman.

Ty could see a bit of her profile. Her dark hair hid the rest. His heart began to pound. She resembled Darcy. The woman was speaking so softly, he couldn't make out the words.

Why would Darcy be here? Ty was puzzled over the possibility. Could she be undercover? Working on an investigation? Something clicked in his mind. Could she be here because of the robberies he'd read about on the internet?

He strained to hear, but all he could make out before the woman stepped away was Nikki Wright saying, "Let me know if you hear anything helpful."

"Oh, I will." The woman turned, saw Ty in the hallway, and locked eyes with him. Her short dark hair accented her sharp features and deep, dark eyes. She smiled.

Darcy.

Ty's eyes widened. The break-up with Darcy had been bitter. She'd been venomous in her correspondence. But years had passed. She couldn't have recognized him, she'd merely been smiling at a stranger. He'd aged. Not to mention the scars …

The woman flipped her hair off her face and then muttered to Sissy Patel. Knowing how Darcy acted when she was undercover, he imagined it was something like "f'ing police." The scent of lemons lifted into the kitchen as the younger woman scrubbed the sink with a cleanser.

He remembered that the name Darcy often used when working undercover was *Chloe Sessions*.

He blinked and turned toward the living room. More people had come into the party, some wearing elaborate costumes, others with a mask concealing part of their face.

Instantly, the tightness in his chest loosened. No one here had any idea he was not who he claimed to be. He didn't need a mask to be unrecognizable.

Ty stepped through the side door at the porte-cochere and nearly collided with a young, uniformed valet. His name badge read 'Carter.' Scrawny with curly brown hair down to his shoulders, a rhythmic beat sounded from the earbuds pushed deep into his ear canal. He pulled one out as he looked at Ty, then fingered his hair, pushing it behind his ears, combing through it with his fingers. A faint marijuana smell clung to his uniform shirt. "Sorry man. Just parking cars."

Ty nodded, then ambled around the house to the circle drive and up to the front patio. Off to one side, a man who looked to be in his mid-twenties was equipping a valet station. A tall, narrow table, draped in black, held a board with key hooks and circular numbered tags. The man looked up and assessed Ty with clear blue eyes as he passed. Acne scars dented his cheeks.

"Great weather. Parking cars won't be a bad gig today," Ty said. He glanced up at the cloudless sky and the leaf-filled canopies of the tall trees.

"Not a bad day. I've already parked four or so. Did you park your car in the street?"

"I'm in the back. Came in yesterday." Ty nodded toward the street. "Are you local?"

"No. The temp agency pulled me up here for this gig. I live in Oklahoma City."

"Good to know. Hope you get lots of tips. Looks like a good crowd for that." Ty nodded and then stepped toward the front door where a man stood, his hands folded in front of him. A security guard. They nodded at each other.

In the living room, a woman was setting up the bar. Slim, with long dark auburn hair falling to her waist, she looked up as Ty entered the room. A cooler with bags of ice sat on the floor behind the bar with a small refrigerator nearby.

"What can I get you? I've got beer, most liquors, and champagne. Soda pop in the frig lemonade, orange juice ... name it."

"Nothing for me right now. Just wandering around until this party gets started." He smiled and reached up to smooth the hair on the top of his head where a cowlick often went astray.

"I'm DeeDee. I bartend in Stillwater three or four nights a week. Have I seen you there?"

"Doubtful. I'm not a drinker, and I don't socialize." But Ty knew it was possible. He'd been out to the bars with Jerry a few times, early in the evening before the crowd got rowdy. Ty and the bartender chatted about life in a college town until they were interrupted by new arrivals. He stepped away, scanning the room, looking for Kyra. She wasn't there.

Disappointment pinched his stomach. What was it about her? She didn't care much for him. Was even avoiding him. So why did he care? He doubted he'd have the opportunity to learn any more about her. It wouldn't matter after today.

Ty headed for Kim and her husband, the only other people in the room he knew. He skirted a group who had come in through the front door. The woman threw back her head and laughed while one of the men checked out the other partygoers in the living room.

The party had officially begun.

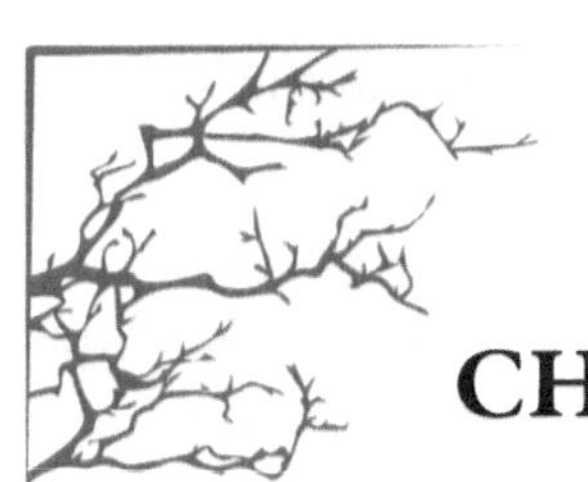

CHAPTER 30 - KYRA

Kyra stared out the window of her bedroom, looking down over the driveway. Cars were pulling in. One man checked in the cars while the other took the keys from the drivers and parked the cars along the street or to the side of the long driveway.

As the people got out of their vehicles, she studied the way the women had dressed, hoping that what she had brought to wear would do. She didn't want to look like a country bumpkin. She purposely avoided that look whenever she was away from the ranch.

Some of the women wore costumes—everything from a Roaring Twenties flapper dress to a 50's Poodle Skirt. One woman appeared in a 'Gone with the Wind' gown, complete with a hooped skirt and a corset that pinched her waist. Another older woman had dressed in formal wear, with elaborate jeweled earrings and a matching necklace. Others seemed dressed for a garden party.

The October day was warm, and Kyra was happy to wear the clothes she had brought. It wouldn't matter if she didn't have a costume. She was an anonymous guest to everyone but the other winners.

In the mirror, her face looked pale. But her thick brown hair shone and curled slightly below her shoulders. She swiped powder blush on her cheeks and forehead and carefully applied lipstick. With a touch of luminous eye shadow, her look was complete. Not bad.

Dawson had called her a 'looker' when they first met, but it hadn't been that way in her early teenage years. She remembered clearly how she'd dreaded leaving the house, dreaded being at school in the hallway with the whispers, or in class with the stares. And then she'd fallen for the worst possible ruse—a cute, popular boy who'd suddenly paid attention to her.

He'd enticed her in the park and sat on the swing beside hers, gently rocking back and forth. Slowly, he'd drawn her out in conversation and encouraged her to share with him the story of her life, of who she was, and how she felt about life and living in Enid.

She'd told him about what it was like to be a foster child. Not loved enough to adopt, no 'real' family to go back to, not even a great aunt or a second cousin who might decide that they 'wanted' her after all. The words had poured out of her, and that boy had listened and asked for more.

She was so unused to the attention, so unused to being asked what she thought and felt. She had read it all wrong, had read into it that the boy cared.

But then, after it had all happened and her second foster family was disintegrating and no longer cared to have her in their home, she'd had no choice but to run away. Two families that didn't want her. Two families that never cared if they saw her ever again. And she didn't care if she ever saw them again either, not even her missing foster brother.

That night she left was the first time that the voice in her brain had told her what to do. *Write a Note that says: I'm ready to be on my own. Goodbye.* She'd done exactly that.

Another runaway. Nothing in the newspaper, and no missing person's report. Just as well. She didn't miss them either.

She glanced out of the window one more time and then went to the full-length mirror hanging on the closet door. Her floral blouse fit her well and accentuated the waist she had worked so hard to keep under 28 inches. Her breasts filled the top out nicely. And her hips ... Well, she'd given birth three times, and there was no way that she'd ever heard of to make her hips any less wide after going through that. Her slacks were sleek and comfortable, and the low-heeled sandals she wore were practically brand new. Her outfit would have to do.

She was no closer to getting the answers she'd hoped to find here. Shimmer was in the house but had not appeared since they'd found Matt Cleary's body. What did his body have to do with her or any mystery in this house? She hadn't liked the man, but then she hardly knew him. Someone had known him well enough to want to kill him. Why?

She'd not heard another word about the mummy. She assumed it had been taken away, but she'd not seen anyone except Detective Wright and the two other officers in the house.

Kyra hated having been the one to discover those two bodies. The morbid nature of it felt like a stain on her soul. Why couldn't it have been someone else who'd found them? Yes, she was overly curious, and yes, she had come here on a mission, but she had wanted it to be a simple discovery, not one that brought in a police detective and a smart security guard who seemed very curious about her.

Kyra stepped slowly down the front staircase, her gaze taking in the interior of the house with each step, imagining that she was someone else and this glorious place was her home. Groups of people stood talking in the front hall, others had moved into the living room where hors d'oeuvres and a bar had been set up.

At the same time, dark memories/dreams swirled. She was in the house at night, the interior dark. She never saw the paintings on the walls or the crystal chandelier in the front hall.

Now, the slate floor shone, and the mid-afternoon light through the stained-glass windows cast a fairy-tale glow on the entry hall.

It was a different place than that she'd dreamed/remembered. She let the current beauty wash away the dim memories, as well as the recent memories of the mummy in the attic and the corpse in the whiskey cellar.

Kim and her husband Richard stood in the living room at the fireplace, and as Kyra entered the room, Kim waved. Kyra started across the room but stopped and looked back when everyone else in the room quieted and turned toward the hall.

Dressed in a slinky white silk dress reminiscent of the opulent Roaring '20s, Danielle Kamber paused at the bottom of the stairs. She wore long beaded necklaces, carried a cigarette in a silver holder, and had a white feather tucked above one ear and into her short black wig. She looked at each of her guests in turn, smiling wide. To Kyra, her blue eyes looked dead, emotionless. Her husband was nowhere in sight.

Taylor McDonald stepped up and handed Danielle a sheaf of papers. After taking them, she beamed at her guests again.

"Welcome." Her voice shook a little. "We have a fun afternoon and evening planned for you. You'll find appetizers here in the living room, as well as a bar serving assorted beverages. Please circulate and meet those you don't know.

"I'll be handing out a sheet of information that you will need if you plan to participate in our scavenger hunt. I hope you will. Please note that the basement hallway is not included as part of the hunt. Neither are the backstairs to the basement. Feel free to use this stairway behind me to access the lounge in the basement during the party this afternoon. Have fun." She moved across the room smiling, greeting each person, and handing them an instruction page. She didn't stop for conversation.

Danielle ignored Kyra and the other winners until the pages were distributed, and then she made her way across the room to Kim and Richard. Kyra joined them. Moments later, Jerry and Andrea stepped up to complete the group of raffle winners.

"If I could have your attention for one more minute. I'd like to introduce the winners of the county-wide raffle we sponsored for this event." Danielle gestured to the winners. "I want to thank each of them for coming and for their contribution to their local charities. I'm also giving each of them one of these sheets. Consider them experts. My husband took them on a tour of the house yesterday, and they spent the night here. Feel free to ask them questions related to items listed in the scavenger hunt. They have also taken pictures around the house and would be willing to share them with you." She smiled at the little group. "Correct? Please share your photographs. Now, everyone enjoy the refreshments and the hunt."

Kyra glanced down at the paper Mrs. Kamber had distributed. The front side included a list of objects to be found in the scavenger hunt, with a blank space beside each to be filled in with the location of the item when found.

A note at the bottom of the page read: Please do not move the items after you find them. And do not enter any areas that have been roped off. The west yard is included in the scavenger hunt. Again, avoid roped-off areas such as the greenhouse.

She flipped the page over and read:

Interested in an evening activity? Join your friends for MURDER at the MANSE –

Gather in the Basement Lounge after the afternoon Scavenger Hunt.
Check the back of your nametag for your group number.
Information will be supplied when you enter the Lounge.

"Hmmm," Jerry Newcomb said to them. "First I'd heard of this. A murder mystery? Think I'll pass. I plan to enjoy the food and then head home to Medford."

The others stared at the printed sheet but didn't mention their plans for later.

Murder at the Manse? Kyra folded the paper and tucked it into her crossbody bag. Enticing aromas from fried foods and aromatic sauces floated about the room. She wasn't hungry. People circulated, carrying plates covered with finger food, fried or on sticks. A few of them stopped to talk to her, remembering she'd been introduced as a winner. "Lucky you!" was the usual response.

Keep smiling.

After seeing Matt's bashed-in head, she couldn't bring herself to eat. The image appeared, over and over. It was hard to be tempted by the skewers of grilled shrimp in cocktail sauce as they passed by, piled high on six-inch glass plates.

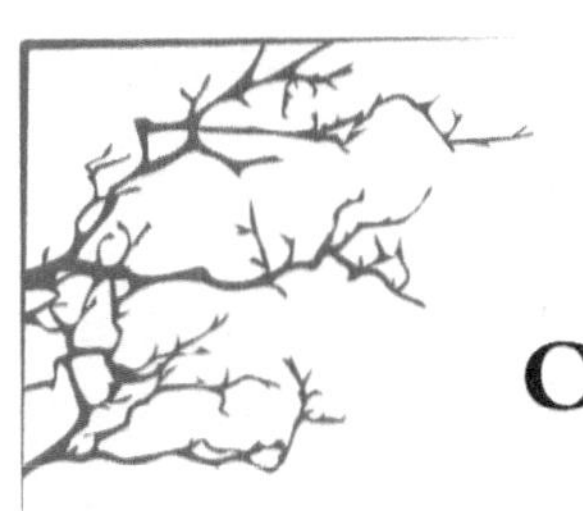

CHAPTER 31 - TY

Ty Harper stepped through the door under the porte-cochere. The outside air felt warm compared to the air-conditioned mansion. A breeze tousled his gray hair, and he closed his eyes for a moment, getting his thoughts in order.

A murder mystery. That was the last thing he needed to take part in. Nowhere in his world was murder a game. He'd almost lost his life 'playing' that game, and he continued to feel that he was slowly losing his mind.

His friend Jerry had meant well when he offered him this opportunity to stay in the mansion and attend the party. Jerry had repeated several times how badly Ty needed to get 'out of his head' and do something interesting, something not related to his former job or his military service. Both men had thought this might be just the thing.

Jerry knew more than anybody what Ty's childhood and youth had been like. He was empathetic but didn't let Ty wallow in his unfortunate past. Not that Ty was prone to that. The past was past, and when he began his adult life, he rarely mentioned that past to anyone. His ex-wife knew; they'd talked about it one night when neither one of them could sleep. Their marriage was fraying, and it was an attempt to put everything on the table and find the cause of their difficulties, especially his insistence on no children. Maybe his youth had created a need in him to feel an adrenaline rush, but at that time, the rush had come naturally, due to his circumstances. How could that have created an addiction to dangerous situations? And maybe his alcoholic father and mean stepfather had ruined his thoughts of fatherhood. He and Sydney had never had a similar conversation. She didn't care about getting to the root of his problems. In the end, she only wanted them to go away.

Ty looked around the yard for a destination. He'd return to the party in a bit, but for now, the late October sunrays shining through the numerous windows had called him outside. The greenhouse occupied a large section of the Kamber acreage. It stood west of the house, and although there was no doubt it had once been a crucial part of keeping the estate beautiful, it appeared abandoned now. A few plastic trays and broken pots remained inside, abandoned on the cement floor where Ty was sure there had once been tables holding flowering plants, seedlings, and bushes for beautifying the property.

He stepped inside the floor-to-ceiling glass walls of the t-shaped greenhouse. Dirt and detritus had accumulated beneath the windows. He focused on those piles and moved along the perimeter of the building, looking for anything out of place. As he moved, he examined the walls as well, and the floor on either side of his path. After he'd completed one circuit, he started around again, this time closer to the middle of the room. Finally, he stood in the center.

Other than the exoskeletons left behind (dead mealy bugs and grasshoppers) he found a few things that had survived the decades: marbles that had rolled into the corners, an arm from a plastic doll, a tire from a model car, a railroad coal car, a rubber band, a plant identification stake, and a dog's rabies vaccination tag from 1984. He left them all where he found them.

Ty opened the collar of his golf shirt and took off his jacket, then checked his watch. He ought to return to the party, but the 75-degree temperature of the air was too nice not to enjoy. He walked out of the front door of the greenhouse and lifted his face toward the afternoon sun.

The adjacent kennel caught his attention, and he peered through the chain link fence. Mouse droppings were piled in the corners. He opened the gate and peeked inside a cabinet at one end of the largest dog run. The shelves were empty except for a battered dog dish and a worn leather dog collar.

Ty walked the outside perimeter of the kennel and the greenhouse. Leaves and small branches littered the ground. He found no signs of disturbance by either animals or people and nothing to show that anyone had been messing around on the property near the abandoned buildings. A gnat buzzed his face, and he wiped his forehead.

Ty traipsed around the greenhouse and the kennel again, farther out into the yard. Bare patches persisted beneath the leafy canopy of the huge old trees, except for places where fescue grass had survived, nurtured through dry spells by a sprinkler system.

Kyra had mentioned that she grew up in the area. A foster kid. She might have had her name changed once she aged out of the system. Kids often did when they wanted to put those years behind them. Doing that didn't make her a bad person; it didn't make her a criminal.

A signal buzzed in the part of his brain that thought like a detective.

That woman was as secretive about her past as he was. They both had their reasons. After today, they'd both go back to their respective lives. Her secrets didn't matter to him, and his secrets wouldn't matter to her. That was the way it was.

But he would remember her. There was something about her that persisted.

CHAPTER 32 - HUGH

Hugh stepped soundlessly down the attic stairs to the second floor and then moved into the governess's apartment. Once inside, with the door closed, he crossed the small living room and entered the bathroom where he pulled a small backpack from the cabinet shelf. Two nights ago, he had altered the top shelf, creating a false back with a piece of cardboard so the shelf offered four inches of storage space behind the folded towels and yet invisible from the front. From the backpack, he pulled three tightly rolled bundles.

He unrolled each one, laying the clothing items flat on the floor in a pile: black sweatpants, a short-sleeved black t-shirt, a black balaclava, and a black windbreaker. Slowly, huffing at the arthritic pain in his joints, he took off the stinking clothing he'd worn for the past three days. Then, he put on the clean set but tucked the black ski mask into a pocket of the windbreaker. He'd pull it over his head and face later.

He sat down at the kitchen table to get his breath. Everything was going according to plan. Soon, the havoc would begin. The invitees were arriving. Nicholas was out of commission.

The tall muscular man had been no match for the baseball bat. One whack and he was out. Hugh had trussed him up and bundled him into a sleeping bag, stashed him in one of the attic rooms, and then locked him in with his own set of keys. His rescuers would have to batter down the door to get to him. If Hugh hadn't killed him before then.

Hugh looked around the apartment, seeing no evidence of the reporter who had intended to occupy the room the night before. The police had already been there and taken the man's belongings. Traces of fingerprint powder remained on the kitchen counters, table, and doorknobs. More powder traces showed in the living room on the coffee and end tables and in the bathroom on the sink fixtures. But the man hadn't been in the apartment long enough to have touched much the previous evening.

Hugh had worn gloves but still been extra careful when he'd knocked on the apartment door late the evening before, and once he was inside, he'd made sure not to touch anything.

"Hello, Matt! Great to see you again. Nicholas told me you were up here, and I had to stop in to say hello. Not too late, is it? Are you usually in bed by 9 p.m.? I'm a night owl. Always have been." He'd stepped into the room, pushing past Matt at the door, and heading inside to the sofa. He made himself at home, sat down, put his feet up on the coffee table, and stretched his arms out to either side. Matt had peered at his black clothing and gloved hands and studied the elderly man's face

"Who...?"

"Oh, hey. Sorry about the way I'm dressed. Just came from a Halloween party down the street. I'm a burglar! Pretty good, huh? And I'll leave the gloves on. Arthritis. The copper lining in these gloves helps with the pain. It can be bad. Forget gardening, and I'll tell you I don't spend much time on the computer. Have you had any trouble with it?"

Although Cleary hadn't recognized him, Hugh insisted they'd known each other in the army. Cleary peered at his wrinkled face and white hair, looking for something he recognized. Good luck with that. They'd never met, although Hugh had seen him around at meetings and places where he might be able to put together a 'story' for the Enid media. He figured the reporter found him familiar because of those same meetings. Familiar, but unidentified.

Hugh knew there was more 'meat' to most news stories than Cleary ever wrote about. The reporter before him at the local media outlet had done a piss-poor job of covering his boy's disappearance twenty years ago. Cleary had been a coach at the high school back then. Years later, when he took the job at the paper, he'd never dug into the case after he was assigned the police beat. And Hugh had asked him to, lots of times. His son's case had been botched. The cops were stupid, and Cleary was just as bad. Unsolved cases. Innocent men in jail.

Matt's curiosity about Hugh's identity increased as they lingered in the living room of the small apartment.

"How do we know each other?" Matt asked.

Hugh muttered a reply, his face turned toward the wall so that Cleary couldn't make out the words of his answer.

And then minutes later, "Who was that army buddy we both knew?"

Hugh laughed and turned the laugh into a cough. His answer was lost in the hacking noise of his throat.

"When did you serve?"

Hugh finally told him that they didn't know one another. But added that he always read Matt's news pieces.

Matt didn't throw him out. They sat down and talked about Enid, about the Kambers, about the house, and about whiskey. Cleary seemed to enjoy a good whiskey just like Hugh did.

Hugh told Matt that they should begin their friendship with a shared bottle of Kamber's finest whiskey, maybe a Macallan single malt. There was bound to be a bottle in the whiskey cellar downstairs. Nicholas Kamber would never even notice it was gone.

Matt agreed and led the way out of the apartment and down the stairs to the cellar. They'd found the door closed, but not locked, and Matt had been the one to pull the handle to open the heavy, safe-like door. They'd entered the whiskey cellar where Hugh had suggested that Matt look for his favorite whiskey on one side of the narrow room, while Hugh checked the shelves on the other. Matt bent over to read the labels of the bottles on the lower shelf. When Matt had searched about most of the shelves, Hugh had decked him with a full bottle of Johnny Walker Gold.

Hugh grinned.

Had anyone found the body yet? He'd been unable to tell if the police had joined the partygoers in the house. Still, even if they had, his plan would go ahead. Kamber would be dead before nightfall.

After he was dressed all in black again, he left the maid's apartment, carefully checking the corridors in all directions before he made his move down the backstairs. He had to be cautious, but nonchalant. His cat burglar costume fit right in with the party theme. No one would stop him or ask who he was.

On the first floor, Hugh continued down to the basement, anticipating a cop to have been posted outside the whiskey cellar. He cupped a small spray can of mace in the palm of his hand as he stepped off the bottom step. The corridor was empty. He moved on to the mechanical room, where he emptied the backpack and stowed the pile of clothes in a corner, behind one of the furnaces.

Hugh had checked the room out the night before and knew exactly where the electrical panel was. Once he flipped the master switch, he'd have two minutes to get back to Kamber's office and the hidden safe in the wall. The rest of his gang would be keeping everyone busy. No one would be in the office.

When he flipped the main switch and darkness fell, the guests would be stunned, not sure if it was part of the planned events or an electrical outage. His people would know that the mission had begun.

He'd already messed with the backup generator, increasing the amount of time until it turned itself on. He'd need at least seven minutes in the dark to do his job in Kamber's office. Then, when the lights came on again, his people would have boobytrapped rooms with smoke bombs. They would explode when someone came in. Everyone would be upset.

He'd spent 15 years of his life in jail, and he'd already lived every minute of this mayhem in his mind a thousand times. He'd waited long enough.

Exactly seven minutes later, he'd be walking out the glass door of the salon, the contents of Kamber's safe—most likely jewels and cash—tucked into the backpack he'd retrieved from Cleary's room. And Nicholas Kamber would be dead. He may not have been the one who killed Warren, but there was no doubt in Hugh's mind that the younger Kamber had a hand in it.

CHAPTER 33 - TY

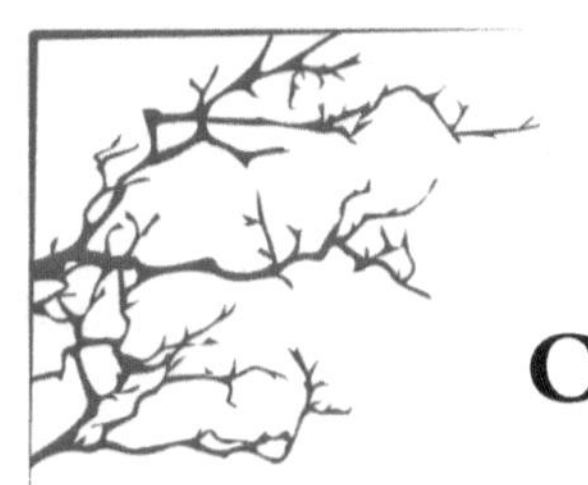

Ty reentered the house and found the party in full swing. He noticed several non-costumed people standing along the walls and watching the guests throughout the first floor. Surveillance mode. He picked out two in the entry hall, another in the music room, and three sets of watchful eyes in the living room where the food and drinks had been set up.

All this surveillance because of what Kyra had found in the attic? He didn't think so. Something bigger might be about to happen.

He made his way through the people around the food tables. Most of them held small plates heaped with hot hors d'oeuvres and crudites, as well as a glass of champagne or a cocktail. About half of the crowd wore costumes, while those not wearing Halloween garb were dressed casually, the men in slacks and sport coats, the women in silk blouses and slacks or nice dresses. His stomach rumbled.

Ty crossed the hall and stepped through the mansion's front door. The two valets had moved all the cars off the long circular driveway, and parked them along the streets of the neighborhood, beside the facing park.

He crossed the driveway and looked back at the mansion. The guests were too far inside the house for them to be seen from outside in the afternoon light. Lamps would soon come on in the interior rooms, and the windows would glow, making it clear by evening that the party was at the Kamber's mansion.

A minute earlier, as he'd passed through the party, glancing at the guests and the wait staff, his phone had beeped with a message. His buddy Jerry, checking in most likely. Now, alone and standing at the curb in front of the grand house, he pulled out his phone.

Ty blinked and did a double-take after reading the message.

The strangest thing just happened. I thought I saw the New You at a party in Enid. Right, what are the chances? You don't do parties and I don't think you live anywhere near here. Anyway, I sometimes think about you and this incident was a reminder that I do have fond memories, despite what you might think. Hope you are well.

He reread the message three times, then swallowed the saliva that had accumulated in his mouth.

So, the woman in the kitchen, working as a server/kitchen helper, HAD been Darcy. Why was she here? She had to be undercover. What was going on?

His mind flashed back to the news article he'd read about recent robberies. This party must have been tagged as a possible target. What were the chances? As if it wasn't strange enough that Darcy had recognized him.

A lot had happened in the years since they split up. For one thing, he'd met and gotten engaged to Sydney. Then he'd left the FBI for the Special Forces, and nearly died in a bomb blast overseas. He'd had facial reconstruction on his shattered face, had lost sixty pounds, and his hair had turned silver. Not to mention the emotional scars and PTSD he was dealing with. He was a very different man from Darcy's former husband.

He glanced up at the late October sun, hanging low in the western sky, casting long shadows across the lawn. Then he studied the young men in conversation at the table off to the side of the front door. They looked bored. The older valet said something the other thought was funny, and both laughed. Ty ambled over.

"Everything all right here?" He shoved his hands into his trouser pockets, hoping he looked more casual than he felt.

"Under control." The young man's face took on a serious look. "You another cop?"

"No. Not me. Just a guest. I'm not good with crowds. Needed a breather." He glanced around at two dozen cars parked on the streets around the mansion. "Bunch of cars."

"More than expected, I think. How does that happen?"

"Party crashers?" Ty guessed. Funny thing, he could be considered a crasher. He hadn't been invited personally. "You guys are on top of things. Hope you keep it that way." He lifted a hand and turned away.

Ty hiked the perimeter again, eventually making his way to the west side of the house and the porte-cochere. He entered the mansion. From the hallway, Ty stopped and peered into the kitchen. Darcy was not there; she was most likely at the bar in the living room. The younger woman was rinsing dirty plates and placing them in a dish carrier. He passed the kitchen and moved down the hall to Kamber's office. The door stood wide open now, and two party guests were snooping around.

Although the top of Kamber's desk was clear, knick-knacks were displayed on shelves and on the top of the wooden file cabinet. As he watched, the two guests tried to open file drawers without success. They fingered picture frames and looked behind them, pulled the curtains aside, and ran their fingers along the windowsills.

What a nightmare. Kamber would have a fit if he knew how people were riffling through his things. He hoped there was nothing to the idea that a gang was planning to rob the Kamber's mansion and the guests at this party. Processing that crime scene, with more than thirty people leaving their fingerprints on everything, would be a challenge.

He saw no items of great value on display. The home barely looked lived in, at least not the parts of it he'd seen. He'd noticed vases, landscape paintings, and Persian rugs that had some value. But the Kambers had let six people spend the night with them in the second-floor bedrooms.

Ty turned away from the office doorway and hugged the wall as two laughing women, each with a glass of champagne, stepped past him and up to the office doorway, waving their instruction sheets in the air.

He sidestepped to pass between more groups standing in the entry hall. Everyone was carrying their papers and heading in different directions. Ty scanned the crowd, looking for Kyra. She was not in the area, but Mrs. Kamber hovered at the bottom of the stairs. Despite the smile on her face, she looked anxious. Her hands were clenched into fists.

When Ty drew near, she reached out for his arm. "Are you one of the detectives? Have you found him yet?"

Ty grabbed a glass of water off a tray as a waiter passed by and considered a possible response. Kamber was missing?

"No, Mrs. Kamber, I'm a raffle winner. Enjoying your party. I ...um... you said someone is missing?"

"Oh, I'm sorry. I mistook you. I'm sure it's all fine. He'll turn up. Never mind. Go enjoy the party."

"Is your husband missing Mrs. Kamber? Is there something I can do for you?" He looked intently into her blue eyes.

"This isn't like him. He should be here, by my side, greeting guests, bantering with the men. Where is he?" She whispered, pursing her lips, and leaned slightly to the right to peer around Ty and down the hallway to the office.

"He'll turn up, ma'am. No doubt he's off somewhere with one of his friends, talking business." Ty smiled reassuringly.

"This isn't an occasion for discussing business. I need him here, beside me. He's the host of the party. There's no other place he should be."

"I'll keep an eye out for him and will let him know you need him if I see him. Talk with your guests. That will help to keep your mind off things." He muttered, "Excuse me, ma'am," to Mrs. Kamber, and turned away.

The party guests who now occupied the living room were finishing the last of their hors d'oeuvres or having a second, or third, drink. Darcy was bartending and did not glance at him as he entered the living room. Kyra and the others formed a loose group around one of the sofas.

CHAPTER 34 - KYRA

"**K**yra, can I get you to stand over there by the fireplace with the other winners? There's Jerry, finally. I'll snag him." Kim took three steps and grabbed his arm as Jerry crossed the living room. He pulled away, smiled as she explained, and then walked with her to the fireplace. He seemed a bit wide-eyed and uncertain, but his stride was more confident than it had been earlier.

Kyra scanned the room as she moved toward the fireplace. Quite a mix of people. One man was no doubt a farmer, his face burnt by the sun and wind. He'd left his collar unbuttoned and his tie unknotted. Although he wore slacks and a jacket, the necktie was overkill. The woman with him was younger and looked around the room with bright eyes, her look lingering on the more elaborate costumes. She was trying too hard, Kyra thought. Both people were uncomfortable but curious. She was certain she did not have that same excited look. Maybe she'd felt that way yesterday, but not today. Too much had happened. Another guest wore denim jeans and a nice short-sleeved shirt that looked like a Bass Pro brand.

Kyra stepped close to the group of winners and smiled as Richard took a picture. Beside her, Jerry coughed into his sleeve just when the picture was snapped. He kept his head down as Richard snapped more pictures. Camera shy?

"Ought to be Matt Cleary taking these pics for the local papers and online mags. Where is he, anyway? Haven't seen him all day. I thought he was assigned to do this. Isn't that what he said yesterday? Has anyone seen him?" Kim asked.

Andrea shook her head, and so did Jerry. Kim frowned and peered around the room. "I've half a mind to call his editor. I know the Kambers wanted good publicity out of this party, and frankly, I'd like some for my community, too."

Someone tapped a glass and the room quieted.

Mrs. Kamber stood in the doorway close to a side table laden with a huge floral bouquet of fall flowers in a crystal vase. She placed one hand on the table. For support?

"Could I have your attention, please? I hope you have all had a chance to work on the scavenger hunt, and that you have found many of the interesting things we have around the house."

Mrs. Kamber looked tired and not as excited about her party as she had been when people first arrived. Nicholas was conspicuously absent. Another reason for the frown around Danielle's eyes?

"Thank you again for coming. I hope you've enjoyed the refreshments. We will be making our way to the downstairs lounge now, where we'll be congregating for entertainment." She looked at the floor and then back at the gathering in the room. "A murder mystery. A light dinner will be served in about an hour, as part of the performance. So now, please—"

Sergeant Murray stepped up to Danielle Kamber. His six-foot-four-inch frame dwarfed her. "Mrs. Kamber, sorry to interrupt."

Mouth agape and eyes wide, she looked up at him. "What are you doing?"

He frowned.

"If I could have your attention. I'm Sergeant Murray, director of Kamber Security. Earlier today, an invited journalist, Matt Cleary of the Enid News, was found in the house, deceased." The sergeant paused as the crowd reacted to this news. Mrs. Kamber's face blanched. She grasped his arm with one hand. Her other hand clasped the long strands of white beads around her neck. The strands broke. Beads pelted the carpet and bounced in all directions.

Beside Kyra, Kim Spaeth gasped. She clutched Kyra's arm.

"If you could all move in an orderly fashion down to the lounge in the south basement, please. The police have arrived and will be conducting interviews, taking fingerprints, and perhaps DNA samples to eliminate all of you from the suspect pool." Murray scanned the crowd, frowning.

Voices murmured around the room.

"Are you canceling the mystery supper? Can you do that, without my permission?" Danielle Kamber hissed at the tall man beside her.

"There will be an investigation, Mrs. Kamber. It will be as orderly as possible." The Sergeant's loud voice silenced the crowd. He looked around the room again. "To repeat, proceed in an orderly fashion down to the lounge. Do not leave this home. Guards have been posted at the outer doors. The police will process you as quickly as possible."

"What?! We can't leave? This is outrageous." One man's face reddened as he clenched and unclenched his hands. "We are all suspects? This death probably happened before I even got here." He glared at Murray.

Kyra patted Kim's hand as she dug into her purse and pulled out a tissue. Dabbing her eyes, Kim moaned. "I can't believe it. Surely not."

Kyra could hardly believe it either, and she'd seen the body with her own eyes.

And then, as Kyra looked around the room at the groups of people absorbing the news, someone smiled. "It's part of the murder mystery setup," someone whispered a little too loudly.

Some guests visibly relaxed as those whispers circulated.

Murray cleared his throat and looked sternly around the room. "After you have been interviewed and fingerprinted, you are free to leave the premises. I apologize to Mrs. Kamber and all of you for the indignity of this experience and I assure you that this was in no way anticipated. I'm sure that both the Kambers and the Enid Police appreciate your willingness to cooperate with the investigation."

Kyra glanced at the smiling guests.

Part of the mystery setup? She didn't think so.

She'd seen Matt Cleary's body.

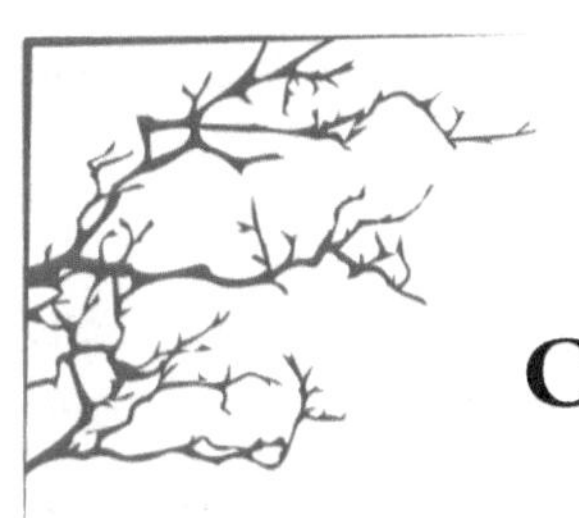

CHAPTER 35 - TY

Ty hung back and watched the crowd begin to move out of the living room toward the basement gate and the narrow stairway that led down to the lounge. Kim and Richard led the way with Andrea beside them. Kyra trailed behind. Ty hurried to catch up with her.

"This is a surprise. Did you know about the murder mystery?" he asked.

Kyra shook her head and shrugged. "First I heard of it. I thought we were just having a scavenger hunt and all this food seemed a little over the top to me. And now a dinner with a murder mystery? Maybe that's just me. Danielle must be very upset."

Ty nodded. Upset was putting it mildly. If her husband was truly missing, she must be beside herself. A man was dead in her house and her husband was nowhere to be found.

Andrea dropped back to walk on Kyra's other side. When she whispered in her ear, Ty strained to hear, leaning closer to Kyra as he walked. Something about the attic? A mummy? Ty had no idea what Andrea was talking about. And he didn't want to know. The event would soon be over. He was ready to go home to his cabin and solitude.

On the other hand, Ty wanted to learn more about Kyra and what she thought about the Kambers and this mansion. He would have liked to find out what her life was like on the ranch. Probably quite different from a life of solitude like his in the old farmhouse/cabin beside Lake McMurtry near Stillwater.

Ty stepped into line behind the others and followed them down the stairs and into the ballroom-like lounge. Once in the room, the guests divided themselves into small groups clustered around scattered square tables. Some people dragged chairs from one table to another.

"Hey, we need those chairs for the four in our group," one woman groused as a chair from her table was taken.

"Don't you get it? We're not doing the murder mystery anymore. There's been a real murder," the woman dragging the chair retorted.

"Hah!" A man yelled from the next table over. "That's what you think. It's all part of staging this murder mystery. Nobody's dead. It's a gimmick." The man, of medium build with curly black hair and yellowed teeth, turned toward Kyra and the group of raffle winners. "I bet they know the truth. It's part of the game, isn't it? Bet he was 'supposedly' found someplace like the wine cellar, wasn't he?"

Ty hung back as Kim's husband Richard took the fourth seat at the winners' table.

"Jerry, pull up a chair," Kim said with a sideways glance at him.

"Rumors seem to be circulating." He grabbed a chair from an empty table and pulled it over. "What do you think? Has there been a murder?" He looked at the others, then let his gaze rest on Kyra.

She pinched her eyes shut and looked down, avoiding his question.

Did she know something more about Matt Cleary?

Richard cleared his throat. "I think something has happened. For one thing, Mrs. Kamber was upset, truly blindsided by what the security chief said. Only a professional actor could have pulled off that reaction, and I don't think she has ever acted."

"So, you're saying poor Matt Cleary really was murdered, and the mystery play they had planned to present is not going to happen. This place should be swarming with police, and I haven't noticed any. Have you?" Kim asked the group at the table.

Kim's husband tilted his head. "At least a half dozen. I think the police officers will begin taking witness statements shortly."

"A half dozen!" Kim looked around the room. "Oh, there's one. In the corner with his hands folded. Dead giveaway."

"Hah!" Richard scoffed.

"Witness statements?" A slight man at the adjacent table said. "None of us saw anything. The party's just beginning folks." He turned to another man and cuffed him on the shoulder. "Okay. I'll play along. I'm Michael Bayes, soon to be elected Congressman from this district, Enid's also my hometown." The wiry man leaned his chair back, so it balanced on two legs. He crossed his arms.

A woman seated at the table next to him sat up straighter. "I'm Melissa Woolery. I'm the curator at the Chisholm Trail Museum here," said a fifty-something graying blonde with a shoulder-length pageboy and bags under her eyes. "I certainly hope no one has died, but really, it would be cruel to lie to us about something like that."

"And I'm Patsy Beard, from the mayor's office," said another middle-aged woman at the table beside her. "Mr. Bayes, the Mayor is with the police now. When he returns, he'll confirm that there has been a death." The silver-haired woman in a business suit nodded at the museum curator. Her look swept across the crowd. "This isn't a game." Ms. Beard looked pointedly at the congressional candidate.

Bayes shrugged. "That remains to be seen."

More people filed into the room, filling the space with murmuring voices.

Ty crossed his arms and sat back, listening to the conversations around the room. The crowd appeared split between believing a murder had happened and believing it was all part of an entertaining murder mystery the Kambers had cooked up.

"I've been dying to see inside this mansion forever," Ms. Beard huffed. "Mrs. Kamber is on the board of directors at the museum, and she was kind enough to extend to me an invitation. I'm so disappointed that we won't be allowed to wander around more. But I completely understand if someone has died. They need to investigate."

"I'm sure they are investigating," Kim Spaeth said to the mayor's staffer. She glared at Bayes, the next table over. "You are welcome to look through the photos I've taken of the house. Perhaps you can at least get a feel for the other rooms, even though you can't visit them personally." She handed Ms. Beard her iPhone and invited her to scroll through the photos.

Bayes let the front legs of his folding chair drop back to the ground. He stretched his legs out in front of it. "Where's that journalist? He's in on this. Out to make a buck. Here for a story, right?"

Kim protested, "That's not right. I know Matt Cleary, and I can tell you for sure that he originally came here to tell the story about this house. It's historic, it's huge, and it's interesting to people. No reporter has been in here for decades, and even though this sounds trite, we'd like to see what they've done with the place."

Ty kept his look on Bayes for a moment and then glanced around the large wood-paneled room, his look encompassing the thirty-plus people who waited, standing and sitting, for their turn to talk with the investigating detectives. His gaze lingered on the huge stone fireplace, black andirons in place, and then swept over the parquet floor and back to Kim. It was like no room he'd ever been in before. A great location for a party, or some kind of dance. It had been years since he'd danced. He doubted that he still remembered how.

"Keep trying to convince me," Bayes said loudly. "More likely, if there's not a story, he'll dig one up. For instance, the story of the moment is Matt Cleary. You say he's been murdered, but we haven't seen any proof. No one has officially made that announcement. They stuck us all down here in a basement rec room, or whatever this is. It's all part of the mystery murder game. Tell us it's going to happen one way, then change the rules. Take one of the crowd off to a backroom to stay in seclusion behind the scenes and tell everyone else they've been murdered. Then interview the participants one by one. Who knows what the 'interviewers' are going to tell us, but it won't be the truth. It's all part of the game."

"You're cynical," Kim Spaeth said slowly in a low voice. Tears glinted in her eyes.

Ty suspected that Kim had known Matt Cleary personally. She might be hoping Bayes was right, and that Matt was alive. It would not be long before they would find out the truth. The questions that the police would ask would make it clear that Matt had been killed in this house. Possibly by someone in this room.

"I'm the voice of experience talking," the candidate's voice echoed in the large room. He had everyone's attention and wanted to keep it. "I know how this works. I know how journalists manipulate the facts and pick what to share and what to hide. It's a nationwide con job. Why don't you admit it? Stop acting all innocent and offended."

He smirked at Kim, and then his look swept the group.

Ty frowned and watched. The man needed to shut up. Ty scanned the crowd and saw red faces and shaking heads. Bayes wasn't going to win the votes of any of those people.

"You're full of it," Andrea said. "You're saying you don't believe people can be honest, that you don't trust what anyone says or does? That the news media is lying, conning the American people at every turn? I completely disagree."

"I used to believe most people tell the truth, ma'am. Not anymore," Bayes said, standing by the table and pounding on it with one hand. "With age comes wisdom. Look behind those spouting the so-called truth. See who the Wizard of Oz is pushing the gears and levers. Tonight, I think that Wizard is Nicholas Kamber. He has an agenda. He wants the publicity, the sensationalism this event will bring him. Otherwise, why subject his dear wife Danielle to such public humiliation? Believe me, she'll be sacrificed on the altar. Let's talk about the Kambers. Any takers?"

Kim locked eyes with Bayes. "What I'm wondering is why Nicholas and Danielle Kamber invited you in the first place. You're only here to make trouble. It's not an election year, is it? It doesn't matter what you say in a crowd this small. But those of us who are here will remember."

"Maybe Kamber invited me because he didn't want to offend me, thought it would appease me. Instead, it stoked the coals. He shouldn't have turned it into a circus, claiming that a man has died. And I have it on good authority that something sinister was found in the attic upstairs last night. A mummified body."

"Who told you that?" Kim asked in a low voice.

The candidate looked pointedly at Kyra and Andrea. "Talk to those two about it. Both were involved. Weren't you?"

Ty watched this exchange and mentally took notes. He could think of several possible explanations. Someone in the house had known about the mummy in the attic, maybe put it there themselves. He recalled the few words he had overheard Andrea say to Kyra as the guests moved down to the lounge after Sergeant Murray's instructions: 'Attic,' 'Mummy.'

The lights in the large room flickered.

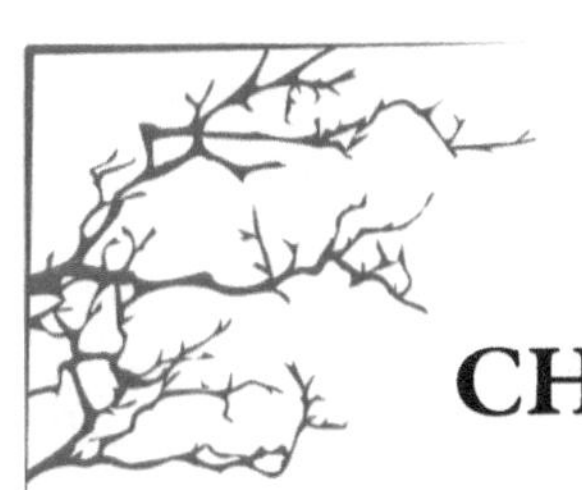

CHAPTER 36 - KYRA

Kyra reached out to grab something, vertigo hitting her as soon as the lights dimmed. At home, she kept a small nightlight burning in every hallway and room. Dawson had asked her about it early in their marriage, but she didn't tell him why. She had shrugged and made light of it. "A quirk of mine. I don't want to bang into walls and furniture if I get up in the middle of the night."

The night terrors that a dark house brought weren't easily explained. Her sadistic foster father had used darkness to cloak the terror he created. She couldn't overcome the dread of darkness that living with that man had instilled in her.

Her husband didn't dig into it. He agreed that nightlights made it easier to navigate the hallways. He didn't wonder if there was anything more to it, and Kyra didn't tell him that she also feared the memories of other things that might cloak themselves with darkness.

For a moment, she stood quietly, breathing deeply, and listening to the worried voices of the partygoers. The lights kept flickering.

Her memory threw her into the past. With her real parents, when she was small, the lights often went off in the house. She didn't know then that it happened because the electrical bill had not been paid for several months.

Sometimes in that dark house, someone would call out for her. Her mother? Then, an angry voice growled and yelled words her child self couldn't understand. Distant sobbing would stifle the scream. She'd huddle in her bed, hoping that no monster came into her room, that no one came except her mother. But Mommy didn't come. The next morning, Mommy's eyes would be rimmed in red and there would be purple marks on her cheek and neck at breakfast. Later, the marks would disappear after Mommy 'put her face' on.

The next morning, she would run to the mirror to check her face for purple marks. She was glad she hadn't inherited any from her mother. Daddy had told her often that she had inherited Mommy's brown hair and brown eyes. He said even more after Mommy disappeared.

One day when Daddy was drunk and watching NASCAR, a man and a woman came to the house. They asked her what she had for dinner. She couldn't remember; it had been a couple of days since then. Daddy told them he'd forgotten to fix anything. Their pantry was empty, except for beer and chips. The couple took her away and bought her breakfast for dinner.

The foster home was supposed to be better. She found out quickly that scary things roamed the hallways in the darkness. No one protected her when something grabbed her neck, poked, and prodded her.

Kyra shook her head to cast away the demon memories, drew in a ragged breath, and let her arms drop to her sides. It was all in the past. She'd made sense of most of it eventually, but she couldn't shake fearful memories of the dark. Bad things happen when the lights go out.

"Are you okay?" Jerry asked. He had moved closer as the light flickered. She was comforted on one hand but also wanted to shove him away. There was no guarantee that he could keep something bad from happening in the dark. He might even cause it.

Jerry was being kind. He seemed interested in her as a person. Should she confide in him? Sometimes she hated masquerading as the rancher's wife. She wanted to be who she was. She needed to talk about it. She needed to put the bad memories to rest.

It's safer to keep your mouth shut.

No arguing with that. She wasn't going to talk about her past to the police detectives when she was interviewed about this murder. They'd write it all down in a police report, where anybody might be able to hack in and access it from the internet.

Shivers traveled across her back. It had been hard to hide for all these years. She couldn't imagine what it would be like if that man found her after all this time. He blamed her. He would never forgive her. When he was in prison, she hadn't been so scared. But he was out now, had been for several years, and she imagined that her name was on his 'To Do' list. The only way she could feel safe was to stay on the ranch, stay quiet, and stay lonely.

She should not have bought that ticket. She should not have come. The lights stopped flickering and went dark.

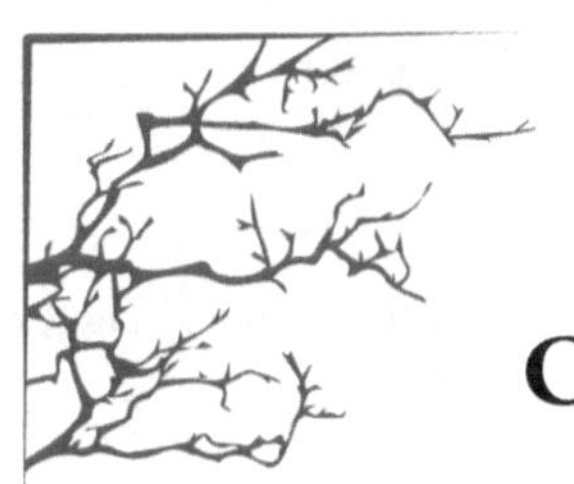

CHAPTER 37 - TY

Someone groaned, and another person gasped. Footsteps crossed the room; table legs screeched against the floor.

In the few seconds before phone flashlights began to click on, Ty strained to see in the darkness. Soft light invaded the room from the ventilation wells that had been built to supply air circulation and light into the below-ground rooms. The sole purpose of the wells was now to allow natural light into the lower floor. But night was falling outside. There was no light to let in.

"Honey? Oh my God—." Kim Spaeth's voice croaked and abruptly went silent.

"Kim?" Kyra asked. "Where are you? Is everyone all right?"

Ty imagined her reaching toward Kim's frightened voice. Across the room, a flashlight beam flicked on.

"The lights will be back on momentarily. I'm sure they have a generator." Ty couldn't make out Kyra's silhouette. More phone lights flashed on. "Who's missing?"

"Kim," Kyra said in a breathless voice from somewhere to his left. "Richard?"

Kim's husband did not speak up.

Ty's eyes adjusted to the dim light of a half dozen phone flashlights around the room. "Kim? Richard?" he called. No response.

He scrutinized the dimly lit crowd of people, trying to catch a glimpse of either of them. "Kim?" he called louder.

No one answered. Voices murmured around the room.

"Maybe they left the room to talk to the police," Andrea suggested from nearby.

"In the darkness?" Kyra's voice was soft. "Without telling us they were going? Wouldn't we have heard the police call for them?"

"Maybe they stepped out to find a bathroom." Andrea offered a second suggestion.

That could be, Ty thought, but why at that moment, and in the darkness?

"Everyone stay put. The main lights will be back on in a minute." Bayes shouted.

"How can you know that?" Andrea's voice was snarky.

"Back-up generators. People in big houses can't stand to be without electricity. In another few seconds, it will click on."

"I hope you're right," Andrea replied in a softer tone.

Ty studied the people who stood around him in the semi-darkness. He didn't like this one bit. Lights off and nearly forty wealthy people gathered in a single room. It was a prescription for crime. A heist could be underway.

He knew from experience that people do weird things when the lights go out, when they felt unseen. It could go bad fast.

"Surely that kitchen next door has emergency flashlights. I'll go check," Ty offered. He stepped closer to Kyra Blackwood. "I'll be right back."

Her face was in shadow, but fear radiated from her in waves.

What was she so frightened of? He was used to the dark. He had memories of wandering in the dark for hours as a child. Nothing to it, unless you knew something was hiding there, something that liked to hurt people, especially children.

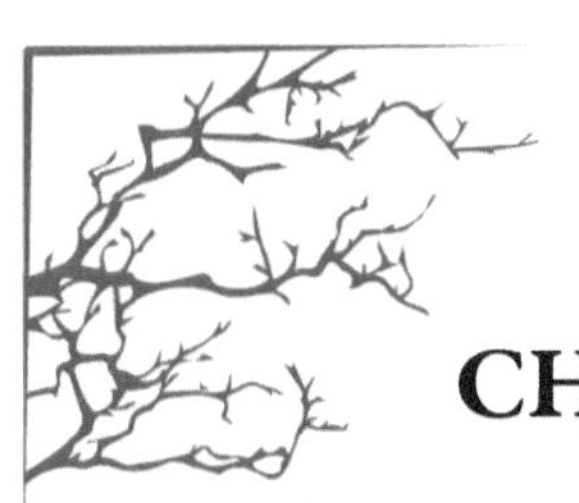

CHAPTER 38 - KYRA

Minutes after Jerry left, the room lights came back on. Phone flashlights clicked off.

"Do you see Kim anywhere?" Andrea asked.

Kyra checked the room. "No." Icy fingers touched her neck.

"Bathroom, most likely," Andrea suggested.

The partygoers spoke in low voices to one another.

The lounge door opened, and Taylor McDonald carried in a box. The guests noticed him and quieted.

"Your attention, please," McDonald said. "We had a brief power outage, but everything seems to be okay now. I have flashlights here if you don't have a phone light with you." McDonald pulled a flashlight out of the box and laid it on the table. "The backup generator is working properly. The police would like to begin interviews. After your interview, you are free to leave. Questioning will begin with those on my left. The first group of four, come this way, please."

Four people who'd been seated at the table closest to the door rushed over. McDonald ushered them through the door to the anteroom, where a uniformed police officer waited. Then Taylor closed the door and stood with his back to it.

Kyra made her way through the tables and across the room to him. "Kim Spaeth and her husband left while the lights were out. Did she talk to the police officers?"

"I don't know anything about the Spaeths, Ms. Blackwood. I've been busy upstairs. Haven't seen her." Taylor McDonald glanced around the room.

"Kim was upset about Matt Cleary's death. Should I go look for her?"

"I was told to keep everyone in here who wasn't being interviewed. That includes you." McDonald frowned.

Kyra frowned back. "I want to make sure she's all right. And I need to use the restroom, with or without your permission."

His frown turned to a glare. "Wouldn't want you to have an accident. Go." He opened the door, and she slipped out.

During the tour, they'd passed the restrooms in the hallway on the other side of the anteroom. Beyond those doorways, crime tape now stretched across the basement hallway. A large placard with the word CLOSED written on it blocked access.

Kyra tried the doorknob to the first bathroom. Locked. She tapped on the door. "Kim? It's Kyra. Are you there? Are you all right?" She waited for a response, but none came. She tapped again. "Kim?"

She tried the second restroom door and found it locked too. Once again, she knocked and called out, with no response.

Gooseflesh raised on her arms. She glanced down the hallway. Shimmer stood at the far end, past another CLOSED SIGN that prevented access to the wine and whiskey cellars. The ghost dog smiled; her tail wagged slowly back and forth.

"Shimmer? What is it?" She whispered. The dog's tail wagged faster. The ghost animal turned and trotted toward the back stairway.

Kyra glanced behind her at the lounge. The anteroom and the hallway were both empty. Shouldn't there have been a guard posted in front of the whiskey cellar? Maybe there was no need; the door appeared to be securely shut. Matt's body had probably been removed.

When she had no response after rattling the bathroom doorknobs one more time, she glanced again down the hallway. Shimmer had disappeared. She hurried to the stairway, went up a few steps, and looked again. Shimmer was waiting on the landing.

"Here we go," Kyra muttered as she climbed the stairs. "Why are you here?" she whispered. The dog's fluffy gray and white tail curled over its back. "I wish you could talk." She stooped to pet the animal but as usual, her hands passed through empty air instead of touching a furry back.

In her mind, she remembered the dog as a puffy puppy, a stray she'd found abandoned in the alleyway behind the house where her second foster family lived. She'd taken it in with her foster mother's permission, and it had followed her everywhere. She'd even taken the pup to school, tucked inside her backpack in place of her textbooks. Although her foster mother had seemed to understand her need for the puppy, her foster father had not. The pup was banished to the backyard and the small wooden doghouse in one corner.

Her foster brother told her the family had previously had a dog or two, but that none of them lasted for long. He'd shrugged his shoulders as if he didn't care, but the ashen look on his face gave her chills. It wasn't an adequate warning. She couldn't have done anything to prevent what happened.

Shimmer paused at the first-floor hallway, and she paused, too. People were muttering in the kitchen. Another group was huddled together, talking, in the front hall. If any one of them turned, they would see her as she went up the steps to the second floor. She wasn't concerned. If they saw her, so be it. Chances were no one would stop her. If anyone did, she would tell them she was going to her bedroom.

Kyra rounded the corner and continued up the stairs. The man standing in the hallway at the kitchen door had his back to her, and the police officers in the front hall had their heads down in a conversation.

Quickly, she caught up with the ghost dog again. "Shimmer, where are you going?"

The apparition plodded forward. The attic? She didn't want to go there. If the lights went out again she wasn't sure she could keep her thoughts straight in that room. Not only had she found the mummy up there, but thinking about it made her head hurt. Memories crowded in.

Kyra's mind flashed. Her bedroom at the second foster home had been in an attic.

She climbed the last few steps and paused before reaching for the light switch. Mustiness, not to mention the place reeked of sweat. Why did it have that smell? No one in the group of winners had body odor. On the tour, they'd stood shoulder to shoulder in many places, and she'd never noticed a smell.

Her memory jumped in. Someone in her past had that kind of body odor. He took pride in it, a sign of his manliness. That man had terrified her.

She insisted that Dawson shower the minute he came in from working outside.

Another memory flashed. Those rooms in the Kamber's attic: she knew them. She'd been in those rooms years ago, long before she followed Nicholas Kamber and the others up there yesterday afternoon.

She'd thought it must be a dream. Now she knew she was remembering. This was why she was here.

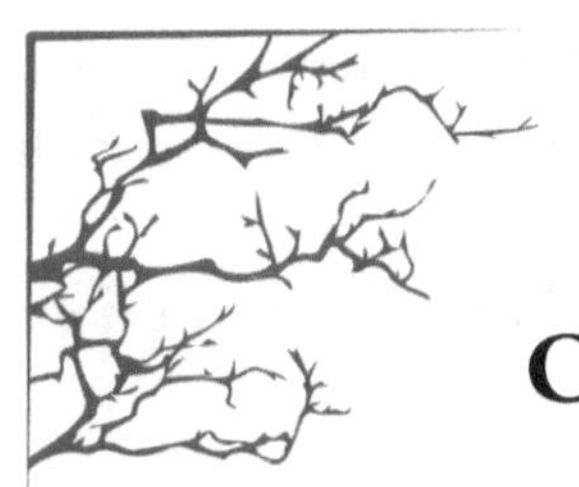

CHAPTER 39 - TY

Moments before, Ty had found the box of LED flashlights in the small kitchen next to the anteroom and had started back into the lounge with it when Taylor McDonald clattered down the stairwell.

"Flashlights?" he'd asked as he took the box from Ty's hands "I'll take it in. Not really needed now that the lights are on."

"Any obvious reason they went off?"

"Probably a breaker. The wiring may be a little out of date, especially in the kitchen. We may need to add a breaker." McDonald took a step back and peered at Ty. "We were introduced I believe. A raffle winner? Jerry?"

"Yes. From Medford." Ty nodded his head and hoped he looked convincing.

McDonald studied his face. "Right. Have we met before? There's something …"

"Been to Medford recently?" Ty asked, chuckling. "Didn't think so. I own the Dollar General store there." He needed to nip that memory in the bud.

"Oh. I hear business is good for those franchises. Well, I'd best get these in there and get the interview process started. If you're in a hurry to get away from here, go upstairs. They'll check you in and do your interview."

Ty was glad to be dismissed. He didn't want to be stuck in the lounge. But he was not completely ready to leave. The instincts that had made him an excellent investigator had kicked in. Something was going on in this house.

He was bothered most by the fact that his ex-wife, Darcy, was here on assignment. He didn't think she was here because of the mummy that Kyra had found last night. She was here with the FBI either because of Matt Cleary's murder or to prevent a crime.

He started up the stairway. McDonald had left the door to the lounge ajar. His voice carried out into the anteroom as he explained the process being followed to interview guests. Ty did not want to be interviewed yet. What he wanted was to check outside to see if someone had tampered with the wiring to the house.

When he reached the top of the stairs, he turned toward the exit door under the

porte-cochere and stepped outside.

Dusk had fallen, but solar yard lights lit up the back drive and the carport, as well as the garage and side entries. Nothing moved around the shadowy greenhouse and the vacant dog kennel. He glanced up at the power lines leading into the house and followed them to the electric poles. On the pole, the transformer hummed.

Ty looked for other wires leading into the house, and when he spotted one, he followed it first to the pole, and then back to the house. The electric wires all entered the house from the rear, and there was no sign of sabotage from outside. Ty continued his search around the north end of the building and then to the front of the house. At the front door, a police officer leaned casually against the stone façade of the house.

The unmistakable pop of a gunshot rang out from somewhere inside the house and was followed by more rapid pops. Ty felt as if an icepick had been shoved into his brain.

"Active shooter on site," the police officer shouted into her radio.

As Ty dashed past her and through the front door into the house, the woman called for backup.

Ty instinctively reached for his gun with one hand and his radio unit with the other. Both hands grabbed thin air. With a jolt, he remembered. He was not Special Forces; he was not FBI. His hands shook.

Inside the house, chaos had broken out. Costumed partygoers ducked behind the furniture while the police officers clustered together, listening to the radios on their shoulders. Ty's heartbeat thundered as he crossed the hall and turned toward the stairway that led down to the lounge. The muffled gunshots must have come from the basement.

Footsteps rushed up the stairs. He stepped to one side. Someone rounded the corner. Bayes, wide-eyed and out of breath, stopped beside him and grabbed Ty's arm.

"Oh my God." The man's voice shook. "I don't want to die."

"No one's going to shoot you up here. You were in the lounge, right?" Ty spoke in a raspy, low voice.

"We were all in that room... Someone fired a gun ... There are dead people down there... I ran out. The shooter's still in there. Oh, God." Bayes bent over, hands on his thighs, and gasped.

Ty took a deep, steadying breath. The edges of the room blurred.

Sirens sounded in the distance. Their screech blared across the entry hall and through the open front door.

More people pounded up the basement stairs. The two women looked to be in shock, with pale faces and shaking hands.

"There's a shooter. He's still down there." Another man pushed past Ty.

"Go around the corner to the living room," Ty instructed. His voice sounded calmer than he felt. "The police are there. You'll be safe."

"What if the shooter ...?"

"You'll be fine. But you need to move out of the way in case..."

Another shot rang out from the basement level. Ty's vision swirled.

One of the women wailed.

"Move. Now. To the living room." He spaced his feet wide apart after the people in the hallway stepped around him.

One woman sobbed as the group hurried toward the living room.

Screams echoed up from below. Ty put his hands on the walls and moved toward the basement stairs. At the top stair, he paused to let his eyes adjust to the level of ambient light and to quiet the vertigo. Then he started down the stairs, moving quietly on the balls of his feet, one hand on the wall, the other on the banister. His cell phone buzzed against his thigh from his right pants pocket. His heartbeat sounded in his ears. The saliva vanished from his mouth and throat.

Gunfire sounded below him.

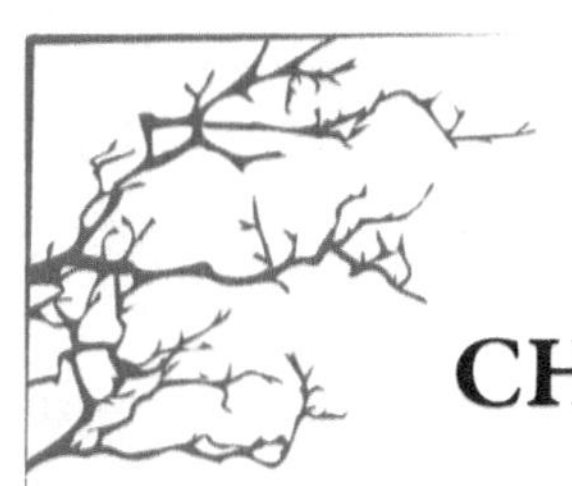

CHAPTER 40 - KYRA

The ghost dog waited beside her at the top of the attic stairs. The animal was close enough to touch but if she reached down, she knew her fingers would stroke empty air. The dog had brought her here. The rest was up to her.

She stepped into the attic. Uneasy, Kyra unzipped her crossbody bag, pulled out her phone, and pushed the flashlight button. She didn't trust the overhead lights; they were too few and too far between. She needed to see her surroundings.

Kyra paused to get her bearings, listening. A low voice muttered from the other end of the attic, near the room where the mummy had been. Kamber? She took another step into the huge space, letting the flashlight beam skip over the furniture and random items stored in the room until it found the unfinished train village. The muttering stopped.

Somewhere below, popping noises erupted. Screams and faint cries reached her ears. Her blood chilled. Gunfire. Someone was shooting in the house.

Her chest tightened. In that large open basement room, people were sitting ducks. Were they being murdered below while she cowered in the attic? What was happening?

The police were in the house now investigating Matt's murder in addition to trying to learn more about the mummy she'd found up here. But their visible presence had not prevented whatever was happening. They'd made it worse by herding everyone into the same room. If the gunfire continued, everyone would soon be dead.

She should go down the back stairs and out the back door. To freedom. To safety.

But before Kyra could turn around and start for the stairs, a weak voice called out. The garbled words sounded vaguely like 'Help! Anybody?'

She pointed her phone flashlight once again into the lightless room. The beam moved from one doorway to another as she stepped further into the attic. Kyra stumbled over something. She reached out and touched a chair, then used it for support as she reoriented herself.

The gunfire stopped. The shooters were either out of bullets or everyone was dead. Whoever was firing the shots might leave the basement to search for more people.

Maybe the police had taken out the gunman. If so, they would search the house for survivors. All she had to do was stay here and stay silent. She would be safe as long as no one knew she was here.

Someone knows you're here. The hairs on her neck bristled.

Her nose detected a now-familiar smell. Sweat. Close by.

Something crashed into her head. She had a sense that she was falling. Blackness descended.

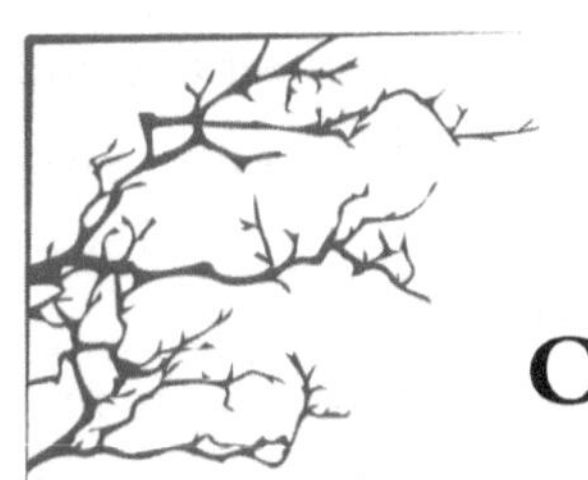

CHAPTER 41 - TY

Screams continued to echo up the stairwell as Ty cautiously descended the steps. Below him, someone pounded on the door to the lounge at the bottom of the stairs and shouted. "Let us out! Open the door."

Ty reached the bottom step. All was silent now. Where was the shooter? He or she could have left the room and gotten away down the long basement hallway. They could be headed up the backstairs, looking for the Kambers. If the shooters were members of the gang he'd read about online, there could have been several shooters. Ty inhaled deeply, then inhaled again. And again. The world around him steadied. His racing heartbeat began to slow.

Ty reached the basement anteroom and moved across it to glance down the basement hallway. Empty. He studied the door beside him. What would he find when he pulled the door open? He imagined the scenario. Blood-smeared bodies. Crying, hysterical people. It might look like a war zone. He breathed deeply, preparing himself. So far, he'd managed his PTSD and had not allowed it to take over. If he concentrated hard enough, he could push past it. He had to. What good was he if he couldn't deal with this kind of event? He had to get past it.

He gritted his teeth, blew out a deep breath, and jerked the door open.

Someone inside the room screamed.

"You're safe. You're safe!" Ty shouted. He surveyed the room. People huddled on the floor, many with their hands over their heads. Couples stretched out, lying atop one another. But he saw no blood. The air smelled of chemical gunshot residue. No smoke lingered in the air. Had it already dissipated? As he scanned the room again, he saw no blood, and no obvious fatalities.

Taylor McDonald was huddled under a table. He got to his feet, brushed himself off, and hurried toward him. "Jerry. What a madhouse."

"Is anyone hurt?" Ty asked. Several people got up from the floor to stand in groups near the tables, their arms clutching each other. He heard voices muttering, but no one called out for help.

"Did the police get the shooters?" McDonald asked.

"I don't know. Is everyone all right? What exactly happened down here?"

McDonald recounted how the lights had flickered and then gone out just after he'd brought in the box of flashlights. The shooting had started suddenly, striking all areas of the room. Then, a minute later, just as suddenly as it started, the shooting stopped. The door opened and closed. The room went quiet.

Ty nodded, spoke loudly to the room, "Before anyone leaves here, I'll make sure there's no longer any danger. I'm sure that the police officers in the house are doing their jobs. I don't know if they have located the shooters, but I'm betting those persons won't get out of this house. They'll be apprehended."

Ty stepped back to the doorway and closed the door. Around the room, excited voices slowed and calmed. Six people crossed the room to where he and McDonald stood. They clutched one another and wiped their white, tear-stained faces.

"Are we safe? Is the shooter gone?" One woman called in a shaky voice.

"Do they know who did this? What were they after?" another man asked.

Ty spoke loud enough that everyone in the room could hear, and his voice held steady. "We will hear from those in command soon. Meanwhile, we should wait. Mr. McDonald and I will make sure that no one enters this room. Is anyone injured?"

The crowd muttered, and low voices spoke up.

"I'm okay, just scared," one woman said.

"I thought I'd been shot, but there's no blood, no bullet entry hole. Still hurts, though," one man said. Another person said the same.

No blood. No bullet holes. Ty frowned. The shooter had been shooting blanks. In that case, there would be wadding on the floor, evidence that blanks had been used.

"The shooter was likely shooting blanks," Ty said. "There was no intent to hurt any of you. For now, I need you to stay here. Remain calm." He walked slowly through the room, inspecting the floor around and under the tables.

The muttering grew louder. He didn't blame people for being upset. They wanted out of this room, and away from this mansion before anything else happened. He doubted any of them still believed the murder mystery would play out. And some of them needed to consult a doctor after this experience.

HE needed to consult a doctor after this experience. At least he had not had a full-blown PTSD episode. He'd been able to control it. Now these people needed someone to take charge. Taylor McDonald wasn't doing it.

"Can I ask those who experienced pain during the staged gunfire, who may have been shot with a blank, to please come to the doorway? Medical personnel will want to make sure you have not been injured." Ty watched as people got to their feet and headed for the doorway where he waited.

Taylor McDonald peered at him, his eyes narrowed.

Ty could read the other man's thoughts. *Who is this guy?*

He wasn't going to get out of here without revealing at least part of his history. He might as well get prepared for it.

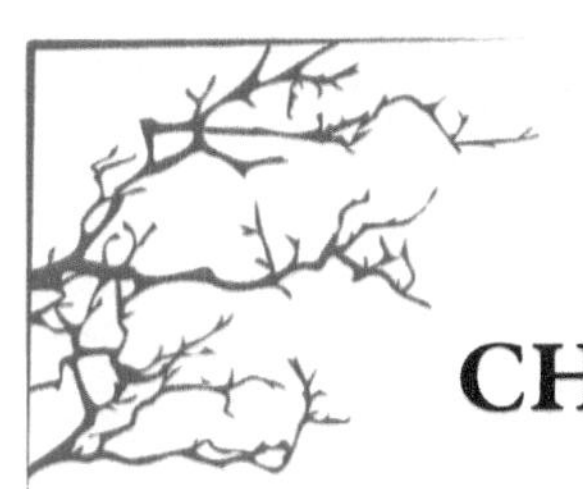

CHAPTER 42 - KYRA

Kyra opened her eyes to blackness. She focused and blinked as she fought to make out shapes. Where was she? Instead of blackness, she could see light seeping in around windows. Her head pounded. She reached up and felt a lump on the back of her head. Her fingers came away sticky with blood. Her face felt gritty, and her back and neck muscles screamed.

Her mind raced. Her mind remembered.

A chill shook her.

Shadows lurked around the room. One shadow became the trunk where she'd found the half-mummy. Andrea, the history teacher, had told them about the man who claimed to have killed Lincoln, the man whose mummy became a carnival attraction. Had the mummy she'd found really been a person at one time? No one had said anything about that mummy today. Not even 24 hours later, that experience in the attic had been pushed aside. With her discovery of Matt Cleary's body, everything else that had happened seemed unimportant.

Had Matt Cleary, with his head bashed in, really been lying in the whiskey cellar?

Her thoughts swirled; the room spun. She braced her hands on the floor to keep from toppling over. Where was she? Someone had hit her over the head. Had they intended to kill her, like Matt Cleary? Who had done this?

She was aware of an emptiness in her stomach, and a dryness in her throat. A thought swirled into her head. She could turn into a mummy if someone didn't find her soon. It was hot up here, and the air was dusty and dry. When someone found her, would they recognize her shriveled and dried flesh? Would she look like the aged hydrangea blooms in her flower beds back home at the ranch?

The would-be Congressperson said that journalists were greedy liars who didn't want the truth. She wanted to know what had happened in this house

187

today. She wanted to get it out there even though people didn't want the truth. They wanted the fairy tale, the good story.

She wanted to know why she dreamed about this house and this attic. There had to be something here to prove her nightmares were not just her imagination. She had tried to figure it out, tried to piece together a good story. She'd taken pictures all over the mansion and could have helped someone solve the scavenger hunt mystery. Why hadn't anyone asked for her help? Danielle Kamber had worked so hard to create that hunt.

She closed her eyes to the darkness and swayed again. She thought she might vomit. She fought the urge. Her stomach was empty anyway.

She pictured the mummy. Another puzzle. Half a body. Who was it? Why and when had it been broken in half, and the upper portion been stuffed into that chest with the Kamber initial? Someone in this house knew more than they were saying. Unbidden, Nicholas Kamber's face came to her mind.

Soon after, Matt Cleary's face moved across her thoughts. Who had he angered so much that they would kill him? Again, Nicholas Kamber came to mind.

Despite the heat, Kyra shivered. Her head hurt, her stomach ached, her throat burned. Was she going to get out of the attic?

If she didn't, her family would never know who she was, and what she had endured in her early life. She wanted the chance to share it, and she still wanted more than anything to resolve the mystery of what had happened to her foster brother. Could she do that alone?

A spider swung from a strand of silk as it built a web in the little beam of light coming from the edge of the window frame. She struggled to clear her mind, to straighten her thoughts. If she was where she thought she was in this attic, the moon wouldn't be shining in from that direction. She was in the south gable, where she'd found the mummy. Someone had locked her in hours ago, hours without drink or food or bathroom. Her bladder ached. She would have to relieve herself soon or explode. When someone found her, she would be soiled and stinky.

Her vision blurred again, and her stomach roiled. Kyra clutched herself, forbidding the nausea to rise into her throat.

She didn't want to be found in a puddle of urine and vomit.

No one would love her then.

She fought with that childish thought. She could hear a voice repeating, 'No one loves you'. It was the mantra of the dark, the mantra of her childhood.

She shook her head, denying that message. Real men love their wives despite everything. Dawson loved her. He would still love her. He would take her home where she'd have a bed to sleep in. Here, she had no bed, only the hard cold floor. No blanket, no pillow, no place to rest, to close her eyes, to get a wink of sleep.

Would the door ever open?

When it did, light would flood the room. She'd be rescued, and Nicholas and Taylor would remember who she was.

Otherwise, she'd be here alone forever. The room swam around her as she grabbed breath after breath until she was dizzy and faint. She slumped to the floor, hugged her knees, and slowed her breathing.

Her eyelids drooped. She had to stay awake. She would fight her captor. She'd get away and run screaming down the stairs to the police. They were in the basement investigating who smashed Matt's head and left him in the cold whiskey cellar.

"Let me out." Kyra's voice sounded pitiful to her ears. No one could hear her.

"Let me out!" She squeezed the words out, louder.

"Please come and let me out," she sobbed. She hiccupped. Kyra squinted into the dark room, looking beyond the thin beams of moon light peeking in. She felt for her phone and the flashlight it could provide but did not find it near her on the floor.

Where was Shimmer? She needed to hold her. She needed her comfort. The dog had been so sweet. Her companion, her friend, when there were no others. Her mother had disappeared; her father had neglected her before he died. And the foster homes were worse. There were too many children for the mother to love. She was an extra mouth to feed, and more money for the foster father to spend on booze and cigarettes. Never mind the second foster mother's ex. He snuck around, tormenting his kids, promising them the moon, and then laughing when he couldn't deliver. Teasing her, berating her.

There was no comfort in this old house. There was nothing here but her past. It was here, in this room, with her.

Kyra sat up. She saw it then, what she had pushed far to the back of her mind. She'd thought earlier about children being locked in these rooms. Only it wasn't children, it was her.

Why had she been in this house? Had someone locked her in one of these rooms?

She rubbed her head, trying to remember through the pain. In her mind, she could see his face, his eyes. Nicholas. He had befriended her. At school, when her foster brother teased, Nicholas stood up for her. At the park, when she'd been alone, he'd come to her, leaving his friends as they played football, coming to talk with her.

She'd followed him home when he offered her a snack. She'd been hungry. He led her into the mansion. She'd gone willingly, hoping that others from the school might be there, that they would see her. That they would SEE her. She wasn't a nobody.

There was a bang on the wall, inches from where she sat in a huddle in the dark room.

Kyra pulled herself away from the racing memories. A knock? Who would be knocking on the wall?

Her thoughts swirled in unreasonable directions. Was it the spirit of the mummy she'd found yesterday? Shimmer was a spirit, and she was here. There could be other spirits. Like Matt's? Like Warren's? Had Warren died in this house?

Her fault. It was all her fault.

She listened, holding her head in her hands as dizziness and nausea battled with her mind and body.

Spirits were ephemeral. They couldn't knock on walls, could they?

If knocking was impossible for them, it was not the spirit of the mummy or the boy. Whoever had knocked on the wall was alive.

Her captor wouldn't be knocking on the wall. Her captor would leave her here until she was rescued, however long that took. Her brain flashed a memory—a girl, waiting alone, in the dark. In this attic.

Dawson and the kids knew where she was, and they expected her home tonight. How long before Dawson reported her missing? Tomorrow, most likely. He loved her, wanted to be with her, and wanted their family together. He would be glad when she made it home. This weekend was the first time she'd left him in total charge of the kids. In his mind, she was the caregiver. Dawson supported the old philosophy that caring for children was women's work. They'd argued about it off and on for most of last week. Then, he stopped throwing words at her and resorted to the weapon of silence.

Kyra rubbed her forehead. She didn't want to think about all of this, didn't want memories to pound back into the front of her thoughts. She had experience with silent houses. Surviving in one was easier than treading on broken glass, trying to keep a powder keg from exploding at a single word or look. Broken glass shreds your soul, she'd learned as a teenager.

Kyra scratched her suddenly itchy arm. Dawson would call the police. They would find her here, in the attic. But what if he didn't call them? What if he assumed that she'd run away?

That would not happen, she argued with herself. Dawson didn't know she'd run away as a teenager. Hadn't she told him she loved him, and told him so before she left home yesterday after lunch?

How long could she survive in this attic if he didn't call the police? What if everyone else in the house was dead, killed by a mad gunman? Three days without water. After that, her internal organs would shrivel, and her blood supply evaporate.

She was so thirsty. The attic was too hot. The warm October day had held hot air beneath the slate roof in the attic with no way for it to get out, or for cooler air to get in. The space was like a giant oven.

How could her mouth be so dry when she had to pee so badly? It didn't make sense. Not a drop of water in sight. Her tongue stuck to her teeth, and she thought about squatting in the corner to relieve the pressure in her bladder.

The knock came again. Kyra scooted closer to the wall and pressed her ear against the thick boards. "Hello? Is someone there?"

Through the wall, she thought she heard words.

"Who's there?" Kyra's heart quickened. She asked again, "Who is this?"

The soft garbled words made no sense. If they were words. If someone was speaking.

"It's Kyra. Who is this? Are you alone?"

More nonsensical words.

"I can't understand you." She spoke into the wall and waited for a response. Minutes ticked past without another word from the other side of the wall. Maybe she'd imagined the voice. Maybe it had been a trick of the heat and the silence.

Remember.

Her memory swirled and deeply buried memories took over again. There'd been two of them imprisoned here before. Two. In the same room.

Her headache boomed. The lump on her head throbbed. She strained, trying to remember. what her mind did not want to remember.

She had been locked here in an attic room of the Kamber Mansion once before.

Why had the universe brought her back? She hadn't rigged the raffle and hadn't wanted to come here. And she hadn't planted the mummy or killed Matt Cleary or had anything to do with those shooting in the mansion now.

Matt Cleary. Had he been in the wrong place at the wrong time?

A breath of cool air licked her arm. She closed her eyes to block out the little bit of light that reached the room through cracks and crevices. She listened, opened her senses, and allowed her sixth sense in.

Shimmer? She needed the ghost dog's help.

Years ago, the dog had appeared in the middle of the highway, in the center of an intersection she was approaching in her car. Going straight would have required her to drive through the dog. She turned the corner. Miles down the road, sirens blasted behind her. On the news that night, she'd learned a high-speed chase had blasted through that intersection. Two pedestrians had been killed as well as the driver of a car on that street. Shimmer had saved her.

"Shimmer?" she whispered. "Come."

Cold air enveloped her, and when she glanced down, Shimmer looked up at her with gleaming eyes, tongue lolling. Her cell phone lay at the ghost animal's feet. The dog lazily got up, stretched, and padded to one corner of the dim room.

Kyra grabbed her phone. The battery indicator showed half battery life. She poked the flashlight function, and the light came on.

The ghost dog nosed at the wall, looked back at her, and then walked through it.

"A secret passage between the walls," Kyra whispered. "I knew it was there." And she could see it clearly in her memory, going through the passage, following the light of a flashlight.

She pointed her flashlight at the wall where the dog had disappeared. She scooted across the floor to the wall and then ran her hands carefully across the dusty, rough walls, seeking a hidden door, a way into or out of a passage.

Kyra eased along the wall, moved slowly toward a corner, and then along the adjacent wall. A slight air movement stopped her at a seam in the wall panel. She pushed and prodded at the seam, then let her fingertips brush the panel. There had to be a latch that allowed the panel to tilt or slide open.

When she pushed on the bottom edge of the panel, a latch popped. A dark space opened in the wall in front of her.

Cautiously she ducked through the short door and eased inside. She shone the light of her phone on the floor and eased her foot down. Kyra gingerly took a step; the floor was solid. She moved forward, watching carefully for signs of decay or a hole in the eighty-year-old floor. If the boards gave way, she would fall to the next floor, or all the way to the basement forty feet below.

She trembled as she scooted along the wall, touching it lightly every few inches, hoping not to encounter a web, a spider, or a rodent. The beam of her flashlight guided her, hopefully, to a way out.

Kyra lost her sense of direction in the dark. Was she moving along outside or interior walls? She glanced back and saw only darkness as if the entryway had closed behind her.

The toe of her shoe slammed into something on the passage floor. When she knelt and focused the beam of her light on the floor, the passage ended in a haphazard pile of boards, bricks, and debris. This passage no longer led to freedom. Kyra didn't want to go back to the room she'd been locked in.

Whoever had constructed this wall had done so quickly. If she pulled down a few boards she might be able to continue along the passage.

Kyra grasped the edge of one board and pulled. With a screech, it moved a fraction of an inch. She jerked on it again. More screeches and more progress. She continued pulling on the board until it was loose from the debris pile. Then, she curled her fingers around the adjacent board and pulled. Once that board had come free, she grabbed another.

Sometime later, winded from exertion, she squatted and forced herself to breathe deeply and slowly. The air was warm and close. She was thirsty, and her bladder hurt. The strong musty smell was laced with undertones of something unpleasant, something rotten. She sucked in a long breath through her mouth and shook her head, trying to keep her mind off the grueling headache and the ache in her lower abdomen.

Finally, the opening through the pile of debris was big enough for Kyra to get through. She pulled in a breath before she crawled through the opening. The beam of her flashlight probed the dark in front of her.

Where would she end up if the passage opened after the blockage? More passages, another room? Her flashlight didn't reach far enough to offer any answers.

Partway through the blockage, she stood on solid ground again. A few feet in front of her was another wall, and behind that, a black hole. Kyra picked up a board and tossed it into the blackness in front of her. Seconds later, it hit the floor.

Kyra squinted into the space beyond the opening. Her eyes registered light.

The wall at the end of the passage contained a small square window. Carefully, she climbed through the remaining debris. In front of her, along the wall with the window, a dark space opened into the floor. Crouching, she approached it slowly. The blackness plunged downward. A stairway hugged the outside wall.

Shimmer was beside her. The ghost dog looked up and then stepped onto the stairway. Descending one step at a time, Kyra followed the dog using her cell phone light to make sure she didn't miss a step.

Kyra let her fingers trail along the wall of the dark stairwell. She heard noises. She stopped. Waited. Somewhere, either above or below, something thumped. Then silence. A minute later, Shimmer began to move again. She continued to follow Shimmer's white tail wagging in front of her.

Where was this stairway taking her?

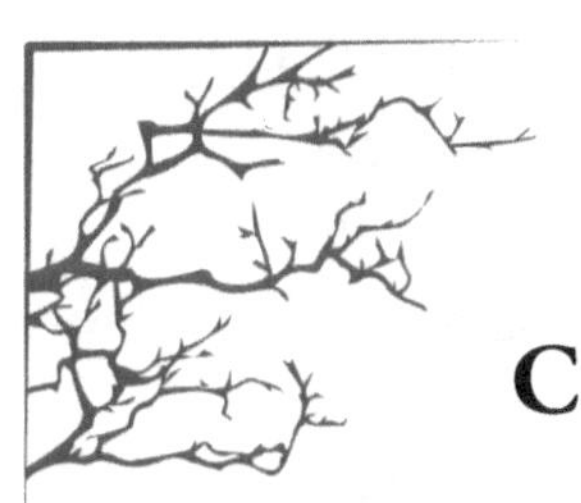

CHAPTER 43 – TY

Ty Harper scanned the lounge for Kyra. She wasn't here. Kim and Richard Spaeth weren't here either. Andrea sat at a table, leaning over so that her head rested on her arms. Like other partygoers, she looked shaken, her face white.

Several guests joined him and Taylor at the door. They showed the two men visible red marks, soon-to-be bruises. Ty knew the bruises were most likely caused by the wadding that was part of the blank bullet rounds from a gun.

"McDonald, have you seen Kyra Blackwood or the Spaeths? They're not here." He grouped Kyra in with the Spaeths, although he wasn't concerned about where they were.

"She left before the gunshots, to use the bathroom, she said. She must not have come back to this room. Maybe she went upstairs to talk to the police." McDonald was not concerned.

"And Kim and her husband?"

"They left before the gunshots, too. You don't suppose there's any chance the three of them have anything to do with the gunshots, do you? We should tell the police."

Ty thought about that. Somehow, he couldn't see Kyra being part of this. He had always been good at reading possible suspects. He was certain Kyra was hiding something, but he doubted it had anything to do with what was happening here. Telling the police would bring him into focus, too. They'd dig into his identity and then they would dig deeper, beyond his FBI experience and his military service. He didn't want that to happen.

"I'll go upstairs to let them know that we need medical personnel down here. Probably should move everyone upstairs now anyway. I'll find out." Ty didn't give McDonald a chance to object. He strode from the room. People threw questions his way, but he didn't pause to answer.

Ty Harper crossed the anteroom to the hallway. Kyra Blackwood had last been seen going down this hallway to the restrooms. Where had she disappeared to? Kim Spaeth and her husband were missing also. Was there a connection? He didn't want to accept Taylor McDonald's suspicion, but it was possible.

At the doorway to each of the downstairs rooms, he shoved open the door, stepped inside, and aimed his flashlight beam around the perimeter of the room. "Kyra? Kim?" He checked the closet and storage spaces before moving on to the next room.

In the mechanical room, two uniformed officers were examining the fuse box. Ty acknowledged them with a quick wave and then backed out into the hallway to continue his search.

Ten minutes later, in the craft room at the north end of the hallway, he paused long enough to wipe his face and flex his fingers. The room had a lingering odor of mineral spirits or paint thinner. He flashed his light around the room and found plaster figurines and paintbrushes along with oil paints. When the a/c cycled on again, the moving air would dissipate the smell. Meanwhile, the door should remain open. He had developed a headache.

Ty climbed the back stairs to the first floor. He checked the salon and then the office. When he found them both empty, he glanced into the formal dining room and then knocked on the door to the study. Murray was deep in conversation with a woman and a man; detectives, he assumed. A cool downdraft from the air conditioner vent in the ceiling struck the back of his neck.

"What do you want?" Murray barked.

Ty raised hands. "I came up from downstairs. People are suffering from shock. No real injuries. Luckily, whoever was down there was shooting blanks, not live rounds. Some of them may need medical attention anyway."

"Thanks for the information. We just sent some EMTs down. Ambulances are waiting on the front drive," Murray said. He studied Ty. "You're one of the raffle winners."

"Yes. Jerry Newcomb. I told Mr. McDonald I'd let you know their status downstairs. Have you caught the perpetrators yet?"

Sergeant Murray cleared his throat. "An investigation is underway. Have you been interviewed yet? Proceed to the living room, please."

"Yes, sir."

Ty hurried down the hallway. As he passed through the entry hall, two groups of people came up the stairs and then entered the living room. He glanced in. Interviews were continuing. No Kyra and the Spaeths weren't there either. Darcy didn't look up from the couple she was interviewing. The detectives had their hands full.

Had Kyra gone home? Had Kim and Richard left, too? They should have at least said goodbye. The fact that they hadn't made them all seem guilty. He stepped out the front door.

Both valets were casually leaning against the valet's station table. The two young men straightened as he approached.

"It shouldn't be long before people start requesting their cars," Ty said.

"Finally. What's going on anyway? We heard gunshots, but no one's come out to tell us anything," Javier, the older valet, said.

"Good thing you have stayed put right here. Very helpful to know that you've been watching. Have you retrieved any vehicles yet, or seen anyone drive away?"

"There's been traffic on the street, but I haven't pulled anyone's car around. The keys are all here." Javier pointed at a board with three rows of hooks holding keys and key fobs. There were no empty spaces.

"Me neither," Carter said, looking at his watch. "Glad this will be over soon. We were told we'd be done by 9, and I've got plans."

"Sorry if you're delayed, but your observations can be helpful. Please think back. You say no one has left recently. What about earlier?"

Both men shook their heads.

"Nope," Carter confirmed. "Once everyone got here, there's been nothing to do. Just you and the other police hanging around. Boring day, except for the gunshots. What's up with that? Part of this murder mystery show they're putting on?"

"Not sure. But it's important to know that no one has retrieved their car keys. And you've seen nothing odd? Has anything else happened today or even yesterday that seemed out of the ordinary? Was anyone lurking around? Did anyone ask you to do something that seemed a little peculiar for a valet?"

Javier shrugged his shoulders. "Typical stuff. Except I'm thinking that I should have charged that lady extra for carrying that trunk yesterday afternoon. It was really heavy for one person to carry alone."

"A trunk? For the party? Decorations, glassware? What was in it?" Ty's curiosity was piqued.

"That's what I thought it was at first, but it didn't look like any party trunk I've ever seen. More like a treasure chest. A dude showed up in an old truck and had the trunk in the back. That lady said she wanted it to go up to the attic. Asked if I'd carry it up. Glad I got to use the elevator. She tipped me a twenty. Should have been more."

"You carried a trunk up to the attic for a lady. For Zia? Dark-haired? Fortyish? She's the person you've been dealing with on this job, right?" Ty's mind buzzed. What trunk?

Javier frowned. "No, it was a different lady. I think she lives here. She's the one in charge of the party. She was out here yesterday when the old guy delivered that chest."

"Do you mean Mrs. Kamber? Blond-haired. Nicely dressed?"

"That's who he means," Carter said. "She was fussing with the wreath on the door and the flowerpots yesterday afternoon. When the truck drove up, she walked over when the driver got out. Then she paid Javier to get it off the truck and take it up to the attic."

"Did you help carry the trunk, too, Carter?"

He shook his head. "No. It was a one-man job. Plus, I was busy cleaning up the area for the key station. Funny, though, she told both of us to keep quiet about it. Like it was going to be a big surprise or something. I figured it was part of the party setup, maybe?"

Not quite. But it had been a surprise.

Kyra had found a mummy up in the attic. Had it been inside the chest that had been delivered to Mrs. Kamber?

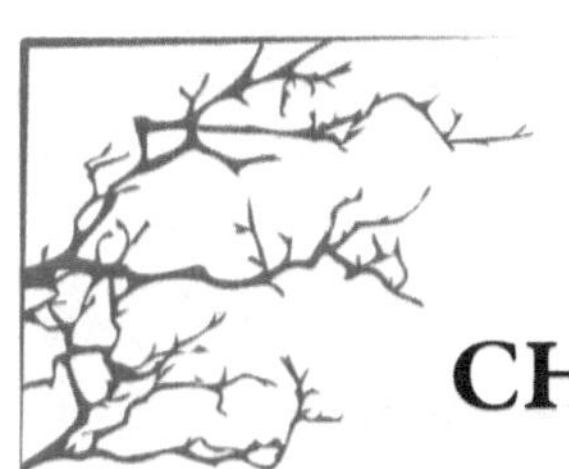

CHAPTER 44 - KYRA

The dark passageway in front of Kyra split two ways. She paused, her hands on the two walls, and pushed her thoughts through the fog in her brain, considering what lay ahead. Where was she in the house? Other than the small beam from her phone, the passageways were pitch black. She felt certain that she had descended the stairs next to an outside wall. One side of the passage had been rough stone, and the other side had been smooth, like sheetrock, or wooden boards.

If she was moving along the outside wall, one passage continued in front of her along the outside wall, the passage to one side must go between two of the downstairs rooms. She shifted her light from the floor to the walls. People were in the house. Shouldn't she be able to hear voices?

Shimmer paused at the intersection, too. But now the dog looked up at her and cocked her head before moving down the passage to her right.

"Where are we Shimmer? Where are we going?" She pointed the beam of her light at the dog's plume of a tail and moved slowly, shuffling her feet as she followed the dog. When Shimmer stopped, her nose to the wall, Kyra stopped, too.

Conversational voices sounded behind the wall. Whatever room that was, people were there. She hoped one of them wasn't the person who had knocked her out and left her in the attic.

Kyra reached out to the wall and ran her hands over it feeling for a latch or something that opened the panel to access the room.

Who was on the other side?

It could be Nicholas Kamber and Taylor McDonald, or it could be the police. Either way, she'd have to explain what had happened in the attic and how she'd found the passage.

She looked down at Shimmer. How could she explain her ghost dog guide? They would doubt her sanity. Not unusual. She doubted it at times herself.

As a teenager, when Shimmer had appeared, she was glad the dog had returned, even as a ghost. Shimmer had kept her from running away from the foster house for many years because she was afraid that the dog was connected to the house where it had died. If she left there, she would lose Shimmer. If she ran away, the ghost animal would be unable to find her, and she would be alone in the world. Back then, that thought had depressed her even more than the current state of her life.

Her memories bloomed in her mind. It was all becoming clear again. She thought about things she'd forced to the back of her brain for twenty years. It made her head and her heart hurt, but at the same time, she felt relief.

A few years after Warren had disappeared, her situation with her foster father became unbearable. She was exhausted from peering over her shoulder, wondering who was behind her, following her, watching her. Her foster parents had treated her like a slave. She'd slept in the attic, locked in at night, awakened every morning by the turn of the key in the door lock.

The day she left, she stuffed a change of clothes into her backpack instead of her schoolbooks. She got on the school bus and a half-mile from the high school, where the jocks got off to go to the gym, she got off too and walked away from the world she'd known in Enid.

Shimmer was waiting for her at the next corner. From then on, Shimmer led the way. Kyra, formerly known as Katie Masterson, followed. It was her 17th birthday.

The voices on the other side of the wall became stronger, and louder. Were they arguing, or was someone giving orders?

She reasoned that it was most likely a group of police officers. After she explained she'd been imprisoned in the attic, they would listen to her story and be sympathetic, she hoped. The reaction might be different if she appeared to Nicholas and Taylor. Either way, she would face lots of questions.

She had to pee.

Her hand bumped a lever, and she could feel a break in the wall paneling, perhaps the outline of a door.

She fumbled with the latch, pushed down, and waited as the hidden door panel shifted.

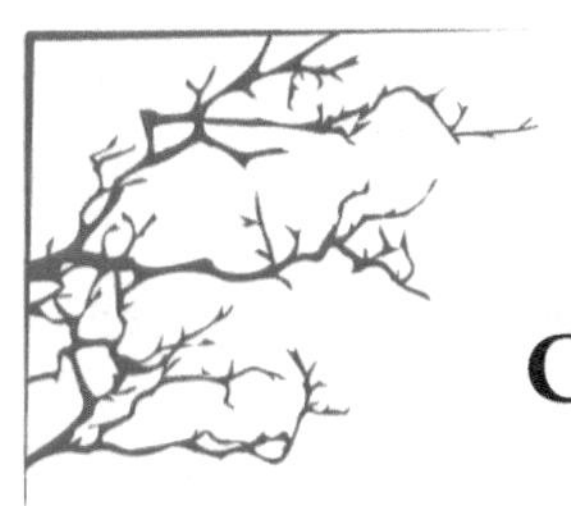

CHAPTER 45 - TY

"You have wormed your way into this investigation. Why didn't that valet share this story about the trunk with the police? Why you? You shouldn't have been questioning them." Sergeant Murray glared at Ty.

Ty pushed himself back into the sofa cushions and looked around the study. He didn't appreciate being verbally attacked by Sergeant Murray. "We were having a conversation. The living room was full of guests being interviewed, so I went outside looking for Kyra, Kim, and her husband. The valets wanted to know what was happening in the house. Then he shared the story about the trunk and Mrs. Kamber. That's all."

"I'm not so sure that's all. While you've been sneaking about, did you happen to see Nicholas Kamber?"

"No. And I haven't seen Mrs. Kamber lately either."

"After the lights came on, she locked herself in her room. She refuses to come out until her husband is found. She doesn't want to see her guests. She doesn't want to address the partygoers again."

"Mr. Kamber is missing?"

Sergeant Murray rubbed his forehead, then reached out and fingered the liquor decanter on the desk. "Forget I said that. And don't share it. My God, this is a cluster," he said gruffly. "I'll get the detective. Stay here." He left the study.

Ty groaned inwardly. He didn't need to be stuck here in the study, he needed to finish searching the house. He flexed his fingers. With every second that passed, he feared for Kyra. She had been missing for over an hour. No one had seen anyone leave the house, but no one had seen them anywhere in it, either. He kept going through the layout of the house in his mind.

Secret rooms and passageways? Was that why they couldn't find Kamber? Was that why he couldn't find Kyra? Something niggled at his mind. His head hurt.

Nearby, something rustled. He was alone in the study, and yet he had the sense that someone else was near. He waited, listening. The faint rustling continued. Where was it coming from? He examined the room, bookshelves, wall-mounted flat screen television, fireplace, pocket doors to the front entry hall, bookshelf, window, window seat, bookshelf ... He walked around the room again, moving in a slow circle.

He was hearing something. Movement. Possibly a quiet shuffle. A step. Something moving along the wall? He stepped closer to one of the bookshelves, trying to pinpoint the location of the muffled sound.

It had to be a mouse or a rat scrambling within the wall. Did the Kambers know they had a rodent problem? It wouldn't be unusual in a house this size and age, to have a nest or two of the animals hidden in the walls.

Something clicked.

As Ty peered at the bookcase, a section in front of him slid open, revealing an opening.

A figure stepped out of the darkness and into the study.

Kyra.

He grabbed her arm, thinking that she couldn't be real. But she was. "Where did you come from? I've been looking for you. Are you all right?"

Kyra stared at Ty, wide-eyed. She swallowed and cleared her throat. "Someone attacked me and left me in an attic room. I found this passage and escaped."

"Are you hurt?"

She rubbed her head. "My head. I must have been knocked out. When I woke up, I was locked in an attic room." Her voice cracked.

Ty released his grip on her arm. Dust and spider webs clung to her blouse and her hair. She swiped at her face and rubbed her eyes. "I'm not badly hurt, but I need, um..., I need a drink, and I ... uh... need to use the bathroom."

"You look like you've been crawling through a tunnel." He brushed a stringy cobweb off her hair, and then wiped it on his shirt to get it off his fingers. "Let's find some water and a bathroom. Then tell me what happened." Ty held the door open for Kyra and followed her down the hall toward the downstairs half-bath.

In the front hall, Kyra grabbed a water bottle from the refreshment table, unscrewed the cap, and took a long drink. The living room buzzed with voices as party guest interviews continued.

When Kyra stepped into the half bath off the front hall, Ty checked out the living room. Darcy was still interviewing guests, still wearing her black-and-white wait staff uniform. A lanyard around her neck displayed her FBI credentials. Her look was focused on the man sitting in front of her.

There's nothing between us anymore, he told himself. She wasn't sure who he was, and he didn't have to admit anything to her. He scratched his head and glanced at the other people being interviewed in the room. Then he turned back to the hall and waited for Kyra.

A secret passageway? Kyra had come out of the opening in the bookshelf dirty and covered in cobwebs. She said that she'd been moving through old passages. Why would she lie about such a thing? And she had appeared behind the wall. He felt certain she was telling the truth.

Had Nicholas Kamber locked her in the attic? He was missing, too, and he'd probably been angry with Kyra for snooping around. What he didn't understand was Kamber's reason for locking her in. Where was he?

Ty had another thought. If there were robbers in the house and she'd stumbled onto them, they could have locked her away to safeguard their plan. Kyra needed to tell the police exactly what had happened.

Kyra caught his eye as she left the bathroom and waited for him near the hallway.

He hurried to her. "Who locked you in?"

"No clue. The blow came from behind. I didn't see anyone." She touched her head and winced.

"Why did you leave the basement?" The question shot out of his mouth before he could stop it. The question sounded like an interrogation.

She frowned at him.

Ty had too many questions. He needed to find a quiet place to talk to Kyra alone.

Kyra took another long swallow. "I was looking for Kim. She and her husband disappeared when the lights went out. Have you seen them?"

"No. They were not in the basement the last time I was there."

"Did I hear gunfire? Is everyone all right?"

"Yes. Just shaken. The best news is that the shooters were using blanks. A few guests have good-sized bruises. No serious injuries."

Relief washed over Kyra's face. They walked down the hall toward the salon.

"You went back up to the attic to look for Kim and Richard? Why there?"

"I looked in the basement, and then ..." Her face went blank. "I don't remember why." Kyra stopped just past the backstairs. "There's someone else up there in the attic. In one of the locked rooms. When I was calling for help, someone knocked on the wall."

"Kim? Or her husband?"

"I can't say for sure. I couldn't understand what the person said. We should go up there."

Ty agreed with her on a logical level. If someone else was locked upstairs, they needed to get them out. But another part of him loathed the idea of going back up to the dark, shadowy attic. It turned his stomach. Going there might trigger his PTSD. It had almost happened yesterday.

"Whoever is locked up there could be injured," Kyra insisted. "Their words were not clear. The voice sounded strange." Kyra chewed her lip. She turned toward the stairs.

Ty swallowed the lump in his throat and sucked in a deep breath. "I don't know where the keys to those rooms are, but if you'll show me which room, I can open the door." Ty patted his pocket and his mini tool set. "After you."

"Newcomb? Where are you going?" Sergeant Murray shouted from the study doorway. He frowned as he marched toward them with two police officers at his heels. "Kyra? Where have you been?"

From the corner of his eye, Ty saw someone dressed in black clothing step from the back stairway onto the main floor hallway between Murray and where he and Kyra stood. Face obscured by a black balaclava, the person glanced to his right at the three men and then charged to his left toward Ty and Kyra. Ty stepped in front of Kyra to meet him, blocking the hallway. He grappled with the figure. Murray and the other officers surrounded the pair as they struggled. One of the police officers grabbed the person's arms and twisted them behind his back.

Murray reached over to jerk the ski mask off. An elderly white-haired man glared at him. "I don't think you're a guest at this party," he growled. One of the police officers handcuffed the man's hands behind him.

The man grunted, closed his eyes, and groaned. When he opened them, he fixed his stare on Kyra. "You," he snarled.

Kyra's face blanched.

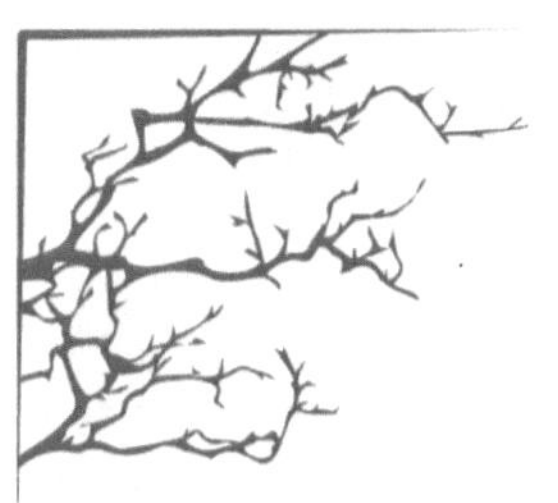

CHAPTER 46 - NICHOLAS

Nicholas Kamber woke up. This time, despite the hammering headache, his mind was clear. He struggled against the cord that kept his hands bound together behind his back.

How long had he been out? The room was dark, but he knew instantly where he was. It was a repeat of all those times when he was a boy. His body trembled. He had to get out.

Nicholas turned all his attention to the locked door of his prison. With his back against the door, he worried at the doorknob with his bound hands, shaking it, trying to turn the screws that held it in place using his fingernails as a screwdriver. The nails broke and bled, but he kept trying until his fingernails were broken, and the ends of his fingers were raw and bloody. He paced the room, grinding his teeth, trying to make sense of what had happened. His jaw hurt.

It wasn't the first time he'd been locked in this room. It was one of his grandfather's favorite places.

The game started innocently enough. "Hide and seek, boys. Let's play a little bit today. You're both always so serious. Lighten up!" Old Man Kamber would say with a chuckle.

The boys were hesitant, but at the same time, yearned for the possibility that the Old Man had changed his ways, that his sadistic streak had been tempered by Grandmama's intervention with the boys' 'discipline' sessions.

Shaking with dread, the two boys had climbed the stairs to the attic. Grandfather knew hiding places that he and Stephen didn't. Until their teenage years, they had no idea of the passageways that connected rooms and led down from the attic to the first floor.

The game would begin casually enough. "I'll count to twenty!" or "You'll count to twenty!". If they were counting, the old man would stomp off, his steps quickly quieting as if he'd taken to the air. They never found him. Eventually, they'd call, "We give up," and he'd walk out of one of the rooms, chuckling.

When it was the old man's turn to seek, he'd call out the numbers, laughing. When he reached twenty, he'd shout, "Ready or not, I'm coming to find you."

His locator sense of their whereabouts was uncanny. He seemed to have eyes in the back of his head. As adults, they learned that their grandfather's extra sensitive hearing enabled him to hear them scurrying around the attic to their hiding places and pinpoint their exact locations easily when they stopped moving. After his second or third turn as the seeker, he locked the doors to the rooms where the preteens had hidden and left them in the dark, sometimes overnight.

Nicholas stuffed those memories deep in the back of his brain, unable to make sense of why that elderly man who professed to love his family thought it necessary to lock them away in these rooms, sometimes for fun, and then, as teenagers, for the slightest infraction of his 'code.'

His father had lived it until he escaped by moving out of town and starting a new life for his family in Pennsylvania. But then, he'd sacrificed his sons when the old man needed someone to practice his tyranny on.

The message from "the Beast" had brought it all back. The real beast hadn't been Warren Switzer, it had been his grandfather. And he didn't have a doubt in his mind that the old man had done away with the teenager, probably somewhere in this house. He'd had a bad feeling when that raffle winner found the mummy and had even wondered in that first minute after seeing the bones if the thing in the trunk was Warren.

But it didn't fit, and he didn't want to consider who it DID fit. The old-fashioned brocade vest, the silk shirt, the wispy white hair.

Besides, everyone knew Grandfather had died of a heart attack and was in the family mausoleum at the local cemetery.

Nicholas snaked his way along, his back against the walls, his fingers searching. He couldn't be sure he was in one of the rooms with a passageway, but he'd find out soon enough. His fingertips pricked when he came across a nail tip, and splinters sliced into his already raw fingertips. But he kept moving anyway, stepping through the familiar dark, hoping to find the way out.

The biggest question on his mind was the question of Who. Someone in the house had attacked him and left him in this attic room. He couldn't think of a single person in his household who would have done that.

Not Danielle, for sure. They had their differences, but she loved him. She was looking for him to make her the city's honored queen, or so it seemed. She wouldn't look that gift horse in the mouth by locking him up here and keeping him away from the party, would she?

And not Taylor. The two of them had been friends since high school. He'd been his first friend in the city, another boy from a wealthy family who was not very athletic and not musically talented with no desire to enter a club for debate or future farmers. That left them with nowhere to go after school but home. They met at Kamber Park where the younger kids played. And their friendship solidified.

Not Zia. Danielle wouldn't allow that, and besides, he and Zia were friends because of Danielle. Zia's world, and his, revolved around keeping Danielle happy, and that meant helping her achieve recognition as a hostess extraordinaire and a leader in the various clubs and organizations she chose to be involved in as a professional.

There was no one else to consider. They hired people to clean and cook, but none of them were employed for longer than six months. It was a way to ensure that no one became too comfortable and that no one uncovered any family secrets that could subject the family to extortion. If there were such secrets.

So, who had done this? Who had knocked him out and locked him in this attic room? Someone he'd invited to his party. Someone he barely knew. Someone who felt that he'd been wronged by Nicholas, or by his family. Had it been Kyra Blackwood? Kim Spaeth? Jerry Newcomb?

Matt Cleary's death brought up the very same questions. Who in his house had hated the news reporter enough to kill him here, in the Kamber Mansion? Was it a coincidence? A crime of opportunity? There were probably multiple people in the community who didn't like the way Matt had handled a news story. Maybe he'd portrayed them in a negative light. Maybe he had ignored critical facts. The possibilities were endless.

He thought of the guest list he'd prepared with Danielle. They'd talked about each person, every husband, wife, and friend. They'd made sure there were no hard feelings in the mix, no reason for them to decline the invitation, and no reason for them to discuss the Kamber family negatively with their friends.

But then, it was hard to know what was happening under the surface, wasn't it?

There was that note from The Beast. That had thrown him for a loop. Someone who remembered what had happened and remembered the teenager who'd gone missing. The so-called bully. He thought about the people he'd invited who had gone to school in this city. None of them would cast any blame on him for the boy's disappearance. And the teenager's family was long gone. Had one of them come back? Hard to believe they would, after all this time. But someone was holding a grudge.

His memory played a tape. Night in Kamber Park. His home lit up with outside lights that shone on the manicured flower beds and shrubs that accented the windows of the house. The best view of that landscape lighting was found across the street in the park.

Nicholas knew he had a goose-egg of a bump on his head. It throbbed, and his head felt wet. He suspected that he was bleeding.

His fingers searched the walls for a hidden switch and the panel that would let him exit this room through the passage.

The trouble was, he couldn't remember much about these passages. He had avoided them for the past twenty years. Too many memories and too much uncertainty about what he might find if he crawled in between the walls.

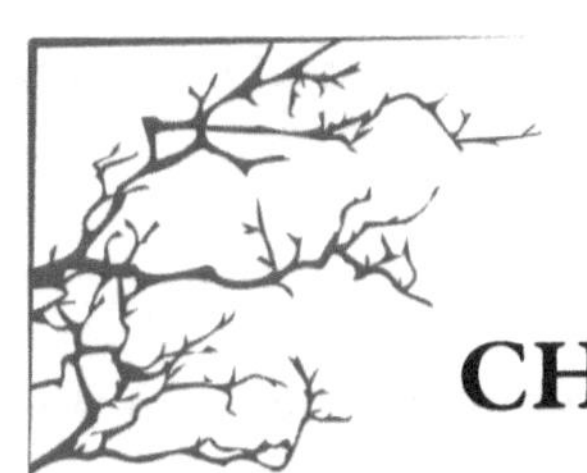

CHAPTER 47 - KYRA

"What is your name?" The sergeant asked the white-haired man wearing black. The man, his face lined with wrinkles and speckled with sunspots, slumped on the sofa in the study, staring at Kyra. A stink of perspiration rose from him.

She turned her back and crossed her arms over her stomach. So, this was why she was here. This was what Shimmer had been leading her to. Perhaps her questions would all be answered after all, just not in the way she had expected.

"Kathryn. It's you, isn't it?" The man ignored Sergeant Murray's question and spoke to Kyra's back. "Katie?"

She didn't respond. She knew what was about to happen. Kyra was going to have to admit who she was as well as her connection to the mansion and this man dressed like a robber. Her stomach twisted.

"I'm talking to you," Murray said gruffly to the man. "You can answer my questions here, or they'll take you down to the police station to answer them. I suspect that you are here to rob the Kambers."

"You can't prove that. I'm a party guest, like everyone else." He coughed.

"Everyone else is in the basement lounge unless they have completed an interview with my security force or the police. Let's cut this short. Who you are? Why are you here?"

"I'm a guest. I went upstairs to check out the second floor. I didn't get a house tour, and after the lights came back on, I thought I'd check it out." Dark blue eyes glared at all of them from a pasty face laced with deep wrinkles. Salt and pepper stubble dirtied his cheeks and chin.

"Right. Name and address." Sergeant Murray picked up the clipboard with the guest list and peered at it before his gaze returned to the man.

The man smirked. "I received a special invitation. I'm not on any list."

Kyra turned back to the room and at once felt the man's steel blue eyes on her. The Sergeant looked at her too. "Do you know this man?"

She faced the security officer. Her heart pounded.

Time to tell the truth.

Maybe, if she told them, the information would go no farther than this room. There were no journalists here, only the Sergeant, two police officers, and Jerry Newcomb from Medford. Maybe they would be the only ones who'd learn who she was and what had happened to her years ago in this house. She had committed no crime. She'd been running from Hugh Switzer.

She glanced at Jerry. His scarred face was further wrinkled by a scowl. Jerry glared at the old man. The hate that radiated from him reminded her of someone else from her past, someone unexpected.

Hugh Switzer stared belligerently at the Sergeant, defiant. He was paying no attention to Jerry. Then he shifted his attention to Kyra, squinting.

"I think I know who he is," she said. "I haven't seen him in many years. His name is Hugh Switzer."

"Hugh Switzer," Sergeant Murray repeated. "The father of the kid who vanished twenty years ago. Disappeared or ran away." Murray's eyebrows raised. "How do you know him?"

Kyra looked at the Persian rug and its swirling pattern of blues and browns. It was time. She'd tell them, and her life would change. She pulled in a breath, and then began.

"When I was a kid, my mother died, and then my father. I was placed with one foster family for two years and then a second foster family. That second family included Hugh Switzer's ex-wife, her new husband, and her children."

Someone pulled in a quick breath, but she didn't search the faces in the room to identify who had reacted. Instead, she kept her look locked on Sergeant Murray.

"You were his wife's foster child?"

Kyra nodded. "I was never adopted into the family. The former Mrs. Switzer and her new husband received money from the state every month to cover the cost of my care, and that of the other foster child in the home, a younger boy. Mr. Switzer showed up sometimes, to visit his kids. I lived with the family until I ran away at 17. That was three years after Warren disappeared."

Switzer scoffed. "Disappeared. Murdered by Old Man Kamber or his grandson. Right here in this house."

Jerry squirmed on the sofa, pale-faced. "You came here to wreck Nicholas Kamber's party?" he asked in a husky voice. "To steal from him? To kill him?"

"I haven't done anything. Party crashing ain't against the law." Switzer shrugged and sat back, pushing into the sofa cushion. He glared at Kyra.

She remained still. Stonily, she met and returned his glare.

"Depends on if that is all you are doing," the Sergeant said. "The police and my men have been rounding up the rest of your 'crew.' I expect all of them will eventually admit to being approached by you to conduct a pseudo-robbery/assault on the guests here at the mansion. They know enough to book you for assault, and other charges. The charges filed will depend on how helpful you are." The Sergeant turned to one side, touched his earbuds, and listened. "Murray." There was a lengthy pause. "I copy." His look darkened. "No danger?" Another pause. "10-4" He disconnected the earbud.

The Sergeant's eyes narrowed as he studied Hugh Switzer. "Forensics is shifting to the basement and the smoke bombs you planted there. Now tell me, why did you kill Matt Cleary? And where is Nicholas Kamber?"

A wide grin spread across Switzer's face. "It's a big house. Secret passages. Maybe you'll find my boy while you're looking for Kamber." Hugh crossed his legs. "And as for Matt Cleary. Don't know the man."

"I think Nicholas might be up in the attic," Kyra spoke up. "Someone else was up there, stuck in another room next to the one I was locked inside."

The men shifted their attention to her.

"I can show you where he is." She nodded toward the door and moved to the edge of the chair seat.

"Detective Wright is on her way. She can go up to the attic. You should go with her, Kyra. And you too, Newcomb." Murray glanced at the two policemen. "I'm sure you have more questions for Mr. Switzer. I'll sit in."

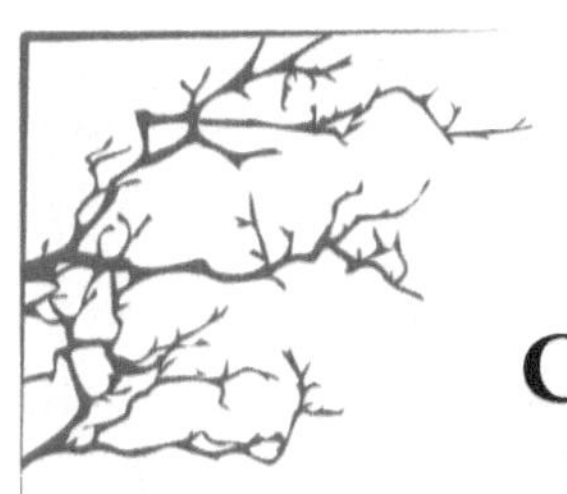

CHAPTER 48 - TY

Ty touched Kyra's shoulder as she stepped in front of him and into the hallway. Detective Nikki Wright joined them.

Ty was numb, too stunned by Kyra's confession to speak. The hallway vibrated around him. He watched the back of her head as she crossed the hallway to the stairs. She didn't say anything, didn't even look at him. But then, why should she? She had no idea who HE was, yet.

Detective Wright followed them up the back stairway, past the second floor, and up another level to the attic. Once in the huge space, Ty flicked on the lights. He tried to ignore the sensation of bugs crawling all over him, and the multi-colored flashes that pummeled his vision.

"Which room were you in?" Wright peered into the dim expanse of the attic.

Kyra pointed toward one of the doors and then crossed the wide central space. "I think I was in here, and that would mean that Nicholas, or whoever it is—it could be Kim or Richard—is in the adjacent room. The passage must run behind this wall, on the other side of the room where I was held." White-faced, she stood in front of the door to the room.

"Are you all right?" the detective asked. "You look a little faint."

Kyra shook her head. "I don't like being up here. Let's find Kamber and get out of here."

Ty swallowed, working hard to keep his equilibrium before he touched her arm again. He put one hand on the wall to steady himself. After pulling his tool kit out of his pocket Ty selected one tool and began work at the lock. If Nicholas was in there, and alive, he'd hear them at the door. They'd know soon enough who had been locked inside.

He'd barely begun work on the lock when a voice sounded from behind the door. The doorknob rattled.

"Who are you?" Wright responded. The mumbled words were once again unintelligible.

Ty carefully worked at the doorknob for a minute. Eventually, the latch clicked. He turned the knob and opened the door.

Nicholas Kamber staggered out of the room, blinking into the light. Face smudged with dirt and clothes filthy with cobwebs and clumps of attic debris, Kamber resembled a hobo more than a millionaire. A bandana had been tied around his head, and a handkerchief stuffed into his mouth. Cords tied his hands together behind him. He spat when the police officer untied the bandana and extracted the handkerchief from his mouth.

"Thank God." Kamber coughed, licked his dry and cracked lips, and rubbed at the angry red marks on his wrists. "I wasn't sure I was going to get out of there."

"You're safe now," the detective said. "And we've apprehended the man most likely responsible for locking you in. He's in custody downstairs."

"That's a relief. Who is he?"

"Kyra identified him as Hugh Switzer," Wright said.

Kamber's look shifted to Kyra. "Hugh Switzer? You don't mean ... Warren's father?" His face twisted into a puzzled expression.

"We don't have all the answers yet, but he crashed the party. Not sure what he intended to do. Let's get you some water. Downstairs," the detective instructed.

Nicholas' eyes widened. He stared at Kyra.

"You ... identified ... him." He blinked, peered closely at her, and then reached for her arm. "That's who you are! I thought I knew you from somewhere. You're Katie. Katie Masterson. I remember you." His mouth dropped open. "Why did Warren's dad come back? And why are you here?" Nicholas' eyes narrowed; he glared. "Did you help him plan this?" His grip tightened on her arm.

Kyra's pale face whitened even more, and she swayed slightly.

"She's not responsible for what Hugh Switzer did," Ty said. "It's just a coincidence that she's here now. She won the raffle, remember?" Ty touched her shoulder. His head pounded. He needed to get out of this attic. He needed to get away from here.

"I would never have come back otherwise," Kyra said in a tired voice. "I couldn't resist the opportunity. I still have nightmares." She crossed her arms and took a step back from the men. "It's been over twenty years since I left Enid. I've never been back."

Anger sparked in Kamber's eyes as he glared at Kyra.

Ty cleared his throat, but that didn't prevent his voice from cracking when he spoke. "Let's go downstairs to sort things out and get Mr. Kamber a drink of water. Your wife is worried about you."

Detective Wright motioned for Kyra to lead the group back to the stairway and out of the attic.

Kyra walked forward and then stopped. "Wait. You know all about the passageways, don't you Nicholas?" She pointed at one of the walls. "Behind there?" She gestured toward one of the walls and then pointed to a locked door. "That's the room I was locked in."

Kamber ran his fingers across his scalp. "It was you that I heard calling. I thought I imagined it." He rubbed his forehead and slumped. Ty grabbed his left arm and moved next to him, offering support. "I can't think. My head." He reached up to touch his head again.

Kyra frowned. "I think Hugh Switzer has been moving around the house in those tunnels. I discovered one by accident in the room where I was imprisoned. Part of that passage had been boarded up. I pulled off a few boards and found the stairwell that goes down to the first floor, and also to the study."

"You're right," Kamber said. "The passageway is behind that long wall, and there's a stairwell that goes down into Grandfather's bedroom on the second floor and another passage to the first-floor office and the study."

Ty imagined the web of passages in his mind. How had Hugh become so well acquainted with the layout?

"Where's Danielle?" Nicholas asked. "She must be frantic with worry. What's happened with the party?" Kamber stumbled as he stepped in front of Kyra.

"Let's go downstairs, Mr. Kamber. We'll get it all sorted out," Wright suggested again.

This time, when she motioned toward the north stairwell, Kyra and Nicholas obeyed. Neither glanced at the other. Ty followed, fighting nausea, and ducking the multicolored lights that shot out from the darkness all around him.

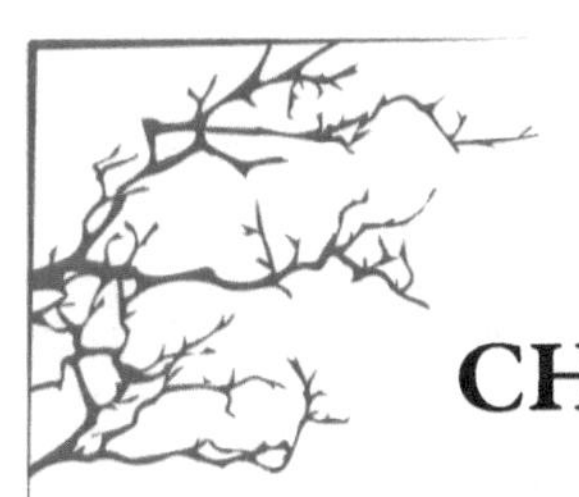

CHAPTER 49 - KYRA

"Is it over?" Kyra asked softly as she stepped into the first-floor hallway. Jerry was behind her. If he heard her question, he didn't respond.

Nicholas pushed ahead of the police officer and into the empty study, with the three others close behind. He quickly turned and dashed back into the hall and then toward the dining room. The others followed.

In the dining room, Danielle gazed out the mullioned front window toward the park and the twinkling streetlights. Nicholas rushed around the table and slipped his arms around his wife. The two of them turned their backs to the room and ducked their heads together in conversation.

Sergeant Murray stood by the sideboard, tapping his fingers on the shiny cherry cabinet. All Kyra cared about at this point was learning the outcome of the day and leaving the mansion. Getting home was her priority. If she was lucky, she'd get out of here before anyone asked her anything about her past, or—heaven forbid––dug up that fateful night when her foster brother had disappeared.

"Did they arrest all the shooters? Was anyone hurt?" Kyra asked.

"Gunmen, such as they were," Sergeant Murray said. "The police have been interviewing partygoers and staff. Several people worked with Hugh to create the fiasco. They were firing blanks, distracting everyone from Hugh as he messed with the generator and kept everyone in the dark. Blanks pack a punch when they hit you. Luckily no one had any serious injuries."

"Have you seen Kim and Richard? What happened to them?" Kyra asked.

Detective Wright pushed her hair off her forehead and frowned. "Richard was involved in Switzer's prank. He retrieved guns hidden in the exercise room and then fired blanks into the crowd in the lounge. He's Hugh Switzer's cousin. Some sort of revenge plot."

"Revenge for what?" Murray asked.

"Only Mr. Switzer knows the answer to that. We expect it to have to do with his son Warren. He disappeared years ago."

"And where's Kim? Did she know what Richard was up to?"

"We caught the Spaeths trying to sneak out of the house together. They are now in custody at the police station."

Sergeant Murray looked pointedly at Danielle Kamber. "Let's go back to the beginning, though. This charade of a party started with the partial mummy found in the attic on Friday evening by Kyra Blackwood. Mrs. Kamber, can you tell us what that was about? I think you have the details."

Danielle's pale face drooped, and her mouth quivered, but her gaze stayed on her husband as she spoke. "I never intended for the mummy to create an issue. It should have been moved to the cemetery long ago. Until it is, I can't help but believe that man's spirit is hanging around this house causing misery."

"Who's spirit? What are you talking about? Danielle, you brought that mummy here?" Nicholas frowned at his wife.

Danielle opened her mouth to say more but before she could, Sergeant Murray interrupted. "Mrs. Kamber, clarify, please. You're saying that you brought the mummy here? Who is it?"

Danielle closed her eyes as she spoke. "My great-grandfather embalmed the body. Here in Enid. He was the local mortician back then, a hundred years ago. I found the mummy in a closet at my father's house when we were organizing an estate sale years ago. I put it in one of the Kamber's chests and left it there. Earlier this month, after my brother and I sold the house, it had to be moved. I had it delivered here and asked one of the valets to carry it up to the attic. I didn't expect anyone to open that chest. I thought it would eventually rot away, or whatever mummies do. I never dreamed anyone would find it, much less make a to-do over it." She opened her eyes to glare at Kyra. "It has colored the whole weekend."

"It used to be a person. It's not just an IT," Kyra said quietly.

"I know. But if you had known the man it was, you wouldn't worry about disrespect." Danielle's fingers worried the folds of dress material in her lap.

Nicholas Kamber touched his wife's shoulder. "You sound as if you knew the man before he was a mummy. Don't tell us you think it's David E. George. He was confused, someone who wanted to be more than he was, even if that meant choosing the identity of a notorious assassin on his deathbed. I don't want to hear that tired story one more time." Nicholas let out a disgusted sigh.

"No, we won't hear it again. Because it's not the truth about this mummy in particular, is it Danielle?" Sergeant Murray asked.

Mrs. Kamber chewed her bottom lip and looked at her husband again. "I...uh. I don't know anything more about that body. It was a vagrant, an unidentified man embalmed out of kindness."

"We know a little more than that, Mrs. Kamber," Detective Wright said. "The corpse is not old enough to be the man known as David E. George or to have been embalmed by your relative a hundred years ago. We've rushed the DNA tests. The results are expected any minute."

Danielle Kamber straightened herself and lifted her head, but her pallor and the downturn of her mouth showed that she was no more eager to tell the truth about the mummy than Kyra was to have to recount one night twenty years ago.

Kyra didn't care who the mummy was. It wasn't Warren. She knew nothing more about what had happened to him than she knew before she came. Now it was too late. She eased toward the door and stepped into the hallway. She might as well go home to the ranch. She'd slip out to her car before anyone could stop her.

As Kyra turned toward the back stairs to retrieve her overnight items, she glanced toward the front hall. Shimmer stood at the foot of the stairs. The ghost dog stepped up onto the first step, her white tail waving behind her.

"Again, Shimmer?" she muttered. "I thought we were done here. What else can there be? I didn't want to see Hugh again. What was the purpose?"

She approached the front stairs as the dog climbed another few steps.

Almost. Don't give up now. The voice inside her head was insistent.

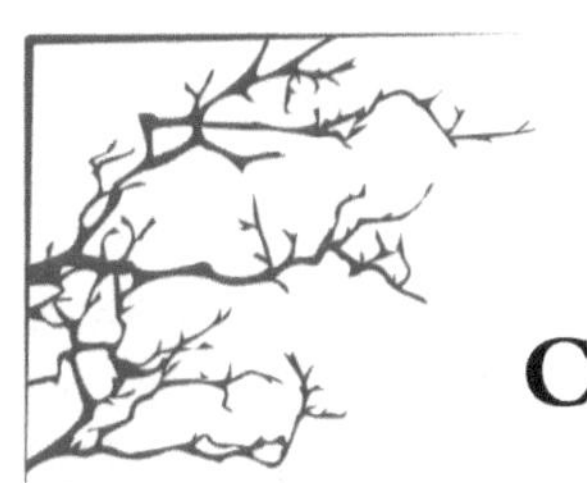

CHAPTER 50 - TY

Ty noticed Kyra step out of the room. He needed to talk to her, but he wasn't sure how he was going to say what he needed to say. He moved toward the door.

"Oh, Newcomb. One of the detectives wants to talk to you. In the living room. Can you go there now, please? She's expecting you," Murray said.

"Sure," he agreed. Darcy? Had she recognized him after all? The breath whooshed out of him, and the world tilted. He could have done without this. Would they come after him if he went out the back door and drove away? The overnight bag he'd left up in his room wasn't important, and there was nothing inside it that could be traced back to him. Toiletries, underwear, the t-shirt he had slept in, yesterday's clothes. But then he realized. There was DNA, and he was in the database

The familiar stab in his gut reminded him that interactions with Darcy had been painful during their last few encounters. But if she knew he was here, he might as well get it over with. He ambled down the hallway and across the entry hall to the living room. This wouldn't take more than a minute. He'd still have time to find Kyra before she could head out of town and back to the ranch.

Inside the living room, amid tables still loaded with food and a fully stocked bar, he found the two valets and two kitchen staff sitting on the sofa. Three of them were handcuffed.

Darcy stood nearby, her notebook in hand. "I think that does it for now. Your cooperation will help, eventually. A van is here to take you down for booking. Your boss, Switzer, is with a detective and will also be taken there within the hour."

"But we didn't—" the older valet began.

"Save it for the interview room. You'll have your say again there. Meanwhile, be good. Okay?" Darcy focused on writing something in her notebook as a police officer led the group out of the room, and out the front door.

When the room was empty except for one plain-clothed detective, Darcy looked over at him and smiled. "Come in, Mr. Newcomb. I'm Darcy Winter. Have a seat."

"Hello," Ty said gruffly. His throat hurt, and it didn't help that the situation made him nervous and agitated. He ran his fingers through his hair and then stuffed his hands into the pockets of his trousers.

"We haven't done your exit interview. You're the last one. Sounds like you've been helping with the investigation. Is there a reason you wanted to get involved?"

He cleared his throat. He doubted she'd recognize his voice. Since his last assignment, and the bomb blast, the timbre of his voice had changed. It was often raspy, his larynx was injured by the chemicals in the smoke from the bomb. Maybe he could get through this interview without his ex-wife identifying him. He had to stick to the facts and avoid looking into her eyes.

"I'm an interested guest. You caught all the crew that was involved in this afternoon's fiasco?" He glanced at her, then dropped his look to the floor.

Darcy tilted her head and studied him. "We think so. Kim Spaeth told us she and her husband weren't involved, but then, under interrogation, the husband admitted to being Switzer's cousin, and agreeing to help him 'scare' some wealthy people. Richard Spaeth was in charge of the lottery tickets in their community. Easy enough to dig his wife's ticket out and claim it to be the winner. We apprehended them loading their bags in their car after the blackout. They still had the pistols with them and some blank cartridges." Darcy frowned as she tucked her notebook inside her jacket. "But I want to know about you, *Jerry*." She emphasized the name and grinned.

Ty rubbed the scar on his cheek, wincing and glancing around the room instead of at his ex-wife. "I own a Dollar General in Medford. Won the raffle." He stroked one eyebrow and studied the carpet.

"So, you say. You've aged a lot, Jerry, since your promo pic for the store." She punched buttons on her phone and then held it up so that he could see an advertisement for the dollar store, featuring his friend, Jerry Newcomb.

"That's several years ago. I've been ill." He coughed and cleared his throat.

Darcy got up, reached behind the party bar, and handed him an ice-cold water bottle. "It's not a scotch, but maybe this will help." She smiled.

Scotch whiskey. His former drink of choice.

"Thank you. And I don't drink the other stuff." He unscrewed the cap and took a long swallow.

She tilted her head. "So, Jerry, tell me why you felt it necessary to help investigate the events here at Mr. Kamber's party."

"I did what seemed right. Not enough police officers here. That's it."

Darcy kept her look on his face. Her eyes flickered. He knew that look. She wasn't sure. She was looking for a 'tell.' He knew his 'tells' and he wouldn't help her. He cleared his throat again and took another long swallow of water.

"We'll need to fingerprint you, and take a DNA swab," she said softly.

He nodded, willing himself not to show any sign of his internal turmoil. His heart sped up and sweat formed on his lip. His leg and the fingers of his left hand twitched. The results of both of those tests would identify him. Darcy would not be surprised. The jig was up.

"Detective Winter," he sighed. He looked directly at her. "You know who I am." His voice was raspy and quiet.

Darcy leaned against the arm of the sofa, her expression blank. "Then, I guess those tests aren't really necessary," she said loudly. Darcy glanced at the police officer standing by the door. "Could you let the Lieutenant know I've finished with Mr. Newcomb, and he's the last of the guests to be interviewed? Thanks." She stood.

Ty stood, too. His heart galloped. His right eyebrow twitched.

The police officer stepped out of the room. Darcy whirled and took two quick steps to stand before him.

"Ty. What are you doing here?" She looked up at him through her long eyelashes. It used to send quivers through his midsection when she did that. Today, he felt no reaction. He let out the breath he'd been holding.

"Filling in for Jerry Newcomb. He's a good friend. He's been helping me out."

"I heard about the bomb. I didn't know how to get in touch with you. They told me you might come back to the force if you could. It's been three years."

"I've been off the grid. Healing. Coping with PTSD. Trying to remember who I am."

Darcy reached toward him.

The door to the living room burst open and Sergeant Murray shoved into the room.

"Switzer is loose. We had a guard posted outside the office. There's another way out of that room. We need to find him before he gets out of the house." He looked at Ty. "I'll get the doors covered. Newcomb, you help search. Take the second floor. If he's gone back into the passageways, he may not be easy to find. We need Kamber's help to cover all the passage entrances. Detective Winter, can you post a guard at every entrance or exit to the house? He could have another trick up his sleeve to complete his mission. We're taking the Kambers from the dining room to the study. They'll be protected there."

"But you know there's another hidden passageway in there. Nothing to prevent Switzer from bursting in and attacking Kamber," Ty said.

"I'm counting on that. Switzer will try to get to Nicholas Kamber. Here's a radio set." He pitched the small radio to Ty. "Get after it and let me know if you find him. Meanwhile, I've got to talk serious business with Nicholas and Danielle Kamber. We got an ID back on that mummy from the coroner. You're not going to believe it."

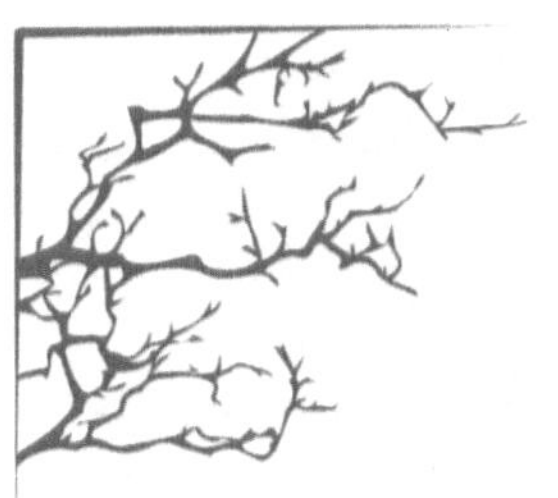

CHAPTER 51 - NICHOLAS

"I'm right outside the door," Sergeant Murray said. "I'll leave you in privacy with the door cracked open. Call out if you need me."

Nicholas sat behind the desk in the study, his head resting on his hands. His thoughts spun. How could this day have gone so wrong? Matt Cleary was murdered, and Hugh Switzer was in his home, running wild. The news media would have a heyday, not only with current events but by regurgitating that horrible story from two decades ago. He could see it now, the next Cold Case expose would be about Hugh's son, The Beast, Warren Switzer. The police would invade the house and tear it apart looking for another body, a body that had been missing for decades. Would they dig up his yard when they searched?

If Kyra Blackwood had not found that mummy, none of this would have ever happened.

He knew without a doubt that Hugh Switzer had left that note in his day planner. Hugh knew the kids at school called his son The Beast. And even though the boy lived with his mother and his new stepfather, his father had influenced him and verbally abused him for years. The seeds were planted that created the monster his son sometimes became.

That monster's teacher had been here, in his house, in the place he lived with his family.

His family. After what he'd just learned from Danielle about the mummy, he wondered if he would still have a family in the coming days. Enid residents would be horrified. The girls would not want to come home from college during semester break after being told what had happened. They would think that he had been part of the coverup and had kept the secret for more than twenty years.

Danielle sat in a chair, facing him, her face pale and her blue eyes on him. She pulled off the short brunette wig she'd been wearing and let her blond hair cascade freely. She watched him as he struggled with her confession.

How could she have done this?

He shook his head and looked at her. "Why didn't you tell me before?"

"I've wanted to tell you, dearest. Honestly, I have," Danielle said, her voice low and matter-of-fact. "The time was never right. I didn't mean for you to find out like this."

"Is that your excuse? Of course, you didn't *mean* for it to happen like this, but it did."

"You knew what he was like. But you didn't know what he was like every time he was alone with me. He never let the rest of you see. But after what he did to you boys, you should have suspected how evil he was. He was evil to me. He thought I was nothing and could be used in whatever way he wanted. You should have protected me." She pouted.

"Don't turn this around and lay the fault in my lap. I'm not my grandfather, and I couldn't be everywhere all at once. You were a grown woman. And now I learn this, what you did after he died. You are responsible for your actions." Nicholas groaned. He had never suspected anything like … this.

Danielle lay a hand on top of his and rubbed her thumb across it.

"After that day in the greenhouse … you remember … Shifty barged in … caught the old man attacking me. Afterward, I couldn't be in the same room as your grandfather. Shifty wanted to do something for me. After the Old Man's heart attack, he saw an opportunity."

"But how did Shifty turn him into a mummy? And where are his legs?" Nicholas covered his face with his hands. He was glad his father was dead so that he didn't have to learn of the desecration that had been done to the Old Man's body.

"No one knew what brought on that heart attack. We had a private service. Unopen casket. I bribed the funeral director to let me have the old man's body. Shifty stuffed it in an old chest the family had left out in the greenhouse. What part of it didn't fit in the chest, he buried in a ditch outside of town. Then, he took the trunk with him and left town."

"Oh my God. Danielle."

"The body had already been embalmed. After a short time in that chest, in the dry heat of the desert, the body mummified."

"How did you end up with it? Why bring it here?"

"Shifty died last month. In his will, he left instructions for that chest to be delivered to me. It arrived yesterday. I had one of the valets take it up to the attic. I never dreamed someone would go up there and find it."

Nicholas rubbed his forehead. He looked at his wife. This was unimaginable. All these years they had been together, and she'd kept a secret like this from him. He didn't know her at all.

"I know my grandfather was awful to you. He was horrible to me. But that mummy was my grandfather."

"That body belonged to a lecherous old man who hated women. Including your mother. And your grandmother. He couldn't abide it if they talked with another man, let alone looked at one." Danielle's eyes sparked.

"That may be true. But look what he built out of nothing. A family legacy, a family fortune." He laid his forehead against the cool wood of the old desk. "Oh, Danielle. I wish you'd told me right after it happened. Shifty wouldn't have had to run off to Arizona, and Grandfather could have been laid to rest properly. As it is now, it's a mess. I don't know how to straighten it out. The police may file charges."

He reached for the tumbler of whiskey and took a long sip.

"Shifty is dead, Nick. Who would they file charges against?"

"You? As an accessory. And the media will find out," Nicholas moaned as he set the glass back down on the desk. "They will feature that story in their news pieces. We'll be lucky if the party and our charities get any media play, between the mummy and all this about Switzer, not to mention that Matt Cleary was murdered in my house. What a mess. Everyone will be breathing down my neck. How can we keep this out of the media?"

A quick knock came at the cracked door, and Sergeant Murray stepped in.

"We haven't located Hugh Switzer, but we don't believe he left the house. I understand there are secret passageways, and that Switzer knows about them. We need your help to find him."

Nicholas sighed. "Yes, there are passages. There's one in here."

Nicholas pushed away from his desk and went to the bookshelf. He pushed the back of the middle shelf, and a section of the paneled wall slid to one side.

A white-haired man dressed in black darted into the room from the dark opening, glaring.

"Where is he? All these years my boy's been here. I know it." Hugh Switzer charged toward Nicholas with clenched fists, his ashen face gleaming with sweat.

"Hugh Switzer. How did you get into my house?" Nicholas met the man in the center of the room, hands fisted. He grimaced at the man's dirty black clothes and the grime that streaked the man's face.

Switzer guffawed. "I've been your gardener for months. This week, I've been pulling your weeds and prettying up your flower beds." Eyes wide and wild, he looked from Nicholas to Danielle and back again. "I'm Warren's dad. You set him up, and your grandfather killed him!" He leaped toward Nicholas, reaching for his neck.

Sergeant Murray grabbed Hugh Switzer's arms and struggled to bring his arms around behind his body. "A little help, please," he shouted. "Stop fighting. It's no use."

A police officer burst into the room, worked with Murray to twist Switzer's arms behind his body, and handcuffed the man.

Hugh Switzer seethed, face red, eyes glaring. "What did you do to my boy? He never came home again. Is he in this house? Where is he?"

Nicholas took in the elderly man, who struggled to stand with his arms locked behind him. It was hard not to feel sorry for him. Switzer had never seen his son again.

And Matt Cleary had withheld a critical piece of information from the police. Had Switzer known that? Had he killed Matt because of it?

On the evening of the day he disappeared, Cleary had driven past Kamber Park. He told the police he'd seen Warren there. What he didn't tell them was that he'd seen Warren enter the Kamber Mansion through a glass door on the north end of the house.

The next day, he took Nicholas aside and told him what he'd seen. Nicholas had begged him to keep that a secret, worried that the police would use that information, as well as the fact that he and Warren had nearly fought at school, to make him a prime suspect in the disappearance. As far as he knew, Cleary had kept his word.

Truthfully, he didn't know if what Cleary said was true. He'd never seen Warren in the house and had heard nothing to indicate he was ever there. His grandfather had not bothered to comment either to Nicholas or to the police when they came to the house to interview them all. "It's a non-issue," he'd said as he perused the *Wall Street Journal.*

Switzer's eyes glistened with moisture. "I raised him to be tough like my father raised me." Switzer took a breath and looked around the study. "I always wanted a place like this. Your grandfather didn't deserve it."

"You don't know anything about my grandfather," Nicholas said. "He worked hard to build his company and this city. You have no right to criticize or judge him. What have you done with your life?" This man would not lecture him about his grandfather.

"Your old man fired me after I'd worked long, hard days, for years. He built this company on the backs of men like me." His shoulders slumped. "And then I caught your grandmother's eye. The old man was jealous. He fired me."

Nicholas peered at Switzer and then looked at his wife. Danielle sat, eyes down, in a chair by the desk. When she looked up, tears filled her eyes.

Had Hugh Switzer been fired because his grandmother liked him?

"My boy must have come here to talk to her, to tell her that I couldn't make it without the job. He never came home." Switzer swiped his eyes. His chest heaved. When he looked up, fire flashed from his eyes again. "Tell me where he is!"

CHAPTER 52 - KYRA

Kyra climbed the front stairway, once again following Shimmer. At the second-story landing where the stairway ended, the ghost dog turned right to the double doors that led to the Kamber's master bedroom.

Shades of the palest blue and glittering silver decorated the luxurious room. Thick draperies hung beside the wide windows, and a satin and lace comforter covered the king-size bed. A floral-patterned rug in blue and cream stretched across a dark wood floor and extended under the bed. Pillows of varying sizes filled the upper half of the mattress, and sheer bed curtains had been gathered at each corner of the four-poster.

She inspected the beautiful room, glancing from the windows to the fireplace, and then to the alcove where Mrs. Kamber's writing desk sat in front of the stained-glass bay window.

Shimmer waited in front of a closed door, licking her paws. She looked up expectantly. Kyra crossed the room and opened the door, revealing a large closet, bigger than her entire bedroom back on the ranch. Blouses, slacks, dresses, and shoes filled the shelves and racks. Danielle's closet, without a doubt.

Shimmer trotted into the closet and crossed the room to the full-length mirror. The ghost dog pushed her way into the clothes hanging from the rods next to the mirror and disappeared.

Kyra turned on the bright overhead light before she crossed the room to shove the clothes aside and examine the paneled wall behind the mirror. Carefully, she ran her fingers over the smooth surface, feeling for a break in the wood. There had to be a hidden panel that opened a secret passage. Did it lead from this bedroom to the attic and eventually downstairs to the office? She didn't care where it led, but she had to find it.

Shimmer had led her here. That could only mean one thing: she needed to find something in this closet, or in a passage that led away from it into the bowels of the house.

Kyra pressed the top of the wall panel directly behind the mirror, then pressed the edges and the bottom of the panel. Nothing caused the wall to move, or to open. There had to be a way. Shimmer had disappeared here.

What if she couldn't find it?

Maybe she shouldn't find it.

Maybe this whole weekend had been a wild goose chase with no purpose.

She dropped down to the carpeted closet floor and sat, hugging her knees.

The thought shook her world. What was Shimmer's purpose for her this weekend? To see crazy Hugh? To remember hideous experiences from her youth, things that had happened in this house?

Her thoughts buzzed. The closet rotated around her. She blinked.

With a jolt, her world steadied. She opened her eyes. No. It wasn't over. Something ...

She scooted the clothing to one side and focused on the lower wall panel where a tiny crack showed in the base of the floor molding.

Kyra fingered the molding, pushing, and prodding. Something clicked. The panel above the molding slid to one side, revealing an opening. Hot, stale air gushed out, heavy with the scent of dust and decay. Spider webs stretched across the passage, and rodent droppings littered the floor. It had been a long time since anyone had been inside.

She pulled her phone out of her bag and pressed the flashlight function. The dim beam barely sliced through the darkness. She was almost out of battery power.

Unlike the other passage she'd moved through, trash littered the wooden floor. Crumpled papers, magazines and newspapers, food wrappers, an old hatbox, shoe boxes, and even faded clothes were scattered on the floor in front of her. All of it added to the smell of age and rot that filled the wide passage.

She paused in the opening. She did not want to enter. Her foster brother Warren could be here, somewhere. She felt certain that Old Man Kamber had never let him out after he'd come here to rescue her. Did it matter whether she saw his body or his bones? She felt him in this house, had felt him here almost from the minute she arrived.

Trembling, she reached behind her into the closet and grabbed an empty hanger, then used it to scrape the webs from across the opening. Kyra entered the passage. Behind her, the wall panel started to close. She grabbed a shoe and blocked the mechanism from closing. She needed the closet light to see inside the passage. Her phone light was too dim.

A few yards ahead, the passage turned. As she rounded the corner, the now dim light from the closet and her phone flashlight revealed something hanging on the wall in front of her. She cringed.

Warren?

On shaking legs, she stepped closer. A pair of jeans and a sweatshirt had been nailed to the wall.

Her memory flashed. Warren and Old Man Kamber fighting. Warren's shirt tearing. These were the clothes Warren had worn when she had last seen him here, in this attic.

The light on her phone blinked out. Kyra's legs gave way beneath her; she crashed into the wall. One of the boards cracked. In her mind, a hole opened. She grasped the edge and held on, her balance compromised. A shaft dropped into nothingness beside her.

Wild-eyed, she looked for something to grab as her grasp on the wallboards failed. Shimmer stood beside her, eyes shining, tongue lolling from one side of her mouth. The dog was ephemeral. A ghost couldn't pull her to safety.

But Kyra reached for the dog anyway. Shimmer's fur bunched beneath her grasping fingers. The animal planted its feet and then backed slowly away from the open shaft.

She held on, and once she felt her balance had shifted and she wouldn't fall, she scooted away from the gaping hole. When she was sure of the solid floor beneath her, she let go of the animal, heart thumping.

"Thank you, oh, thank you Shimmer." She reached for Shimmer again, wanting comfort.

Empty air. The ghost dog had vanished.

Kyra lay on the floor and put her head down on her arms. Dust tickled her nose. She sneezed and closed her eyes.

Her muscles ached, her head pounded, and her body quivered. She wished she was in a thousand other places besides here. Her mind pulled up an image of the tree swing behind the ranch house, the one Dawson had put up for her on the edge of the wood that rimmed the creek. A peaceful place, with a beautiful view toward the west no matter the season. She'd like to be there.

The next time she went there, she would be different. She would truly appreciate that view more than ever before. She would appreciate the life she had. She would no longer dwell on what had happened all those years ago.

For too many years the shrouded memories and the uncertainty of what had happened to Warren had lurked in the back of her mind, burdening her. That uncertainty had tinged everything she thought and did. She couldn't escape the ever-present guilt.

Dawson had never understood her black moods. He had no idea. He didn't know who her birth parents were or what her birth name was. He didn't know about her foster families, didn't know about her foster brother. Didn't know about the man who had mistreated her foster brother Warren, his son, or that her birth father had nearly let her starve before he died.

Her foster brother had been here in the Kamber Mansion for all these years. He had not abandoned her after the rescue, and he had never searched for her. But the fact remained. Warren had come into this house to rescue her, and he'd never come out.

She accepted his death finally. But where were the bones?

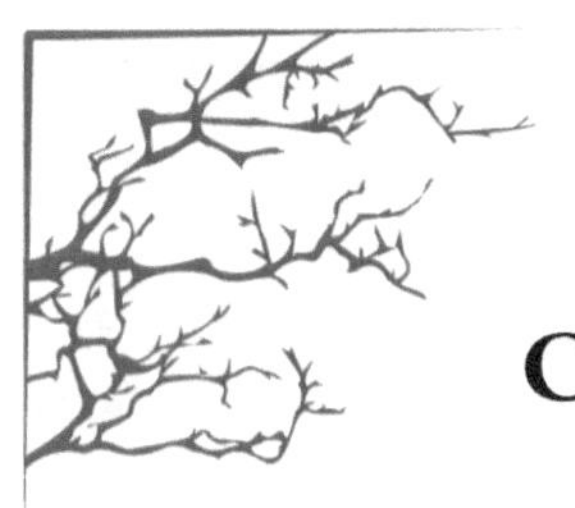

CHAPTER 53 - TY

Ty Harper raced up the front stairway toward the second floor, keeping his look focused in front of him, not wanting to travel back in time again, not wanting to remember. There had to be a hidden passageway on this floor. It seemed likely Kyra was headed there.

A numbness had enveloped his inner core. Her confession, as she named Switzer, had shaken him. If Switzer had managed to get away, he didn't care. He didn't want to see him, didn't want to talk to him. But he did want to find Kyra.

She'd walked away from the dining room, holding her head high, full of purpose. Once she'd identified Hugh Switzer, she never looked at Ty again. What would she have seen if she had?

At the top of the stairs, Ty rounded the corner. The door to the master suite stood ajar. He slipped in quietly and inspected the empty room. If there was a passage on this floor, this was a likely entry point.

The closet door stood open; he crossed the room to the doorway. The clothes on the back rod were askew on their hangers and had been pushed aside so that the wall panels were visible behind.

He stepped farther into the closet. Behind the floor-length mirror was a narrow opening in the wall, held open by a shoe. He tried to open it further by pulling on it, but the wall didn't move. He studied the panel, pushing it this way and that. His efforts moved to the bottom of the panel, and the molding near the floor. Something clicked. The lower part of the panel slid fully open.

Ty flicked on his flashlight as he entered the passageway, stepping over trash and old clothes. At some point in the past, someone had been staying here, eating, drinking, maybe even sleeping. He doubted that Nicholas or his wife had left these things here. He doubted the grandmother had left them here either. Had she even known of the existence of this route through the house?

His mind buzzed. His body began to shake. No. Not now. He pulled in and then blew out several deep breaths. Why was this passageway setting off a PTSD episode? His current memory flickers—darkness, fear, thirst—had nothing to do with the bombing.

Lights flashed in his head, revealing bare boards and beams. Something fluttered in the rafters, something skittered along the floor. His empty stomach ached, needing food, and his tongue and throat hurt, the tissues so dry.

Nausea, but the dry heaves brought no relief. The passage walls around him vibrated and twisted. He wanted out.

Let me out!

Another part of his brain recognized the memory. He opened his eyes wide, focused on the present and the beam of his flashlight skittering across the floor.

NOW. I am here NOW.

He shook his head as if that could shake the memories away, but they remained, and he was existing in both times concurrently. He flicked off the flashlight for a moment, hoping that would stop his world from vibrating, stop the strobing lights. With deep breaths, he gradually calmed and settled into the present.

When he opened his eyes again, flicked on the flashlight, and swung the beam straight in front of him, the tunnel narrowed and turned a corner. He stepped slowly and carefully through the clutter, listening as he moved forward. Something was alive in the darkness ahead. Words. No, sobs.

The passage turned. Ty stopped. Fully present now, the memories fell away. He studied the narrowed walls of the passage and smelled the dust and the scent of raw wood from the timbers that framed it. Three steps farther. He looked ahead. He stopped.

Kyra lay in a fetal position on the floor. Clothing rags hung above her on the wall of the passage.

"Kyra?" Ty moved closer, and as he did, she rolled to one side and looked at him. She pushed herself to rest on her elbows.

"He's not here. Only his clothes. I thought I'd find him. Shimmer led me here."

Ty reached down to help her stand. He scrutinized the passage. A large, familiar white dog stood a few feet farther down the tunnel. The animal's tail wagged, and her jaw opened in a smile.

"Shimmer," Ty whispered.

Kyra's eyes widened. "You can see her? You can see the dog?"

Ty paused. "Yes." He knew the dog. He remembered its grave.

"How?" Unsteadily, Kyra reached out to the passage wall for support. She pushed her hair off her face. "No one can see Shimmer. She's a ghost."

Ty nodded. "Figures." He touched the sleeve of the shirt that hung from a nail in the wall. "Come with me. We need to talk, and I need coffee."

CHAPTER 54 - KYRA

Kyra followed the man she knew as Jerry Newcomb down the front stairs to the living room. Once there, she crossed the room toward a grouping of chairs near the fireplace. Halfway there, she stumbled. She couldn't feel her feet, or her hands. Her mind wouldn't focus. The light in the room dimmed and then brightened. Tears welled in her eyes. She slumped into the chair.

She would never know what happened to Warren. His clothes were there, but not his body. There were no bones. She would never know the truth. All she knew for sure was that Old Man Kamber was responsible for whatever had happened to Warren.

She'd always thought that once she knew the truth, her emotions about everything would change. Over time, her anger would dissipate, her sadness and even her guilt would diminish. But it all hinged upon finding his body.

She had to let it go. No more thinking about it, no more looking over her shoulder, afraid that Hugh Switzer was blaming her, hunting her. No more secrets from her family. It was over.

Jerry sat on the edge of one of the chairs and leaned forward towards her. "What do you think you found up there?"

She looked at the man and searched his scarred face, his thick silvery hair, and his hazel eyes. Her look dropped to his hands, folded in his lap as he studied her. "Clothes. Trash. Somebody lived up there. Maybe my foster brother Warren. I don't know what happened to him. I don't think I will ever know. It's too late to find anything."

Jerry closed his eyes. His limp hands fisted.

A thought pricked at her brain. "Upstairs, in the attic, before we came downstairs. You saw Shimmer." She peered at Jerry Newcomb.

His head jerked. "Shimmer. Your dog."

"No one has ever seen Shimmer but me. She died a long time ago." Kyra chewed at her lips. "I don't understand it. Why could you see her? She's a ghost."

Jerry's lips pulled up in a slight smile. "I can explain that. But first, I'd like to know why you came here. Were you looking for something? Did you have any idea that Hugh Switzer would be here?"

Kyra sucked in a deep breath. She was going to bare her soul to this stranger. HE SAW SHIMMER. That meant something. This man was not her husband, and she was about to tell him things she had never told Dawson, things her kids had no idea about. Was it finally time to talk about it?

HE SAW SHIMMER.

The police would want to know more about her. They would want to know why she came to the house this weekend and whether she had played any part in Hugh Switzer's revenge scheme.

She would talk to the police again soon enough. Meanwhile, Jerry Newcomb leaned toward her and his sorrowful, kind hazel eyes pulled at her. She focused on a lighted sconce on the wall by the fireplace behind him and began.

"One of my favorite things to do as a child was play in the park across the street. Most often, alone. I didn't have many friends. My mother died, and my father didn't take care of me. I lived with one foster family for two years and then another. That second family included Warren Switzer's mother and his stepfather. I lived with them for five years." She focused on the beautiful draperies. She didn't want to see Jerry's eyes change as he judged her for who she had been as a child.

"Did anyone at school know you were a foster kid?" His voice was soft and raspy.

"Nobody asked. It embarrassed me. I didn't make friends easily. Trust issues."

"You were lonely, and people teased you."

"A lot of people did. Including my foster brothers. At home, the oldest one tolerated me, protected me from my foster father at times, but at school, in front of the other kids, he called me a 'Monet.' In kid-speak, that meant someone who looked better from far away than they did up close. It hurt when Warren called me that in public. But home was worse. My foster father terrorized me."

"I'm so sorry that happened to you. It should have been better."

"I dreamed of it being better. I became friends with Nicholas Kamber at the park. He came over to talk to me once, and after that, when all his friends had gone home, he'd sneak me into the house and give me food. Sometimes it was the only meal I had all day. There were too many kids at my foster home. They forgot about me most of the time. But my foster father didn't forget about me. I wish he had."

Jerry's eyes narrowed and he scowled. "I've never understood men like that. I never will. You were a child."

"There was protection when Warren was there. The man stayed away. One night I snuck into the Kamber's house when Nicholas had told me that no one would be home. I did what I usually did there when I had the place to myself. I wandered through the first-floor rooms and went to my favorite spot in the salon, where I could look out into the night. I loved being able to see outside and to know that no one could see me, sitting there in the dark. After a little while, I took the stairs up to the attic and went to a room where they'd stored old books."

"You weren't scared up in that attic?"

"No. I had been there with Nicholas so many times. But that night, I had just grabbed a book and settled into the reading chair when the door swung shut. The lock clicked. I froze. At first, I thought it was Nicholas playing a joke on me. He'd never done that before, but he had told me about him and his older brother getting locked in the rooms by his grandfather. Not long after that, the lights went off. I couldn't get out of the room. A little light came from the attic window. I sat there, alone, cold and hungry all that night and the next day."

Out of the corner of her eyes, she saw Jerry Newcomb straighten his fingers and then bend them into a fist again. He kept his eyes on her face as she talked.

"My foster family didn't report me missing. But the next day, in the late afternoon, Warren came looking for me. He came into the house through the salon and then came up to the attic. He jimmied the door lock there, too, but before we could leave the attic, the old man showed up."

Kyra's mind released the memories in full color. She winced and tried to settle herself with deep breathing. Finally, she continued. "He beat Warren and slapped me across the room. Warren hit the wall hard and didn't get up. The old man ranted— and told Warren to stay away from his grandson. Blamed him for getting Nicholas in trouble, jeopardizing his grandson's future. Then he locked him in that same room I'd been in, pushed me into the elevator, got in, and sent it downstairs. On the first floor, he shoved me out of it. He told me to get out, go home, and not to tell anyone where I'd been. He threatened to send me to jail for breaking and entering. He claimed that he'd see to it that I never got out."

She sat quietly. "I didn't think he'd keep Warren there. But he never came home. I never saw him again. Honestly, everyone, including the police, thought he'd run away. His father, Hugh, was the only person who believed Mr. Kamber had killed his son. Warren's mother never recovered after Warren disappeared. For me, life became unbearable at that house. My stepfather was a sadist. At 17, I ran away. Warren's stepfather moved the family away shortly after. If Warren died here, it was my fault. He was in this house because of me."

"You didn't see Nicholas that night?"

"I never saw another soul until Warren opened the door to that room."

"And you never talked to Nicholas about it?"

"I didn't talk to him at all after what his grandfather had said. I quit going to the park, and I never saw him at school anyway, he was four years older. I had idolized Nicholas. Had Cinderella dreams that he loved me. But all those fantasies vanished after that night in the mansion."

Jerry Newcomb reached over and brushed a strand of hair from her cheek. "How did it all begin? I mean, how did you and Nicholas become friends?"

"The park was usually full of kids. One night, I had to wait for a swing, so I sat at a picnic table until the kids went home, and I had the swings to myself. Nick's friends eventually left too, went home for supper, I guess, and he came over to me on the swings. We didn't talk much, just swung back and forth. He wasn't in any hurry to get home. Then he jumped off and invited me to come to his house for an ice cream bar. I hadn't eaten much that day, so

I went. Truthfully, I didn't know people could buy ice cream bars at the store and keep them in their freezers."

"Yeah, not likely your foster family had those in the freezer," Jerry said, frowning.

"A few nights afterward, I went into the house with him again. He showed me the passages. Made me promise not to tell anyone. And then he bragged about how anyone could get into the house anytime. He showed me how and swore me to secrecy. A couple of times, I went in alone. I would just sit there quietly in one of the rooms. Sometimes I'd read. It was so nice. Peaceful. I could hear a clock ticking somewhere, and birds outside in the trees. It wasn't at all like where I lived, where everyone yelled all the time."

"Quiet, huh? And a little bit spooky. It's a big house. And you never got caught?"

Kyra shook her head. "I snuck in more often with Nicholas. He was kind and funny. It was like being part of a special club or something. I think Nicholas was lonely, too. And I think he wanted to see what he could get away with, how far he could go without being found out."

"In the house, what did the two of you do?"

"We crept through the passages, usually ending up in the attic if other people were in the house. If no one was home, we sat on the floor in the office or study." Her throat tightened. She'd never talked about this with anyone. And now the words were spilling out of her. Jerry looked ... interested. But his face was emotional, the scars like red scratches, more evident than at any time during the weekend.

Kyra shivered. Tears filled her eyes. She closed her eyes, seeing the darkness, tasting the dust, feeling the desperation.

"That night and day locked in that room ... I became a different person. And when I finally ran away from home, I blocked it all out, or I tried to. In the back of my mind, this house loomed. It was the last place Warren had been."

"So, you bought the raffle ticket," Jerry said.

"That wasn't why I bought the raffle ticket. Actually, I'd pushed everything so far back in my mind. I had no idea when I first arrived what I was really here for, but my subconscious guided me. Shimmer guided me. And once I realized what those nightmares meant —that all of it had really happened—I needed the truth. I had to find out if there was anything left of him here."

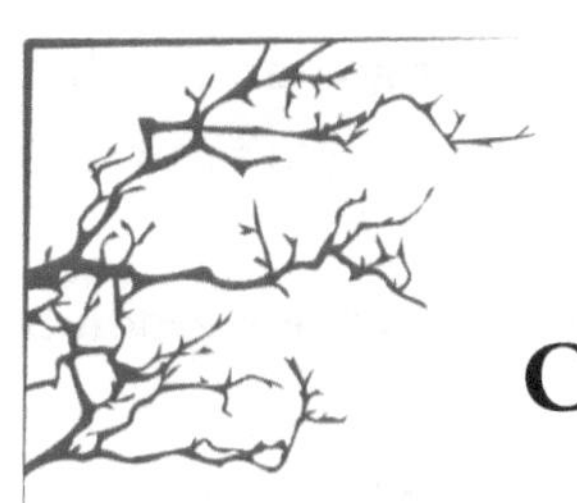

CHAPTER 55 - TY

Ty Harper stared down at his hands. His fingers worked, rubbing each other as he tried to decide how to tell Kyra the truth. She'd been so open with him. His heart swelled with wonder at how she had kept her foster brother in her heart all these years, how she'd hidden her past. For her, the disappearance of Warren Switzer had never been solved, and she was riddled with guilt.

Now, she sat with her eyes closed. Despite the continuing mystery, her face was peaceful and beautiful. Her brown eyes opened and grew wide as she looked at him and then at the floor where Shimmer sat.

"Shimmer?" she whispered. The dog smiled up at them.

Ty cleared his throat. He took a long swallow from the water bottle he'd grabbed from the bar. "I have things to tell you, too. First off, my name isn't Jerry Newcomb. It's Ty Harper. Jerry won the Medford raffle, but he couldn't come to the party this weekend. I've always been interested in this house, and so he asked me to stand in for him. We didn't tell the Kambers. Easier for me to be Jerry for the weekend."

"It wouldn't have mattered, would it? I bet they would have let you come anyway."

"Probably wouldn't have mattered. But I've been off the radar for several years. I worked for the FBI and served in the Special Forces. A bomb blast put me out of commission, and I have Post Traumatic Stress Syndrome. I live alone, in a cabin on the Cimarron River south of Stillwater." He reached out to pet the dog, who sat on the floor between him and Kyra, but his fingers only found space.

Kyra frowned at his movement. "I'm sorry you are dealing with that. It didn't help you to experience what happened here today, did it? Are you all right now?" She scooted to the edge of the sofa cushions and leaned toward him.

"I will be. I'm able to cope most of the time. But I don't go out in public much. Something as mundane as a car backfiring or a siren going off can start things up in my head."

"I don't understand why you can see Shimmer. The trauma of the bomb, maybe?"

Darcy Winters walked into the living room. She crossed the room to where they sat on the sofa. Shimmer vanished.

"How are you doing?" Darcy rested her hand on Ty's shoulder. "They're ready to transport Hugh Switzer down to the station. Thought you'd want to know."

Ty nodded. "Thanks, Darcy. Um, did you meet Kyra Blackwood?"

Darcy extended her hand. "We haven't met, but I've heard a lot about you. Let me get this straight. Switzer was not your foster father, but your foster mother's ex-husband?"

"I lived with his ex-wife and her second husband. But Hugh came around often to harass her and heckle the kids."

"So, you two are having a bit of a reunion?" Darcy smiled at her and then at Ty.

His facial muscles stiffened. Ty cleared his throat. "I told her about my PTSD and subbing for Jerry. We haven't touched on ... the other."

"Oh, then I should—"

"It's all right, Darcy. Nothing you don't already know. And truth be told, I could use the moral support." He reached up and took Darcy's hand, pulling her down on the sofa beside him.

"What is it?" Kyra asked. She plucked at the piping along the edge of the blue sofa cushion. Then she peered at Jerry.

"Like you, I had another name in my early life. I had that name changed before I joined the police and the Special Forces." He took a deep breath. "As a teenager, people here in Enid knew me as Warren Switzer."

Kyra sucked in her breath. She stood up so quickly that she saw stars. One hand covered her mouth. Her face darkened, and tears swelled in her eyes. She blinked and blinked again.

"Warren? That's not possible." She stared at him. "But, what ... happened ... to you? Where have you been?" She choked out the words.

Ty sat for a few seconds, needing the time to recover from what he'd just told Kyra as much as she needed to recover from what he'd said. He began again. "Days passed after Old Man Kamber let you leave. I was banged up. Nose broken. Cheekbones smashed. Shoulder cracked. I guess he knew he'd gone too far. He sent me to a private medical facility in Missouri. Before my release, a lawyer came with papers for a new identity. Ty Harper became my name. Free and clear. New social security number, and a savings account. There was only one stipulation, don't come back to Enid and never tell anyone what had happened to me. I obliged. I started over."

Darcy Winters took Ty's hands in hers. "He told me. We were married for nearly ten years. Lived in Tennessee. He's a good man."

"Thanks," Ty said gruffly.

Kyra didn't take her eyes off his face. "What about Hugh Switzer? He thinks you're dead. That your body is in this house. Are you going to tell him who you are?"

He shook his head. "The right thing to do is to tell him, although I don't think it would change anything in his life. He's lived all these years believing the Kambers killed me. If I tell him Warren never died, I'm the one left to hate. If he ever makes it out of prison after what he did here today, I'll be his new target."

"I'm hoping we can prove Switzer killed Matt Cleary. Then he'll be in prison for the rest of his life," Darcy said.

"Warren." Kyra studied his face. "I can't believe it." She dropped back down onto the sofa as a tear slid down her cheek.

Ty stood and opened his arms. Kyra hesitated only for a moment before she stood up and stepped into them.

The three of them sat in the quiet living room, Kyra on Ty's left side and Darcy on his right. The caterers finished clearing away the tables and putting away the liquor from the makeshift bar.

"Kyra, you're going to need to clear up the records. You took on a new name after you ran away. Did you file official name change documents? Do you have a social security number?" Darcy asked.

Kyra smiled, wryly. "With the help of a man in the small town where I moved—he had contacts who made fake IDs—I got a new social security number and a doctored birth certificate. I didn't want Hugh Switzer to find me. If Warren was alive, which I doubted, I didn't think he'd want to see me after what happened. It was all my fault."

"You will need to take care of legal issues related to your name. Does your husband know about any of this?" Darcy asked.

"No. I need to explain to him what happened so long ago will be hard. So much time has passed. But I'm ready to tell him. I need to tell him. I should have told him long ago."

"Are you worried about his reaction?" the FBI agent asked.

Kyra stared at the floor. When she looked up again, the trace of a smile shone in them. "Not really. He'll be shocked to know the truth, but he loves me. He'll understand why I didn't tell him. At least, I hope he will."

"I'll help in any way I can," Ty Harper said.

"Nicholas and Danielle Kamber, as well as Taylor McDonald, need to be told your true identities. Want to come with me to do that?" Darcy asked.

Ty and Kyra exchanged a look.

"It's been a long day. And I'd like to get home to my family. Why don't you tell them and give them my regards? Okay?" Kyra said.

"And Ty? Are you coming with me to tell them who you are?"

Ty considered doing that. The Kambers deserved to know that the remains of the 'missing' teenager were not in their house and that their grandfather had not killed him. But telling his father that his long-lost son was alive ... Now that his mind had opened again, memories of the pain his father had inflicted, both physical and emotional, swirled in his head.

The possibility of falling over the edge into a PTSD episode hovered.

Darcy took his hand again. Kyra stood up, her eyes on Ty's scarred face.

Ty looked up and saw vestiges of the girl he'd known so long ago. He'd felt so sorry when she had been dropped into his family. His mother had wanted to try to provide a home for her, but his stepfather had only seen another victim. His mother's second husband had been too much like her first. Ty had never understood why she married either man.

Ty stood up smiling. "Kyra, or Katie ... I don't know what to call you. I'd love to meet your family sometime. Back in my teenage years, I was a mess. I hated who I was and what had happened in my family. I was not a happy teenager. When Old Man Kamber offered me a new start, a new name, I was glad. I had no idea that you thought I might have died and that you blamed yourself for causing my death. I'm truly sorry that I didn't try to find you, and that I left you bearing all that guilt for all these years." He opened his arms again. Their hug was tentative, but tender. When she pulled away, he patted her shoulder.

"I'm glad you're still alive. You were brave to start over, Warren," Kyra said. "I'm sorry for everything you've gone through since."

"You were brave, too, Katie."

"Okay, okay," Darcy interrupted. "I think you two will find plenty of time to make amends and to share the happy stories of your lives, as well as to share some of those old memories, but for now, I've got to get back to the Kambers. Are you coming, Ty?" Darcy took a step across the room toward the door.

Ty squeezed Kyra's arm and moved away from her. "Yes." He grabbed a leftover napkin from the table and slipped a pen out of his jacket pocket. "Here's my number. I hope you'll call." He scribbled on the napkin and handed it to her.

"I will. We've got some catching up to do," Kyra said softly.

Ty frowned. "Some of those years are better forgotten. We'll sort that out. Call soon, Katie."

He kissed her on the cheek and followed Darcy out of the room.

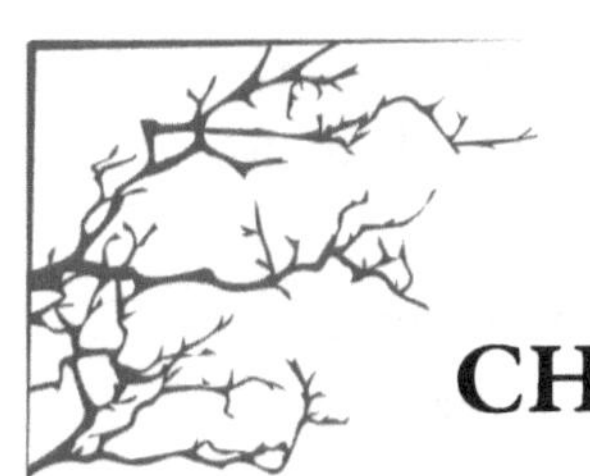

CHAPTER 56 - KYRA

Kyra shaded her face with her hand. The early winter sun shone down from the clear blue December sky causing the Christmas lights in the evergreen bushes around the ranch house to twinkle as if Dawson had already turned them on, although it was early afternoon.

"When will they be here?" Skye asked. She did a little tap dance on the boards of the front porch. "Tell me again. He's your brother. In all my life, why haven't I heard of him before?" She zipped her jacket and tucked her hands in the pockets, then bounded off the porch and galloped in a circle before coming back to stand before her mother.

Kyra smiled and tucked a stray bit of hair back into the braid that she'd plaited for Skye earlier that morning.

"Let's just say we lost track of each other. And when I went to Enid for that overnight in the mansion last October, I found him again."

"I have an uncle. A real live uncle." Skye's face beamed.

A dust trail kicked up at the end of their driveway where it intersected with the county road.

Kyra pulled in her breath. She watched the dust come closer. "I told you about the scars on his face. He's still handsome. And he's kind, and thoughtful and not at all scary. Those scars made him who he is. That's what scars do, you know. Many times, other people can't see our scars. Some of them are inside our hearts."

"Do you have scars, Momma?"

Kyra looked into her daughter's brown eyes.

"Of course, everybody does. One day, you'll have scars too. And you'll still be the most beautiful person in the world to me."

The car rumbled up. Skye turned to face the world as Jerry's black Charger rolled to a stop and parked in front of the ranch house. "They're here!" she called over her shoulder.

Ty stepped out of the car and hurried around to the passenger side to open the door. Arms full of Christmas presents, Darcy kissed his cheek as she got out.

Dawson, Robbie, and Declan came through the front door as Kyra stepped off the porch to welcome the pair to Christmas dinner.

THE END

Other Books by MARY COLEY

Fiction:

The Family Secret Series

Cobwebs: A Suspense Novel. Wheatmark. 2013.

Ant Dens: A Suspense Novel. Wheatmark. 2014.

Beehives: A Suspense Novel. Wheatmark. 2015.

Chrysalis: A Suspense Novel. Moonglow Books. 2018.

The Oklahoma Series

Blood on the Cimarron: No Motive for Murder. Moonglow Books. 2017.

Blood on the Mother Road: No Place to Hide. Moonglow Books. 2021.

The Ravine. Wild Rose Press. 2016.

Crystalline Crypt. Moonglow Books. 2019.

Nonfiction:

Environmentalism: How You Can Make a Difference. Capstone Press: Mankato, MN 2009.

Short Story Collections by ML Coley

Naked Ladies: Seasons of the Heart. ML Coley and Create Space, 2013.

Beneath a Wild Sky: Forest Cat and Other Stories. ML Coley and Create Space, 2013.

Anthology Contributions by Mary Coley

"River Crossing," in Shades of Tulsa, Tulsa Nightwriters. 2007.

"The Soul of a Poet," in Around the Block on Parnell Square, Around the Block Writers Collaborative. 2012.

"Dunes of a Faraway Place," and "The Stingray" in The Jekyll Island Writers, Vol. 2, Jekyll Island Writers. 2016.

"Beach Dogs," in A River of Stories, Tulsa Nightwriters. 2016.

"Pieces of White," in From Behind the Mask, Tulsa Nightwriters. 2020.

"The Thirteenth Victim", in A Collection of Friday the 13th Stories, Vol. 4. 2023.

"Knockers", in A Collection of Friday the 13th Stories, Vol. 5. 2023.

Don't miss out!

Visit the website below and you can sign up to receive emails whenever Mary Coley publishes a new book. There's no charge and no obligation.

https://books2read.com/r/B-A-RKECB-RBWAD

BOOKS 2 READ

Connecting independent readers to independent writers.

About the Author

Mary Coley writes award-winning mysteries, usually set in her home state of Oklahoma. With the heart of an adventurer, she loves to travel and learn new things. Sometimes those things end up in her fiction.

Crumbling Bones is her ninth mystery, and the first to be set in her home town of Enid, Oklahoma. She is thankful that her Enid High Creative Writing teacher, Mrs. Cozart, was always so encouraging.

After receiving her B.S and M.S. degrees at Oklahoma State University, she worked for the Nature Conservancy of Oklahoma and the City of Tulsa before retiring to write fiction. Currently, she spends time in both Jenks and Edmond, OK. She and her husband, Daryl, have five adult children, eight grandchildren and their Dachsund mix rescue, Trixie.

Read more at marycoley.com.